MW00329646

HOLY ORDERS

CAROLYN THORMAN

LONGSTREET PRESS
Atlanta, Georgia

I thank Robert Dublin, Esquire,
Richard Thorman, and
the Maryland State Arts Council

Published by LONGSTREET PRESS, INC.
A subsidiary of Cox Newspapers, Inc.
2140 Newmarket Parkway
Suite 118
Marietta, Georgia 30067

Copyright © 1992 by Carolyn Thorman

All rights reserved. No part of this book may be reproduced in any
form by any means without the prior written permission of the
Publisher, excepting brief quotes used in connection with reviews,
written specifically for inclusion in a magazine or newspaper.

Printed in the United States of America

1st printing, 1992

Library of Congress Catalog Number 91-77188

ISBN: 1-56352-026-5

This book was printed by R. R. Donnelley & Sons, Harrisonburg,
Virginia. The text was set in Sabon.
Book desgin by Jill Dible.
Jacket design by Tonya Beach.

Ite, Missa est.

CHAPTER

1

I made up my mind to quit the Sisters of Siluva. No crisis of faith, no man, my relationship with the Order was over, that's all. And I wanted my grandfather to be the first to hear—provided he wasn't too drunk to listen. So I borrowed the parish pickup and headed out to his farm, eight acres of cabbage on the West Virginia side of the Shackle River.

This was on a hazy September afternoon, sun grazing on soft dry grass. I backed out of the parking lot of St. Michael's Mission and inched around the dumpster piled to the brim with empty boxes stamped "USDA—Commodity Cheese." Two blocks away I waited for the light to change, then clattered onto the planked bridge that spanned the Shackle's glossy orange water and its hard-packed shore, where rows of railroad cars sat rusted onto broken tracks.

The river starts as a clear spring around Clarksburg. Then it winds northwest to Shackle where ten thousand people live in trailers, or in those asbestos-shingle dog boxes that West Virginia realtors call starter homes. Inside, the houses and the trailers look alike. Rooms with no more than one tiny window apiece, walls panelled in dark brown knotty pine: plywood sub-flooring rotting under indoor-outdoor carpet shot through with mold. Outside, the land butts smack up against the mountain. In each backyard there's a spare car stashed among the weeds, kept handy for parts. That's about all the yard's good for anyway since nothing worthwhile grows in dirt riddled with coal chips. I often wonder how the black slivers find their way to the top. Maybe the earth is expelling them, the way the body works a splinter up through the skin. Six inches below the top soil, you hit sheets of solid pink shale. That's why the septic systems are so shallow, and why in wet weather the whole town smells of the sea.

I glanced at a barge moored to cleats inside Number Four Lock where a steamer paced before the concrete gates. I slowed at the yellow blinker by the main entrance of Pittsburgh and Weirton Steel, then wound through the west side of town where I picked up Route Nine. One more red light, and I slipped off my shoes for the forty-mile drive to Cheat Furnace.

The Order discouraged family ties, and during the past ten years I had visited my grandfather only on holidays. Count Vytautas Gediminas Zedonis: I call him Pops. The origins of his counthood were buried in the archives of Lithuania—if there was such a thing. He got a kick out of abbreviating the title as CT after his name, in his tall slanty handwriting, each dot over each i a perfect circle. I have a picture of the Zedonis manor in the old country. It looks like an abandoned plantation house, complete with fluted white pillars and scabs of blistered paint peeling from the eves. I also have a sepia photo of his mother, my great-grandmother Vida—I was named after her—taken in a Vilnius studio. She wears a long linen smock with an embroidered yoke and sits stiffly in front of a broken Greek column. Pops says I look like her and that we both look like Marlene Dietrich. I wouldn't know, the actress was a bit before my time. But I can see myself in my great-grandmother's narrow face, her high cheeks with ax-blade bones, her pale gray eyes, and her heavy blonde hair that she wore braided around the top of her head and that maybe, like mine, would neither curl nor hang elegantly straight.

I figured my grandfather would take my calling to leave the Order right in stride. After all, he himself taught me the Holy Ghost speaks in all kinds of ways and directs us to many vocations, not just to the cloth. People who have never been called must imagine it to be a sound only they themselves can hear, something like a dog whistle. That's not always true. Sometimes the voice can be seen: "Rise up and follow Me." Wind filling a sail. Pops used the story of his life to teach me to recognize the signs and to pay attention.

He had been told to leave Suvalki by a tree. One day while eating a kielbasa sandwich in Donalaitas Park, a hemlock crashed to the ground a foot behind him. Shaken, he moved to a bench in a clearing and watched the park attendants drag off the dead trunk. He had been thinking about America but wasn't sure. He said the sign meant go, don't press your luck, next time you'll be flattened.

He got off the boat and, as he put it, lost one day of his life on Ellis Island and two more in New York City before he wised up and took the train to Cheat Furnace where cousin Druzouskas lived. He was about thirty-five then, my age now, and planning his future. One look at the apple orchards dotting the slopes, and Pops decided the mining town was for him. "This West Virginia has possibilities," he said. "People live in the woods. You might say it's the Lithuania of the United States." He found work as a rock duster at the company everyone calls PAW, Pittsburgh and Weirton Industries.

I rolled down the window and rested my elbow on the door. The breeze had freshened, and what with the blue sky and hint of yellow in the pin oaks, today the Shackle Valley seemed a place where a person could almost live. Wide maple leaves fanned the iron trestles. The sun had scorched the tips of the sumac along the tracks bright red. Pops didn't have a phone, so I couldn't call to let him know I was on my way. But he was usually home, and he liked company—except for the few times a year he took to the toolshed and drank himself blind. Sundays, his radio would be blaring the Lithuanian Melody Hour that played cracked 78s of catchy accordion tunes, some with the sound of horses clip-clopping in the background. A pot of schli would be bubbling on the stove and the house would smell of bay leaves. Pops would be polishing his van or stretched out on the sofa with his old gray cat, Lyda, on his chest and a Lucky Strike smoldering in the saucer on the floor beside him. He was my closest relative. Unless you counted my parents.

My mother, born with no common sense Pops said, was his only child. When Tillie was two, my grandmother Maruta died, and Pops raised Tillie single-handed, as he later raised me. Tillie quit school at sixteen to work the switchboard of Mountain Electric, where she took up with my father, Ralph. In those days she owned pink Capri pants and wore her hair in a long ponytail with spit curls at the ears. Ralph Bowser was short and fat with pouty red lips. Something had gone wrong with his tongue when he was a baby, and surgery rendered it a tiny beached whale on the bottom of his mouth. Lisp or no lisp, he had a year of computer management at West Virginia University, and Tillie's girlfriends agreed he would go far. Pops was amazed that his kid, who he probably suspected was about to go bad, married a white-collar man whose father owned the Cheat Furnace Ford dealership and whose name was easy to spell.

Behind me, the square muzzle of a Mac was breathing down my neck. On Route Nine where dirt tracks lead to mine shafts, the coal trucks jump out at you from the weeds, ready to run you off the road. I pulled over and let this one rattle past, chains whipping the back panel, then I had the highway to myself again.

I was born when Ralph and Tillie lived in an efficiency in Port Shirley. By the time I was four, they had moved to Pittsburgh, then to Cleveland, then back to Cheat Furnace. Nowadays, people would say Ralph was finding himself. Ralph said all he needed was a place where he wasn't picked on like he had been at Westinghouse, Valley

Motoron, Mountaineer Tool and Dye, Proton Five Hundred, and West Virginia Computex, Inc. Too many times I sat across the kitchen table from Tillie, who would be crying into a dishtowel, while unemployed Ralph in his three-piece checkered suit hung out in some highway cocktail lounge. Or worse—the night he spent in jail for what he called his forgetsies—forgetting to zip up his pants in the mall during a Girl Scout Jamboree. After each Ralph-related crisis, I would be shipped off to Pops's while Tillie and Ralph worked it out. Then we would move. I lost track of the apartments, basements, flats, attics, and duplexes we passed through, and I wanted to live in a castle not just to be a queen, but because it wouldn't be rented. When I was nine, Tillie announced we were moving again, only this time she and Ralph couldn't find a place big enough for the three of us so I would stay with Pops. The deal had been cut, no discussion, no nevermind, as if everyone knew all along what would happen. Instead of my family splitting like others, up and down, between mother and father, mine crashed like a tree sawed in half, me being the stump. I used to think of Tillie and Ralph as having one mind between them. Now, looking back, I realize how different they were from each other. Ralph was mean, and a coward to boot. Tillie was none too bright and afraid of standing up to him. But down deep it was possible she had a heart. There was a naturalness among Tillie, Pops, and me, and I often imagined myself as their child. That's not literally true, but I seem to have no Bowser in me—unless I'm stamping out the traces as I go along. In grade school no one cared when I started using Zedonis as my last name.

Every few months Ralph and Tillie drove out to the farm in their latest model Ford, a demonstrator from the Bowser dealership. If they had moved since the last visit, Tillie would jot down their new address and tell Pops and me to keep in touch. Her saying it that way always made it seem chancy: I would wonder if I would ever see her again. When I was twenty-five and about to take final vows, I called Tillie in Steubenville to invite her and Ralph to the Mass. They didn't show.

Halfway up the slope of the mountain, a deer loped across the road and jumped the culvert in a flash of white tail. It got me thinking about doe season, which was coming up, and how Pops would be oiling his .30-30, and shopping for ammunition at K mart. Then it struck me he and I could have lived without a calendar. Time was marked by rototilling the garden, apple picking, and the shift schedule the foreman at PAW posted on the locker room door. Mostly Pops worked nights, so our days were upside down: supper in the morning and black coffee with the late news. He would leave the house before midnight whistling a polka and swinging his metal lunchbucket. Around eight in the morning he would sit down to what was breakfast for me—fried pork chops, potatoes boiled in their dimpled red skins, and cabbage steamed gray and slick with white bacon. Afternoons, Pops napped, chopped wood, tended his still and fought black-backed horned cabbage worms. Home from school, I worked alongside him. One summer, the whole time arguing over technique, Pops and I reshingled the barn, me mounting and layering while he nailed. The winter I was twelve, we raised nightcrawlers in the springhouse and, come June, filled the freezer with skinned, pink-meat catfish. Every fall, right about this time of year, Pops took me to the Knights of Puntuckas Barley Festival. Now and then he threw parties for his cronies, where I played the accordion and kept the glasses filled. Life was rooted, not at all what it would have been had I stayed with my parents, running from the scene of Ralph's latest persecution and watching Tillie paint her fingernails gold. Yet sometimes I wondered if there wasn't a grain of flightiness in me too. Like a virus transmitted at birth that lay dormant in some ganglion and could strike any minute.

Route Nine takes a dangerous curve at the scenic overlook, and I inched around the bend. When the road straightened, I glanced down at Shackle, piled in the valley, a thousand feet below, the jumble of asphalt, tarpaper and tin roofs looking as if a tablecloth had been yanked up and the dishes had crashed to the bottom. The only slate roof topped the old flour mill, now a boutique selling scented candles and Appalachian quilts made in Taiwan. The airport tower, a lighthouse marking the rocky foothills of the mountain, sat beside the runway. I spotted the brick chimney of St. Michael's, and suddenly I felt like two cents. Quitting when there was no replacement for me as director would be shabby—something Ralph would do. I concentrated on the cupola of St. Stanislas, a copper heart turned upside down blazing against the dark pines.

By now, cold mountain air filled the truck, and I wound the window up. A red moon rose on one side of the sky while the sun set on the other. I was trapped behind a truck loaded with timber, a red flag trailing from the end of a log, and by the time I reached the Apache Trailer dealership, the landmark for the turnoff to Jacob's Ladder Road, the afternoon was shot. Just as I crested the hill, my high beams glinted off an orange ball, and I slammed on the brakes. A turtle rose on all fours, stepped an inch toward the center line, then rested. I leaned on the horn. The turtle didn't move, so I pulled onto the shoulder, switched on my hazard lights and jumped from the cab. The turtle drew into its shell. I picked it up, set it in a clump of Queen Anne's lace, then looked down between the trees.

From the top of the rise I got a bird's-eye view of Pops's bungalow. Dago Creek ran between his front yard and the red-dog gravel road, so he had built himself a wooden bridge, truck-width, over the stream. Every few years it overflowed, carrying Pops's handiwork straight into the Shackle and probably all the way to Pittsburgh.

The spotlights on the barn were lit, shining off the new four-wheel-drive Toyota Pops said he won in the Elks raffle. His rust-bucket van with "No Job Too Small" written on the side sat beside the toolshed. Suddenly the porch light snapped on. A Corvette, its exhaust billowing over the porch, idled in front of the house. The front door opened and Pops stepped out, held the screen, and a fat man wearing a cowboy hat waddled out behind him. I walked as close as I dared to the rim of the bluff and broke off a branch blocking my view. Pops paused beside the car, then ducked his head and slipped into the passenger side. The fat man hitched up his pants and, gripping the doorframe, lowered himself into the driver's seat: Sleaze Gobetsky, for sure.

Ex-president of the United Mine Workers local, Sleaze was associated with Shackle Downs, the State Liquor Commission, the Democratic Central Committee, and Videoworld Outlets, a front for one thing or another. Every four years whoever was the new county attorney hauled Sleaze into court for a racketeering. He claimed he lived off his chain of parking lots. Both were always empty. "Why pay that hunky?" Pops said. "The whole goddamn state's a parking lot."

Pops and Sleaze together meant big trouble. Pops by himself could be a pain in the neck. Sooner or later his get-rich-quick schemes would catch up with him. Two years ago after I put my foot down, he had stopped selling rights to the magnetic waves he claimed were under his garden. Then the minute my back was turned, he started selling African ermine pelts, actually West Virginia rabbit. When I was a kid, it had been the whiskey he cooked in the cellar. A sheet draped on a clothesline blocked the view of his mash pot from the basement window. He could undersell retailers, who had to pass on state excise tax, and still net a 200 percent profit. His customers used to be neighbors too poor or too cheap to buy over the counter. Then in the sixties a commune of hippies bought the old Civilian Conservation Corps camp on the north slope of Hazel Mountain, and Pops hit pay dirt. Charmed by his story that the recipe had been passed down word of mouth in the Appalachian hills, they bought cases of what he labeled "Organically-Grown Corn Sour Mash" distilled from mealy potatoes the manager of Kroger sold him half price. He colored the hundred proof alcohol with a complicated formula involving Gravy-Master and cheracol cough syrup. In the old days he put up his stock in empty bottles he collected from

friends. For the hippies he poured it into quart Mason
jars.

The commune was busted for back taxes and child
abuse. Whiskey orders dwindled to where every other
summer Pops made just enough for himself, the Kove-
leskys down the road, and his neighbor lady, Mrs.
Gigliano. He experimented with a new pension supplement, fortune-telling. But that dried up when Madam
Celestial Romany, operating from the van of an eighteen-
wheeler on blocks on Route Nine, aced him out of clien-
tele.

The Corvette bounced across the lawn and onto the
driveway in a spray of cinders and headed toward the
track that connected Jacob's Ladder Road with Route
98. I wondered whether I should head back to Shackle or
hang around the house in hopes Pops returned. I had a
key, and the prospect of a cup of coffee was too
tempting. I drove down the hill, rumbled across Pops's
bridge, and pulled up beside his new pickup. Last visit, I
hadn't noticed the spots mounted on the roof, the raised
wheels, and the stripes. Raffle? I slammed my truck door
behind me. The cool wind bit my skin, and I hurried
toward the house.

Two dormers peaked like grasshopper legs above the
porch. A tree alongside the downspout rose above the
roof. When I moved in with Pops, the elm was a sapling
strapped to a broom handle. Now the leaves brushed the
gutters making the cottage with its flat yard and picket
fence look like a child's drawing of a home. Empty
planters swung from the porch rafters, and a row of
black-stemmed zinnias, gone to pod, lined the walk. Pale
green bugs treaded light around the porch lamp.

A gust of warm air smelling of burning hickory and
roast pork hit me as I stepped into the living room. From
habit, first thing I went to the kitchen and checked the
wood stove. A fresh log smoldered. I opened the damper
an inch, then straightened. Brushing off my hands I saw
Pops must have taken off in a hurry; the pot of schli sat
on the sink top, and Lyda, not allowed in the house alone,

sat on the table licking her paws. I pushed her down and brushed off the newspaper Pops used as a tablecloth. Then I decided to heat the leftover coffee, and I lifted the enamel pot. None of the valves on Pops's gas stove worked right. The fire was either so low it went out when you breathed, or it shot halfway up the wall. To cook, he regulated the distance between the pot and the flame by piling up grids. While the coffee heated on top of three of them, I straightened my veil in the gilt-framed mirror over the kitchen sink. Pops's razor strop that hung on a crystal knob under the drainboard bumped against my knee.

I had seen myself in this freckled glass wearing my hair in two braids. Then, in the sixties, in one long one. Now I checked that my bun was still pinned tight and tucked back the cowlick hairs creeping from under the coif. Velcro or no Velcro, the thing never stayed in place. The Order was flexible about day-to-day dress. A dark skirt or loose-fitting slacks and a sweater or vest. Only the veil was required. Now, of course, for me it didn't matter. By this time next week, the cuff, gabardine—the whole kit and caboodle would be buried in a dresser drawer.

I went into the living room carrying a chipped mug full of burnt coffee and sat on the sofa. But for some reason I couldn't push the picture of Sleaze from my mind. Restless, I rose, set the mug on the mantel, and emptied Pops's saucer ashtray in the wastebasket. Suddenly I felt eyes following my hands. Then I realized I felt watched because I was about to do something I wouldn't want anyone to see—search the place to find out what Pops was up to. Maybe he was back in business and had fired up the still in the cellar.

I picked my way down the wobbly basement steps. The clothesline was still stretched across the room, but instead of the sheet, Pops's union suit sagged on the rope. As always, the galvanized tub he washed his feet in sat beside the drain in the floor. Pops had not taken an ordinary bath since 1952 when he heard about a man in Port Shirley struck by lightning in the tub. A centipede slid over the toilet seat, and I took off my shoe and squashed it beside the coal bin. Then I noticed a tarp draped over something behind the furnace. I lifted a corner of the canvas covering the copper mash pot. It was dusty and tarnished green.

Back in the kitchen, I lifted the Coleman lantern hanging beside Pops's gun rack, took a box of matches from the drawer and went onto the porch. The moon, crisp as an onion slice, was so bright I could read the arrows on the lamp's fuel knob. Pops probably wouldn't hide anything in the barn where he kept the tubs filled with rabbit pelts soaking in his mixture of tea leaves and salt. I unlatched the door to the toolshed. There was the lawn mower, the kerosene heater and the torn plastic couch where he slept off hangovers.

Then I remembered the school bus Pops bought at a county auction. "No motor, but hell," he said, "it seats thirty-five." Pops had raised his rabbits in it until Mrs. Gigliano, next door, gave up trying to sell her rabbit fillets to Spassky, the butcher. She passed on her pens, each equipped with removable dropping trays, to Pops. After he moved out his litters, I tried to talk him into letting me use the bus to raise geese. I was in high school and thought I could earn enough selling holiday birds to buy a car. "Bastards will tear up my seats," he said. He was probably right.

The bus looked the same as it had fifteen years ago, except the words "Hazel County Department of Education" seemed a little more faded. I expected the door, a plywood slab, to be wedged tight against the chassis. But a kick at the bottom corner loosened the top, and I easily lowered it onto the grass. A moldy bag of Purina Rabbit Chow leaned against the steering wheel. I raised the Coleman. A new shelf had been built over the rear bench. On it, three-pound coffee cans were lined up window to window. I made my way down the aisle and set the lamp on the floor. Inside a Maxwell House can was a plastic bag tied with a twister. I opened the sack and wondered why on earth Pops was saving shredded tobacco. When I tipped it to the light I saw the crumbled leaves were actually bright green. I sprinkled a few in my palm.

"Dammit, Jesus, Mary and Joseph."

I slammed the can down on a rabbit pen. Helicopters full of cops were cruising the whole state looking for marijuana fields. German shepherds sniffed out high school lockers.

The first time I smoked grass I was seventeen sitting beside Tillie in Pops's van. She and Ralph were visiting, and after lunch she coaxed me into taking her to the mall. We took Pops's truck because we knew Ralph needed his Ford. For some reason, he would not use Pops's toilet. At least once during every visit Ralph would mumble something about filling the gas tank, slip out to his car and take off toward the Red Head station three miles down the road.

Tillie and I had left Pops in the kitchen canning tomatoes and Ralph in the living room staring petulantly at the Steelers on TV. Tillie had never learned to drive, and something about me taking her shopping always made her giddy, as if she was a teenager out to try on clothes. That was her era of lavender-tinted hair and stretch pants with jackets to match and sometimes a color-coordinated scarf oily with pancake makeup from her throat.

After milling through Penney's, K mart and Hill's, we stopped at a Hardees. We had pulled away from the take-out window and parked beside the dumpster, and I was just lifting my coffee from the bag when she poked me in the ribs. "Look." She held up a lumpy joint.

A good thing the parking lot was empty. "Put that away," I said. She laughed and fished a pack of matches from her purse. I blew on my cup and stared at the reefer. "Where did you get it?"

Her long red nails flashed as she fumbled with the striking pad. "Don't you have these at school?" she asked, the cigarette bobbing between her lips.

I shook my head, and she looked at me with amazement bordering on pity. "Some of the St. John's boys pass them around," I mumbled apologetically.

She took a deep drag, talking fast because she was
holding her breath. "Friend of Ralph's, Darrell." She
exhaled and slapped her chest with her palm. "Wouldn't
Ralph have a fit?" She held the cigarette towards
me. "Don't be scared," she said, as if it were a dare.

"I'm not," I said.

"See, Darrell and me—"

All at once I was curious. "Give it here," I said. Also, I
didn't really want to hear about her and Darrell. By the
time Tillie and I finished, I felt slightly dizzy, probably
from gulping air, and hungry as a wolf.

All told, Pops's cans must have held more than a pound
of grass. Where was he getting it? On a hunch, I left the
bus, carefully replaced the door, and headed into the
orchard.

The apple trees were heavy with dark fruit, and here
and there a ladder leaned against a trunk. I stopped and
listened to the faint whine from the vent-fan of PAW Shaft
Number Two. Then I bit into a Winesap and picked my
way around the gnarled trunks. A thorny wall of Rosa
multiflora hid what used to be the pasture. I pitched the
apple core and finally found the gate buried in tangled
honeysuckle. Maybe too tangled: I lifted a vine carefully
trained around white butcher string Pops saved from
Spassky's. The latch on the fence was rusted shut, and it
took both hands to wrestle it open.

By now my stockings were in shreds, my skirt riddled
with burrs. Why on earth hadn't I worn slacks? I knew
better than to come to the farm in a skirt. I tightened my
raincoat belt and stepped into the clearing.

The meadow was a stage of ballerinas. Graceful, tall
bushes in straight rows swayed in the moonlight. This one
leaped, trembled midair, then bowed low. That one
pliéd. A breeze rustled the serrated leaves, the sound of
tulle brushed by fingertips.

An oil drum sat a few feet away, and I tipped it towards
me. Inside, a pump sprayer lay beside a five-pound box of
Rapid-Gro. Pops always overfertilized. His gigantic cabbage leaves were tough as dishpans, and instead of slender

vines, his tomatoes hung on hairy trunks. I broke off a
branch of hemp and turned back to the house.

Just as I got to the backyard, I saw Pops, tall and
straight as a crowbar, standing beside his van. He wore
high green rubber boots and a checkered shirt. The ear
flaps of his cap were buckled on top of his head. He
waved and yelled, "You okay?"

Of course he would ask that, he wasn't expecting
me. "Just visiting," I assured him. He joined me on the
back porch, and I smelled the whiskey on his breath. Then
he followed me into the kitchen where I tossed the branch
on the counter and said, "You won't get away with this."

"You never took a little smoke?" A slight roll of the
"r"s, and a mixed up sentence now and then, was all that
was left of his accent. He opened the wood stove, then
held out his arm and snapped his fingers, my cue to hand
him a log from the cardboard box beside the hearth. The
wood hit the grate in a shower of sparks. Pops jumped
back, then poked at the fire with a shovel. He frowned at
me, then tightened the damper to where it had been
before I opened it.

"I saw you with Sleaze," I said.

Pops hung his cap behind the cellar door. His hair was
thin and too dark. I knew about the bottle of Roux next
to a matted black toothbrush under the sink. "Whiskey,
rabbit fur, now pot. You sure push your luck."

"The law says a man has the right to what he makes."

"Oh, it does not."

Pops was smart and cocksure, but sooner or later the
police would catch up with him, and I wondered if he
could survive the humiliation. I had the sudden urge to
walk over and put my arm around his bony shoulders, but
we had never been that way. "You have a good pension
and don't need whatever you make from these fool pro-
jects. By the way, what bought that fancy four by four out
front?"

He opened the white metal cabinet over the stove.

"It's not like the whiskey days," I went on. "Now they
have helicopters, dogs."

"Big dogs?"

"Don't give me a hard time."

He stared at me, those calm gray eyes slanting up over high cheekbones. Then with his thumbs and middle fingers, he made a circle with his hands. "My business is my business." As if he had to remind me, of all people, his boundaries were not negotiable.

"Get arrested and it's my business too."

He went to the cupboard and took out two water glasses decorated with football helmets, then reached behind the toaster for his whiskey in a plastic juice bottle. He nodded at the marijuana branch. "You like my beauties? Stalks grew two feet in one week."

I draped my raincoat on the back of a chair. "I keep telling you, nitrogen burns out roots." For a second I had forgotten what kind of plants we were talking about.

"Miss Horticulture would like a drink?"

He knew the Order's rule about liquor. "No thanks."

"Kills the nerve." He set one glass aside and filled the other to the brim. "Meanwhile, what holiday I'm forgetting brings you out?"

I sat down across from him. "I'm leaving the Sisters," I said in one breath.

Pops held his glass mid-air. I sensed his body stiffen. "Boyfriend?"

"No."

His shoulders relaxed.

"They pushing you around?"

"It's over, that's all."

Pops added a drop to his glass. "You never could stand being pushed around."

"Don't start on me. Just don't start."

"Then why?"

I had rehearsed the speech I would make a hundred times wondering if there was any explanation that would ring true in Pops's ears. "The others might have a spirit of community, but I don't. I think we're just a bunch of working women, like in a YWCA. In the old days, before women could get ordinary jobs and live in the world, religious orders made sense."

He seemed to be mulling over what I said.

"Nuns are quaint. Relics. Symbols. Like the changing of the guard at Buckingham palace—like something you'd see in Williamsburg."

"They do good work."

"Except the rules get in the way. I'd do better free."

"Maybe nothing's wrong at all. Maybe you think too much."

"What's that got to do with it?"

Pops tapped his chest, over his heart.

I looked around the room as if to find something to help me. "I'm not just thinking. In Lithuania last year— you remember me being in Suvalki—I felt inside it was time for me to go. I knew—that is—in a way that I was ordered to leave."

"Lithuania?"

"No, the Order."

Pops nodded, and all at once I remembered his Donalaitas Park story. "Sort of like when the hemlock went down."

"What hemlock?"

"Remember how you said you had been thinking about leaving the old country? Then how the tree told you for sure?"

Lyda jumped on his lap, and Pops rubbed her spine and drew his fingers along the length of her rat-colored tail.

"Or be flattened?"

He blew on his hand and watched the short gray hairs float from his fingers. Somewhere in the distance a hound bayed. The faucet dripped once, a click against a pot lid.

Then Pops smacked the table. Lyda leaped to the floor, and he stood. "What did Mother General say?"

"I'm telling her one o'clock tomorrow."

Pops moved around the kitchen, opening and closing the refrigerator and balancing the schli on top of two burners. He set a salami and a jar of horseradish on the table. "If she says you can't?"

"She won't. She'll sign for me to live outside the Order

for three years. When that's over, unless I change my mind, I'll have dispensation."

"What if she says, 'no three years?'"

"She can't. She did it for others. She has to be consistent."

"She don't have to be nothing."

"If push comes to shove I can walk out. After all, it's not jail. Except—."

"I know all about except. Walk out nilly-willy and you're out of the Church, too."

Lyda put her front paws on my thigh, and I rubbed her ear between my fingers. "That was in the old days. I meant to say that I want to leave with good feelings. The days of excommunicating someone for leaving an order are over. For one thing, what with the number of religious leaving, the churches would be empty."

Pops tore a square off a roll of Scott towels. "If you say so." He folded the paper into a napkin, his long fingers with knobby red knuckles shaking as he tucked it under my plate. "You know something?" he said softly. "Your Hollywood bed's still upstairs. The vanity I made with the skirt underneath, your nationality dolls sitting on top like czarinas."

"What's left of my childhood." I smiled.

Pops drew himself up full height. "You were never a child," he said proudly. "Just small."

The skin on my hairline suddenly itched like crazy—it had been doing that lately—and I ran my finger around the cuff. "Only I won't be moving back here. I'm going to Matewan County."

Pops squinted, as if trying to see me in a different light. "Nun work?"

"The County runs a free medical clinic, and I think I'd be best off away from Shackle. For awhile, anyway. Besides, they need a social worker."

"So. You break a promise to God and go with hillbilly miners?"

"You're a miner."

"That's different."

"They're out of work."

"Out of? What's this out of? Work is part of a person. Even President Bush says—."

I held up my hand to stop him before he started in on welfare cheats, his favorite subject.

"You'll get a decent salary?"

"About seventeen thousand."

He whistled. "Big money. How much did it cost you?"

"Oh, come on."

"You think West Virginia civil service hires honest? Like IBM?"

I folded the napkin in thirds, then unfolded it. "Julian Hunting Sun—

"Funny name."

"He's a Cherokee. An Indian. He married Penny Baily, remember my freshman roommate?" I decided not to mention their divorce. "I knew him since college—he's a pediatrician down there." I looked over Pops's shoulder at the wall. "Actually it was embarrassing not to see someone for years, then to be calling him up."

"You pay him direct?"

"No, Hunt's straight as they come. He put me in touch with a county commissioner who, I guess, will be wanting a campaign contribution."

Pops scratched his head. "What about your job at the Mission?"

"Sister Silesia will have to find another director."

"How many nuns are left?"

"She can always hire a layperson."

I reached into my bag and pulled out a check withdrawing my savings. "There's one more thing."

When I had been ten years old, Ralph's father, a grandfather I never knew, died and left me some certificates of deposit. I suppose he felt it was the least he could do to make up for Ralph. "I'll need something to live on. I'm thinking to buy a trailer. Land's cheap there. Maybe I can have a few acres, a garden."

"You always were a loner."

I touched my vest. "Real clothes, a pickup." The new

life spread out in front of me like a calm bright field. Suddenly my eyes burned. "I always wanted a dog."

Pops cleared his throat. "That old van out front," he said quickly. "Take it."

"Let's see what I can find used." I held out the check. "I need you to sign, too."

Pops adjusted the paper the correct distance from his eyes. "The whole thirty-one thousand?"

"Trust me."

He licked his thumb, and slowly reached for the pen in the jelly-jar on the table. His hand trembling as always when he wrote, he circled the dot over the last "i." He raised the check up to the light, then suddenly lowered it. "Want some souri cheese?"

The tension in my jaw relaxed. "Got any rye?"

The first milestone in my leaving had been crossed. With Pops, I was home free. For the time being, anyway.

"Only Mrs. Gigliano's dago-white."

He got up and came back from the counter carrying a round cheese on a meat platter. He cut a wedge and small creamy balls crumbled onto the table like snow stomped from a boot.

"Now only one thing bothers me."

"Cheese too dry?"

I tried to sound casual. "I think of my leaving as being set free. Not being flighty."

Pops held the knife upright, then wiped each side of the slender blade on his shirtsleeve, flexed his elbows, and cut a thin circle of salami. "If you were flighty enough so that it mattered, you would be too flighty to wonder if you were." He dropped a teaspoon of horseradish on the slice and rolled it up. "Take the little shit."

I looked up sharply. "Ralph?"

"You think he ever asked anyone that question?"

All at once light-headed, I smiled.

"Which reminds me, your mother's coming by Tuesday morning. What's-his-name has a new job."

"In Shackle?"

"Somewhere in the south. They're on their way down."

"You think I should be here? Maybe I might as well break the news that I'm out of the Order. As if they care," I added.

"Funny," Pops said thoughtfully. "You being normal again. Think you'll be over the wall by next week?"

"Why?"

"The Knights' Barley Festival." His voice grew excited. "When you're not in Matewan County, stay here. Then at one, two in the morning when you can't sleep, you'll be coming downstairs looking for a beer and a Ritz cracker like you used to."

It was as if the past had crept around from behind and was becoming my future.

Pops lifted the soup pot lid, and steam from boiling bay leaves filled the air. Drops of water slid down the windowpanes, and the fire crackled in the stove. I breathed deep, and the knots in my stomach loosened for the first time in weeks. I yawned and reached for the cheese just as red and blue lights swirled across the stove, the wall, then the table.

Pops dashed to the window. "Police," he yelled. Lyda shot behind the stove, and I struggled to my feet. Men's voices and heavy boots sounded on the porch. Pops ran to the living room, and instinctively I grabbed his glass and rinsed it in the sink, the way we postulants had dashed to the bathroom with our wine glasses when Sister's footsteps tapped down the hall. The front door slammed. I was bracing myself to go into the living room when I spotted the marijuana stalk, and after glancing frantically around the room I lifted my skirt and shoved the branch under the elastic of my half-slip.

Sheriff Harry McAllister, Phil Stotler, Jim Burr and Jamie Stotler, Phil's boy, faced Pops, who stood in the middle of the room with his arms folded across his chest. Harry was reading the last words of a warrant, "felony" and "right to counsel." His hair was all whichway from his Sunday nap. Phil, part-time minister of the Church of the Divine Right, was still in his black suit. Jamie held a shotgun. When Phil saw me in the doorway, he lowered his head and mumbled, "Sorry Sister Zedonis." I ducked my head, the deference shown the veil, in my case entirely unearned, while Harry nodded and Jamie gave me a thin smile. For sure everyone in the room saw that branch.

Jim ordered Jamie to watch Pops, then waved for the others to follow him out the door. Not knowing what else to do, I sat down next to Pops on the sofa. Jamie, across from me in the rocker, polished the stock of his gun on the sleeve of his khaki jacket. I pictured the school bus sitting behind the springhouse plain as day, and the neatly cultivated field. It was only a matter of minutes before one of the men came back with the coffee cans. What was the sentence for growing pot? I should have visited Pops more often, Order be hanged. The stalk pricked my stomach. Was I an accomplice? I cleared my throat and shifted my weight to get Pops's attention. "Not a word until we get a lawyer," I whispered.

Jamie looked up, and I smiled.

The door swung open and Phil strode through the room and headed down the cellar. Pops's face was calm, but his jaw was set tight. I tried to recall if I had Justin Buccalotta's home phone number, or only the number for his law office, and was interrupted when Harry stomped in from the back door at the same time Jim came through the front. "Barn's clean. Except for some old rags soaking in slop," Jim said. Apparently he had never tanned rabbit skins. "You get the shed?"

Harry nodded.

A crash came from beneath the floor.

"Say what?" Harry yelled down the radiator.

"Stepped in a kind of funny big bucket."

Pops, staring straight ahead, smiled and I knew he was thinking about his foot-tub.

"Shit," Phil's voice was muffled, then clearer as he must have moved to the bottom of the stairs. "Give me a hand. I got it."

A minute later, the men huddled on the living room

floor around the mash pot and coils. Jim rubbed his hands together. "Paraphernalia."

"Even if it ain't been used?" Jamie asked.

Harry, on his knees, sat back on his heels and held up a copper valve. "Where's this hickey go?"

Pops slowly closed his eyes, then opened them.

I was so busy worrying about the grass, it took me a minute to realize the search had been over the minute the still was found. Was moonshining all they had on Pops? I pushed aside the saucer-ashtray with my foot and stood. "You're forgetting something." Harry rose and faced me. "I have a right to know what charges you have against my grandfather." I probably didn't, but figured Harry wouldn't quibble.

He reached in the pocket of his padded vest, unfolded a long sheet of paper and read aloud slowly, coming down hard on the end of each word. "Article 6, The West Virginia Code." He slanted the warrant to the light. "Unlawful operation of a plant manufacturing distilled spirits." I waited impatiently while he worked his way through a description and location of the house.

"What's next?" I interrupted.

He looked up and said, "We're taking the paraphernalia." Then from another paper that appeared to be a receipt, he read, "All persons concerned or interested may appear and show cause why said property should not be—"

I gathered Pops would have to fight the county attorney for return of his still.

Phil, Harry and Jamie bundled the paraphernalia in the tarp and hauled it out the front door, while Harry waited for Pops to sign the receipt. He handed Pops a carbon copy, then turned in the entrance. "Don't go nowheres without stopping by the office first."

A minute later, outside, car doors opened, a trunk door slammed, then the men cleared out in a crunch of gravel. Pops and I stood looking at each other. Then he turned into the kitchen. "Where's my glass?" he asked.

I stepped around Lyda, who was eating dried cat-food

from her bowl, and lifted the glass from the dish drain-
er. "Let me call Justin Buccalotta tomorrow. He's got
pull."

Pops took the juice bottle from behind the toaster.

"Look," I said. "They'll have to prove you used the
still. What if you're an antique collector."

He slammed the juice bottle on the table.

"It's not as bad as it could have been."

"A picayune fine," he said coldly. "They haven't arrested anyone for possession of equipment since 1945, and
then it was kicked out of court."

"You keep up with the literature." Instead of the smile I
expected, his lips were a sharp line and he worked at
avoiding my eyes. "Are you mad at me?"

"Let me think."

We sat across from each other at the table, as we had
before the raid. "I couldn't say anything without Justin," I
said as an apology. "Could I? Besides, I was thinking they
had been tipped off about the pot."

"And you were about to spill the beans." He held up
his hand, as if to stop any argument. "Sure you changed
your mind. But it still counts."

I stared at him.

"Near the end when you said, 'you're forgetting something'."

"What makes you think—?"

"This feeling. In my bones."

"You think I even could? Don't you know me better?"

He shrugged. "Vida, yes. This Sister Zedonis, who can
say?"

It took me a minute to figure out what he was talking
about. What difference did a veil make? I sat back
slowly. Of course Pops wouldn't realize I was the same; he
hadn't seen that much of me. Then it struck me that
maybe his thinking I had changed was logical, and that
maybe—had he spoken an idea I had been fighting tooth
and nail—I should have. In fact, another reason I could be
quitting the Order was because it had failed to change me
enough so that I couldn't. The Mother General's silly rules

had had a purpose, to disengage a novice from life's nuts and bolts. For everyone except me, it worked. Her discipline, training, was carefully designed to weaken the earth's pull. I, on the other hand, had gone to spiritual seed. Over the years I had grown further and further apart from the other sisters. They had developed a sweetness, naivete. Compared to them, I saw myself as being hard, weatherbeaten, a person who had been around. Take my reaction to the raid. Not once had I thought to side with law and order. And if that wasn't enough, I hid evidence, clearly the act of an accomplice, moral and criminal. Another thing, although I prayed daily for Pops's health, it never occurred to me to pray for him to go straight, meaning that ten years of daily mass, weekly reconciliation, prayer, hadn't put a dent in my character.

Look at these stockings, striped with runs, a burr riding the calf. I couldn't even keep up a good front. I was inferior to nuns like Sister Cordelia, who wouldn't be caught dead climbing through weeds to get to a field of marijuanna.

I looked up as Pops sliced off the heel of the bread. The loaf lay on the newspaper tablecloth. Maybe my failure wasn't all my fault. One morning I had passed Cordelia's parents' split level house, her father swinging a Weed-Eater along the driveway and her mother setting out geraniums, and suddenly I had known that inside, on the breakfast table, there would be bacon and eggs and Corn Flakes set out on Williamsburg place mats. Cordelia belonged in a place Pops and I did not. Maybe my problem was being too much like him—a person who didn't fit, a hand-me-down.

"It's a terrible thing when blood turns bad," Pops said.

All at once I was tired. Convincing Pops I hadn't thought to turn him in would take too much out of me. "Look at the soup," I ordered.

He turned his head, then looked back.

"I mean stay that way for a minute."

He raised his brows and turned again. I quickly unbuttoned the bottom of my blouse, pulled out the stalk and laid it on the table. "Okay," I said.

Pops turned and stared at the branch. It had snapped in the middle, and the leaves were shriveled and dark green. A black beetle the size of a pinhead crawled along a withered new shoot. Pops half smiled, then coughed and cleared his throat as if ashamed of himself.

"A tree. A branch. The Holy Ghost speaks in many ways," I said softly.

"Except sometimes He's wrong," Pops said, refilling his glass. He started to set the juice bottle aside, then pulled it back. The tumbler he had set out for me before dinner was still beside the cheese. Pops filled it half full, then slid it in the direction of my hand. When he looked up, his cheeks seemed hollow, as if dead leaves had been raked away leaving fresh clean earth. Our drinks were inches apart. He slowly pushed his towards mine with his index finger. The glasses touched without a sound. "Sveikas," he said.

CHAPTER

2

The next morning I knew my luck was about to go bad the minute Justin Buccalotta, the better half of the law partnership of Buccalotta and Blotta, walked into my office at seven a.m. "What's wrong?" I asked, before he even had a chance to say hello.

He reached under his chin to unsnap his motorcycle helmet. "Your grandfather's been busted for pot."

I rose from my desk chair, then remembered I was in my bathrobe and quickly sat down. Fifteen minutes ago Stella, the Mission's housekeeper, had knocked on my bedroom door ordering me downstairs, quick. Thinking I was wanted on the phone, I had hurried to my office, putting on my veil as I ran down the hall. It turned out Justin had been waiting in the foyer. "Where is Pops now?" I asked.

"Out on his own recognizance."

I motioned to the wingback across from me. He sat on the edge of the seat and balanced the helmet on his knees. Your first impression of Justin was that he was immature: tall, thin as a scarecrow, soft brown eyes and pale skin. But the minute he spoke you were struck by the competence in that gentle voice. He and Joe Blotta were the best sports in town for taking pro-bono cases for the Mission. Yet sometimes I wondered if he only volunteered at St. Michael's as a public relations ploy before running for office, in the tradition of Italian lawyers from Clarksburg who controlled their fair share and more of local government. "Sorry to barge in so early," Justin said. "The lady who opened the door told me to wait and she would—"

"What about Pops?"

Justin ran his fingers through his curly brown hair. "Midnight last night I get this call from him at the police station. Seemed the cops had gone out to your grandfather's farm earlier that night looking for whiskey. They confiscated a still. Then went back to get a lighter one of them thought he lost somewhere on the place. They found an old school bus, and in it, twenty-two cans of pot. McAllister nailed the old man on Article 33 of the West Virginia Code, possession sale and use of—"

"Use? Pops never once used grass."

"It's called throwing the book."

I opened my mouth to breathe. The dentist had warned me about gritting my teeth. So McAllister had gone back to the farm after I left. McAllister—Pops called him the shanty Irish sheriff. And I had voted for the little shit anyway—God forgive me Jesus, Mary and Joseph.

"Worst is, before I can shut him up, Mr. Zedonis allowed as how he grew the stuff." Justin said. "Claims it cures sinuses, swore he only gave it to friends and never sold an ounce."

I thought of Pops climbing into Sleaze Gobetsky's Corvette. "Do you believe him?"

Justin took off his wire-rimmed glasses, blew on the lens, then polished them on a corner of his pin-striped vest. "He's my client." He held the glasses up to the light, put them back on, then, always thorough, launched into the relationship between the West Virginia Code and federal statutes on controlled substances.

The only thing I heard was this time Pops was in over his head and me right along with him. Here at the Mission, on the second floor, all three of the homeless men were kicking addictions of one sort or another. Manny

Gigliano, a cousin of Pops's neighbor, was seventeen and on probation for selling crack in the Trailways parking lot. Pavel Kostick was on community placement from Chafin State Psychiatric Hospital. At one time he had spiked his Thorozine with speed. And Vinnie Le Clair, fifty-seven, running a generation ahead or behind the others, depending on how you looked at it, on Sunrise gin. Now who in this town would resist speculating if, say, Manny had gotten his first high on a Zedonis bumper crop. Family business. Pops got them hooked. I shored them up.

Justin was telling me how he had driven Pops home, Pops riding the rear bumper of the Suzuki.

"Why didn't you call me sooner?"

"Because Mr. Zedonis made me swear up and down I wouldn't tell you until it was over."

"It's over?"

"No."

Justin went into trials, appellate rights, and I got the message that keeping Pops out of jail wasn't going to be easy. I tried to pay attention to the legal maneuvers and to put Pops's predicament ahead of my own. But why today, of all days? My meeting with the Mother General, Sister Silesia, was at one o'clock. Ten years in the Order and today was the day I was hanging it up, and now this.

"A protracted struggle," Justin was saying. "Court costs—"

"Send me the bills," I said. Not that I was sure how I would pay them if the going got rough. The check Pops had signed last night was every nickel to my name.

Justin glanced at the photo of Cardinal Ratzinger behind my desk, then at the wall, as if talking fees made him uncomfortable. Or maybe it was the cardinal. He lifted his helmet. "I've got a deposition to take," he said, getting to his feet. "Charleston's a good three hours."

I adjusted my coif.

"The court will go easy on an old man," he added. "I'll cut us a deal."

Seeing Justin out would mean standing up in full view. I

folded my hands on my day-at-a-glance calendar. "Thank you for coming," I said quietly.

He crossed the room and opened my office door. Stella Ripalas faced him dead on. She held a rag in one hand and a can of Kwik-Clean in the other. Not fat, she was more sturdy and compact. A white cotton scarf covered her head and was tied at the nape of the neck. She wore one of the housedresses she whipped up on the treadle machine in her second floor room. Today's was patterned with orange flowers and bright blue leaves; a bibbed apron hid most of the foliage. Justin stepped aside and motioned her into the office, but she pointed to the frame around the door. "Fingerprints," she said to me.

Justin turned and said, "If it weren't for Charleston, I wouldn't be here this early. I tried to call but no one answered, so I said to myself, since they live here at the Mission." He shrugged.

"It rang like a house on fire," Stella said. She aimed the nozzle and shot a pillow of white foam onto the woodwork. "I had to turn down the button. Sister has too much on her mind."

I made a mental note to reset the volume and to warn Stella to keep her hands off it. "Let me know what I can do," I said to Justin.

He waved and disappeared into the hall. I waited until the front door slammed, then asked, "What's with the Kwik-Clean?"

Stella stood on tiptoe and snapped the rag at the molding. "Why didn't you tell lawyer Buccalotta you were out to Mr. Zedonis's farm last night?"

I got up and rounded the corner of my desk. "Because what you don't say can't hurt you."

Outside, Justin's engine sputtered, then kicked into a deafening roar. I closed my eyes as it passed the window.

"Isn't that against the law?" Stella shouted.

A typical Stella all-purpose question, designed to trash Justin, or me, depending on how I chose to interpret it. "I'm going to get dressed," I yelled above the din.

A few minutes later, I was watching the gray September

light filter through the window of my attic bedroom. I drew aside the sheer curtain. Vapor spires split the shoulders of Mt. Sorry Dog. The Shackle flowed flat and black beneath a fine mist.

I crossed myself. Dear Mother of God, he's an old man, don't let him be arrested again, humiliated, pushed around in a long drawn-out process of procedural—. Justin's words, "court costs," came back at me, and the prayer died. The only asset Pops had as far as I knew, aside from that new truck, was his house and the few acres it sat on, worth about sixty thousand, all told. If he had to sell out, where would he live? In a senior citizens sheltered housing project? "Blessed Mother, he would be miserable," I whispered.

In my bag on the dresser was the check for thirty thousand. Maybe I should set it aside for him. Which would mean I couldn't afford to quit the Order. Could the arrest be a sign I shouldn't leave? I felt, rather than knew, the answer right off. God does not send a sign to one person through the pain of another.

All at once the wind kicked up, and a few branches clicked against the pitted gutters waiting to be relined. Instinctively I glanced at the roof, then at the driveway below. Sure enough, another shingle bit the dust. The radiator hissed and slowly the window turned milky white. I would have faith in my decision, faith in Justin, and blind faith that Pops would not be indicted. If events took a turn for the worst, I could work an extra job or borrow against my salary. God hadn't failed me yet.

I dropped the curtain and briskly adjusted the folds so that it hung properly. Then I crossed the room, opened a drawer and pulled out a chemise. Last year I had given up brassieres, buying Stella's argument that they caused cancer. Down deep I didn't quite believe that, but of all the underwear in the world brassieres were the most hideous. Probably invented by a man. I opened a lower drawer and took out a blouse. It was new, the linen stiff as cardboard. I slipped it on, then shoved a few more hairpins around my braid and picked up the veil. Lately I had been draping it over the lampshade at night, a new technique to hang out the wrinkles. I fastened the Velcro on the back of the cuff while standing before the glass. The Order allowed mirrors, but to be used only as necessary, like sleeping pills. Preoccupation with one's reflection was a First Commandment offense. I kept my eyes on the dresser.

The long, low 1950s monstrosity had curved edges and ornamental pustules on the face of the drawers. It had come with the matching nightstand and headboard, donated by the diocese, and was nothing I would have chosen. Getting dressed, I moved from the closet to the chest of drawers. In fact, nothing around me was mine except for the books—Bible, Teilhard de Chardin, Kazantzakis—piled on the shelves. This room itself was reason to leave the Siluva's. No one can live without the intimacy of place. Without people, yes, but not without place. To live where there's no earthly proof of one's self is to have no self.

Which is why I would have my own house and my own land, no matter how modest. There would be a period of adjustment. But I was lucky to have a job waiting. Sister Claudia, who had resigned last year, had had a rough time relocating. I had taken her advice and made plans. Since I had no intention of getting married, or getting rich, keeping the Rule while waiting for final dispensation would be simple. Sister Silesia would probably sign for my interim freedom this afternoon, provided she had the blank papers (for some reason an indult was always referred to as "papers"). I had vacation time coming, and one unspoken custom of the Order was that when a sister left, she left fast. No farewell dinners. No rotten apple to spoil the rest in the barrel.

I buttoned my vest and straightened the string bow tie on the blouse. I would do the best I could to conserve the money in case Pops needed it. Meanwhile, Justin's parting shot—that the court would go easy on an old man—rang in my mind. I slipped into my loafers and found my missal under a pile of *Faith-Styles*, Bishop Crumrine's diocesan magazine, then headed downstairs.

Theme music of "Hey There, West Virginia," drifted from the kitchen. The light was out in the dining room, and I ran my hand over the flaking paint, feeling for the switch. An upright piano with the ivory peeled off middle C flanked the wall. A plywood slab on two horses served as a table for the fifteen old people at noon. Stella covered it with kerosene-scented yellow vinyl. Samsonite chairs, sentries, guarded the window and the African violets on the sill. A horn groaned from a barge on the river. I swung open the kitchen door.

Stella was halfway up a ladder propped against the wall. "What on earth?" I said.

She twisted around. From where I stood I could see the varicose veins she refused to treat choking her calves like wild purple vines. Pantyhose were for movie stars, she said, and garters caused varicose veins. Stella's stockings were knotted in tight balls behind her knees. Something like a tablecloth hung over her shoulder. "Pudding—" she took a thumbtack from her mouth. "Putting up his flag."

I reached to the top of the enamel cabinet and snapped off the TV. "What flag?"

"Remember, Sister? Novotsky's shut down his so-called bar and grill. Remodelment, he says. So you promised Vito us Knights could meet in the kitchen."

Vito was Stella's boyfriend and the current Grand Master of the Knights of Puntukas, a fraternal lodge qualifying itinerant workers for group life insurance. The little I knew about the secret organization I had picked up from Pops, a charter member. St. Stanilaus, the only Lithuanian parish in the Shackle Valley, more or less sponsored the local chapter. Stella snapped open the cloth. "Catch that end."

"I'm off to Mass."

"Hold the end is all I ask."

I held the banner while she tacked a corner of it to the wall. She stepped down from the bottom rung. "Watch out, please." She moved the ladder a few feet, then climbed up and adjusted a tack. "Now check me for straight."

I stood back. "An inch lower on my side."

Embroidered figures covered grainy white linen. Knights on horseback advanced toward a dome suspended above the Vilnius skyline. On the top left, a tower of Gediminas castle split a pink cloud. A blue cloud held a cross-stitched figure of a vidalete, keeper of the sacred fire. Dressed in her long tunic, she fed a branch to a flame curling from a stone. A brown chain-stitched line was almost hidden among ruta leaves. I leaned closer. A snake, smiling, and wearing a crown, snake's head size, glided in front of the knights as if pointing the way. I turned to Stella.

"Ozier," she said, gripping the ladder as she stepped to the floor.

"What's he doing?"

Stella brushed off her hands. "Leading us to the Holy City."

Vito had gotten the idea, from goodness knows where, that he would organize a crusade to recapture Jerusalem for the pope. Of course only knights knew the details of this hare-brained scheme. But it was no secret the lodge was having a terrible time raising money to carry it out.

Stella frowned and ran her hand over the cloth. "I know, Sister, that you can't believe in us."

"It's not that I can't—"

"You have to believe regular."

"It's just that I can't see how he's going to pull it off," I said, feeling silly discussing the idea as if it made sense. But I couldn't hurt Stella, who did seem to believe in Vito's crusade. Or at least in Vito.

She pressed a tack in deeper. "An international cartel, that's how."

I pictured Vito, a wizened little man, his worn gabardine overcoat, his watery blue eyes red-rimmed from Four Roses. "Cartel? The pope doesn't want Jerusalem anyway," I told her for the hundredth time.

Stella raised her eyebrows. "He said that?"

"Some would say the whole notion's absolutely crazy."

"No crazier than anyone else's crusade." Then she folded down the paint-can platform and slapped the ladder shut. "Let's get this to where we won't trip. Manny can haul it down the cellar. Lift the feet for me, please."

We jockeyed the ladder through the door and onto the rickety back porch. Then I followed Stella back into the kitchen. She lit the gas under an iron skillet and instantly the air filled with the smell of fried bacon. I crossed the room and looked over her shoulder. A slab of salt pork crackled in a shiny pool of grease. "How about we skip the cholesterol. Vinnie's heart, remember?"

"You know what your problem is?"

I steeled myself for her daily attack on my character.

She pulled a pack of Luckies from her pocket. "You think people can be wrapped in cotton." The cigarette dangled between her lips as she fumbled for a match. She stepped on the garbage can pedal, and the lid flew up and banged the hot water tank. The matchstick landed on a lettuce leaf. "Let Mr. Le Clair choose his own poison, my sausage or my oatmeal."

"Anyone else up?" I asked wearily.

"Manny took off in the van to get gas. Pavel's on the phone. Mr. Vinnie Le Big-Shot hasn't shown his face." She nodded at the rags on the radiator. "Orange-cat hauled home a dead bird. He's out front picking his teeth."

I lifted my raincoat from the gnarled joint on the plumbing beside the door. Lead pipes ran from ceiling to floor, some thick as kielbasi, others slim as pencils. A Mason jar caught the leak under the windowsill. Slowly I buttoned my coat. Every morning I coaxed Stella to come to Mass. Every morning she refused, our exchange itself becoming a litany. She said that during the Second Vatican Council, the church had made a deal with the president of the United States and had turned Protestant.

"Are you too busy this morning to—"

"For sing-along, always," she said.

I had explained that singing hymns did not make a Catholic a Lutheran, or a Methodist. She still insisted we had turned from God. The new liturgy—Father facing the congregation instead of the altar—drove her crazy.

"Come to Mass with me," I said.

Stella waved a fork in a circle. "Not until my Church turns backwards again."

I opened the door, then paused. "Change your mind?"

She shook the skillet back and forth. "My mind is a brick."

The sky was black, and a warm wind howled down the mountain. I cut across the lawn and headed towards St. Stanislas, three blocks away. I remembered the fallen shingle and turned, walking backwards against the wind and looking up at the Mission. Turrets on both wings made the gray stone mansion appear to be sitting on its haunches guarding its asphalt parking lot along one flank, its basketball court along the other. Behind the house a shale hillside led down to the river. In the distance, on the opposite shore, PAW's smokestacks stood like sooty organ pipes.

A sharper gust; I faced it and flipped up my collar. The neon clock on Spivak's auto-body shop window was stuck on five—a memorial to whatever day, year, it had stopped. Joe Spivak, leaning on a rake, watched a pyramid of tires smolder in the vacant lot. The rain had settled into mist hiding the cupola of St. Stanislas. It almost hid the rectory yard. The lawn sloped down to the front steps so that the frame house, situated in a gully, appeared to be fighting its way up to the street.

As usual, the church vestibule smelled as if it had been hosed down with Pine-Sol. I crossed myself, then noticed the green scum in the holy water font was back. Once more the Women Aglow Society had slipped up. Eight years ago the original St. Stanislas had burned to the ground. Just this summer the parish had raised enough money to pay off the new building, install the recessed lighting and cover every inch of floor, nave to vestibule, with beige weather-beater carpet.

Someone touched my elbow. "Sister?"

It was Clotilda, the old woman who volunteered to

clean the rectory and iron the altar linens. Every parish
has one like her, in a crepe-de-chine dress and soft black
shoes with flapping soles, a hunched-backed squirrel scur-
rying between the exit door and a pew up front. Today
her frayed coat was unbuttoned, and an ivory fist with the
index finger and little finger extended hung from a chain
around her neck. "Please, Sister, go see my Angela for me
this week. It's my gallbladder," she said dramatically,
clutching her collar. "Tomorrow I go under the knife."

"Will you be in Shackle General?"

Clotilda nodded and I made a mental note to collect
from Father Kozakas for flowers.

"Don't think of me, it's Angie."

Clotilda's youngest had been in Chafin State Mental
Hospital for some months, depression, borderline schizophrenia. I put my hand on the old woman's bony shoulder. "I usually make Chafin visits on Wednesdays. Of
course I'll go see Angie. And pray for you."

A group of teenagers flooded the vestibule. Clotilda
blessed me and hurried down the aisle.

I knelt quickly alongside the last row in back, crossed
myself, then slid along the bench and groped for the
kneeling pad. I drew my rosary from my bag and kissed
the Crucifix. Raising my eyes, once more I was struck by
the ugliness of this new church, the freshly painted cinder-
block walls, the mural behind the altar depicting a sun
surrounded by a crown of magenta thorns. The Women
Aglow Society had substituted a standing chrome electric
candelabrum for the old wrought iron tier of votive candles. I closed my eyes.

3

Last year the Order sent me to our convent in Lithuania to study ethnography and syntax. A month after I arrived, I suspected the real reason for sending me there was to perfect my tolerance for suffering. The Second Vatican Council, which blew the roof off the American church, breezed lightly over Eastern Europe. The Siluvas, being an institute of diocesan right, was overseen by the Bishop of Warsaw, and American or not, as a Sister I was under his medieval thumb.

When Pops was born in Suvalki, the Sudova region of Lithuania had been a gubernia administered by the Czar. After the First World War it became Polish, then German, then Russian again. When Pops and Mama Birute left, Suvalki was back in northeastern Poland, thirty kilometers from the Soviet line, its twenty thousand souls still exiled by another shift in borders. Nevertheless, Lithuanians went on building their roadside shrines, raising stringy chickens and beets, and living much as American Indians live on a reservation, minding their own business, surrounded by strange people.

My flight from Warsaw landed at dawn. I had been told I would be met at the airport. It turned out the Order's laywoman chauffeur whipped a black Polski sedan onto the runway and waited, motor running, while

I struggled down the steps of the Illyusha jet. February wind tore at my coat as I opened the car door. Sister Jagellonia, director of apostolic affairs, and another nun whose title I translated roughly as "Sword of the Siluva Word," made room for me in the back seat. They wore the full-length habits the teaching sisters at St. Alphonsus had worn in West Virginia when I was in high school in the sixties. I sat beside Sister Jagellonia. The stiff bonnet that circled her face hid her profile. All I could see were pale slim hands, the X of blue veins on the backs, her gold ring of the Blood of the Lamb loose beneath her ivory knuckle bone. I looked down at my dark gray cuticles. Last week I had mixed a bucket of concrete to patch the cracks in the Mission's front walk. My own gold ring was cemented in swollen, chapped skin. Had Sister noticed my Nikes? I had hoped they would keep my feet from swelling on the seven-hour flight from New York. My coat was open, showing the drop of mayonnaise that had dried on my street-length gabardine skirt. Slowly, so as not to catch Sister's eye, I slid my muffler over the spot. I wondered how she saw me. I thought of the B girls back home Sleaze Gobetsky hired for the Pink Venus, his cocktail lounge in the Shackle Valley Mall. I turned and stared out the window, hoping Sister Jagellonia would do the same.

The Polski crawled along the narrow highway cut between rows of tall evergreens. The high boughs drooped like moustaches over the road. The lower branches had been sawed off, and you could see deep into the forest where shafts of dusty light filtered between smooth trunks. Cars were parked along the shoulder. Mushroom pickers carrying baskets, the handles curved over their arms, glided in and out among the trees like ghosts of Saint Zita. The chauffeur rolled down the window to pitch her cigarette, and even before the fresh air hit me, I knew it would be damp and smell of resin, mold, and diesel fumes. Then I realized nothing in the landscape was unexpected, as if I had been in this woods, on this road before. Each fork in the highway was marked by a shrine: a simple birch cross; a statue of the Holy Vir-

gin of the Seven Sorrows, a wire ringed with metal stars
circling her face. We wound through villages. Each had its
log cottages, church, closed restaurant, and closed gas station. Then we were back between the trees. Soon we were
passing brick buildings and signs pointing to Suvalki,
dead ahead.

The city had been in most of Pops's stories. Every Friday the Zedonises had driven their flatbed cart to market,
Pops sitting cross-legged on the logs lashed together with
rope. He said the sidewalks had been lined with wire
cages filled with chickens, their heads sticking through the
portholes. Wooden crates were layered with crusty dried
herring. Sauerkraut, packed in white hailstones of rock
salt, was sold straight from the crock. Jewish merchants
drove their horse-drawn barrels full of Christian babies
through the streets, the barrels studded with nailheads,
points hammered in. When I asked Pops if the Jewish part
was true, he had crossed himself and spit over the porch.
Yet for all his stories, Pops had never gotten around to
telling me what the city itself looked like. I could have
been in Leningrad: wide streets bordered with Peter the
Great buildings, some even painted pale blue like the Her-
mitage. A few years ago in Russia, I noticed that the
streets, lamposts, doorknobs, were too big—bolshoi—as
if built for a race of giants. A McCormick reaper could
have passed through the doors of Suvalki City Hall. A
statue of either Neptune or Lenin stood at least thirty
feet. A fence of rusty bars as wide as elephant legs surrounded the park.

During the drive neither Sister Jagellonia nor the Sword
of the Word spoke. Then I saw a mule tethered to a parking meter. A log cart was hitched to the animal's flanks. I
touched Sister's arm, pointed, and said in my best
Lithuanian grammar, "My grandfather had one of
those." The bundle of dark wool did not speak or move. I
wondered if she heard me. I spoke louder. "He was from a
small estate nearby."

The pale hand closest to mine slid to the other side of
her lap.

"He and my grandmother went to the United States, Cheat Furnace, West Virginia, after the Second World War."

No sign of life.

Look at me, I wanted to shout. I could not feel her breathe. Maybe I should grab her shoulders and shake her; say I wasn't just some tourist carrying a camera and a Mediterranean fruit fly in my luggage that would wipe out the people's cabbage crop. I pressed my back against the far corner of the seat. I belonged in this world as much as she did.

While we waited for a light to change, I watched a stocky woman in galoshes and a housedress topped by a man's jacket, sweep the gutter with a short-handled broom. True, Pops and Mama Birute couldn't wait to get out of Europe. Maybe Sister was bitter because she had been left behind. Or maybe she resented Americans like me, thinking we could come back any old time and reclaim our heritage, just like that, when we never had to wait in line to buy rotten potatoes or eat spoiled meat. She had a point.

Through the front window I saw a banner draped across the facade of a building. The Byzantine eagle, a branch in its talons, was looking east and west at the same time. What had I expected? That the old country sisters would fall all over me because I knew a few words of the language and how to cook borscht? Maybe I had been naive, expecting too much. I pulled my gloves from my pocket. Just because I needed roots didn't mean the earth had to shift to make room.

The driver turned and said something I couldn't understand. The Sword answered, and the car swung into a wide alley behind a row of cinder-block buildings with rickety fire escapes zigzagging down their flanks. Dented trash cans sat on matted weeds. The sky hung low and dark. Snowflakes blew against the windshield, stuck, then slid down the pane. The Polski slowed. I thought of convicts being hustled into Lubianka prison. Without warning I felt dizzy and desperate for air. I wanted to be back

in Shackle, out of this city and out of this car. I saw myself
unlatching the door and running down one of the dim
corridors between the walls, bullets whizzing over my
head. I saw the Sword, black cape flying, hot on my tail.

We pulled up to the convent, a five-story townhouse
once owned, I learned later, by Count Bialiki. The sisters,
one on each side, whisked me through a Shackle-style
courtyard cluttered with galvanized tubs, inner tubes, an
old bicycle, and a power lawn mower sitting on concrete
blocks. Then through the kitchen, a blur, and up the
winding staircase and into what was to be my room. A
wimple and a pile of yellowy underwear lay on the dresser. The Sword stepped ahead of me and opened the closet
door. A long black cassock swung from a coat hanger. I
got the message. Dinner in a few minutes, Sister Jagellonia
announced in part English, part Polish. Alone, I struggled
to assemble dress shields, a garter belt that buttoned on
the side, and black stockings as sheer as Ace bandages. It
took me a few minutes to figure out that the goathair rope
went around the waist. Special loops held a huge wooden
rosary. The beads hung to my knees and clicked like marbles when I walked.

At dinner I sat among the forty or so other nuns. We
kept silence as we ate. Not that it mattered, since they
spoke no English and I spoke poor Lithuanian and no Polish at all. I never did learn their names or what their work
was. The wide floppy sleeves of my habit skimmed the
butter. The round starched bib beneath my chin caught
grease from the mutton stew. I leaned back and carefully
scraped my soup spoon against the rim of the
bowl. Somehow I would have to learn to manage the
weight, the heft of this cloth.

And as the winter progressed, I did get the hang of it. I
was beginning to enjoy rounding a corner feeling like a
Radziwill princess, the soft cassock swirling at my feet,
the cape catching the wind like a black spinnaker. Then
came June and I discovered there was no summer habit,
the theory being dark fabrics blocked the sun. Maybe
woolen robes did save the Sahara Bedouins from

hypothermia. But the damp Suvalki air, heavy with pollen and dust from the sawmill, turned our cassocks into coats of mail.

If the habit wasn't bad enough, no nun was to be seen on the streets or in a car unaccompanied by another sister. No driving. And never, under any circumstances, was a Siluva to be alone with a member of the opposite gender. (I cannot recall the words man or sex ever being used). My room was vast as a San Sebastian cave. In winter the stone floors deflected the cold straight to the marrow of my bones. In summer the floor gathered enough noon sun to boil the night air straight through till dawn. The one bathroom was a mile from my door. Narrow corridors like interstate entrance ramps fed into the hall perpetually clogged with nuns holding thin gray towels and toothbrushes. Nevertheless, I tried to adjust to the Province and to the daily routine.

Each morning plump Sister Maria Sophia and I would hurry down October the 12th Street to the ethnographic museum where classes were held. After lectures Sister and I had permission to go into the city square—the deal being she could weigh herself on the scale outside the chemist's shop provided we kept our eyes on the cobblestones. For a few minutes while she fiddled with the weights, I held her books and took in the flower sellers sitting among cut roses and daisies, the shoppers carrying string bags, the pigeons that for no reason rose in flocks, circled, then landed at the shore of the same puddle they had left. I wanted to browse through the books in the stalls, buy coffee and sit on the base of the statue of Vytautas the Great. But a turn of my head and Sister would snap at me in Polish to look sharp and not be distracted by wordly affairs, the devil's lure.

When classes were over, the student nuns studied before the crackling fireplace in the library with its high-vaulted ceiling, its Jan Matejko mural of decapitated Turks, aerial view. When the weather warmed, we moved to the flagstone terrace furnished with round tables and spindly plastic chairs. Dinner, sparse and quick, came at four-thirty. Prayer until vespers, then to bed at nine. Breakfast was at five in the morning after Mass. For exercise we took turns scrubbing the marble foyer or waxing the spiral staircase, the energy equivalent of painting the Brooklyn Bridge.

In America I had been curious to learn what our old world Order was like. I had been growing more and more restless and dissatisfied with the emptiness and lack of spiritual values of the West Virginia Siluvas. I was hoping Suvalki would bring a renewal of my commitment. I had been looking forward to the peace and security of a sheltered convent. And peaceful it was. But in spite of the calm empty days, my skin seemed to be drawn taut, too tight for my body. I began losing sleep worrying that I would forget a declension, or to return the paste wax to the hall cupboard. Then I worried I would oversleep and miss Mass. There was no one to talk to. Conversation consisted of smiles, and "Have a nice day," in my broken Polish.

Then I discovered the gap between the others and me was more profound than language alone. One evening Sister Yolanda sidled up to me in the toothbrush line and pulled a glossy book from under her arm, titled in English, "Microwaving the Whole Bit." She pointed to a glossy photo of a woman standing on a deck above what looked to be Big Sur. The model wore a white apron over a black leotard. One hand touched her tumbling red hair. The other held an artichoke in front of a black-doored oven resting on the teak railing. I looked for the cord; goodness knows where they had hidden the plug. Sister asked something to the effect of was this what America was like. I nodded, yes. Then she pointed to me. I gathered she imagined that was how I had looked back home in Shackle. I smiled and shrugged. Even if I knew the Polish words I wouldn't know how on earth to explain Shackle, the trust territory of gun racks, snow ball bushes, and Wonder Bread sandwiches of commodity peanut butter and cheese. I patted her arm and handed the book back. Then a thought hit me. I wasn't from America as the world knew it. And I didn't fit in Suvalki. So who was I, and where did I belong?

About that time my eyelashes started to go. Not all at once, but my lids seemed to be getting slimmer, like autumn branches dropping leaves day by day. Mirrors were forbidden, so it was hard to track the disintegration rate. Of course my lashes had never been anything to write home about. When I was fifteen, Tillie had bought me false ones and talked me into wearing them to school. The next morning I found myself in the girls' room with Sister Florenza tapping her foot while I peeled off the adhesive. I still had those fake lashes in my dresser drawer, lying curved, asleep in their plastic case.

I wondered if anyone noticed that my face seemed bare, bigger than it was when I arrived. There was no one to ask. What type of cancer started this way? Maybe I was going crazy. Madness starts with obsessions, delusions. Yet the hairs were leaving one by one. Were my eyes safe? While I studied, I would blink against my index finger, trying to count the number of bristles brushing my skin. By late summer I was depressed, miserable, convinced I was losing both my eyesight and my mind.

August had been the hottest on record, and so humid I felt I was living underwater. The cassock itched like poison ivy. I took to doing what many of the sisters did but never discussed—holing up in their rooms stripped to their muslin underwear, rereading dog-eared Conrad novels. I tried to struggle on with pronouns, and to keep the banister polished to a high gloss despite the heat. But on the day before the Feast of the Assumption, August 14, I cracked.

That morning, like every morning for the past month, the sun barreled out of Russia at four a.m., a cossack aiming a blowtorch. The stone floors seared the soles of my bare feet. The lecture on the subjunctive dragged, and I tried not to doze. After class, I was the only one studying on the terrace. Dinner was inedible: molten lava chicken broth, hard-boiled eggs and day-old bread. In my room I tore off the woolen shroud and the loathsome stockings, then passed out more than slept. Slick with sweat, I woke up a few hours later, my mouth dry and my head pounding. Not stopping to think, I stumbled to the closet and dug out my American habit, last worn on the flight from New York. Even before it was buttoned the blouse stuck to my skin. I stepped into the short blue skirt, then groped for my Nikes on the shelf. I pinned up my hair by touch. Escape. No matter that I had no clothes except those on my back, or that I had dollar bills instead of zlotys. I dug out my book bag decorated with Hebrew letters, the one a friend brought me from Jeruselum, jammed my wallet and passport into the top pouch, then opened the door.

The setting sun slit the elephant footprints of the hall Bokhara. My legs felt cool, for the first time in months naked in outdoor air. I walked, then half-ran past the closed doors, a row of square oak soldiers. To this day I don't know what I would have done if a nun had stepped from her room. And, mirable dictu, the bathroom corridor was empty. The kitchen was silent too, but for the hum of the walk-in freezer. I went into the courtyard overgrown with goldenrod.

The rickety bicycle was still there, bolshoi, rusty, leaning against the wall as if catching its breath, its kickstand long gone. The pedals were wide as oar blades, the fenders could have covered tractor wheels. Then I noticed it was built for the opposite gender. Had there been time to think, I never would have worked up the nerve to run along beside the bike, hop and swing my leg over the seat.

Bakalarzewska Avenue dozed in a muggy stupor. Sweat dripped from my chin. My hands slipped around the metal handlebars, there being no rubber grips. I pedalled fast, faster. Soon the street widened and there were highway signs, Bialstok, Warszawa, Olecko, Olsztyn, 250 km. Now and then a truck rattled past. Men in a beat-up Moskvitch shouted at me and roared by in a cloud of engine fumes. Hunched over the bars I didn't care where I was going. The wheels tore along at their own speed. I crossed the bridge over the Czarna Hancza River: the blue water shone around black rocks. A sailboat in irons bobbed on the lake. Not a breath of wind stirred. Soon the buildings grew further apart, and tall silver birches lined the road. I slowed and sat back on the padded seat, which was broad as an ironing board.

Since I hadn't shown up for vespers, by now I was in deep trouble. Sister Marie, in charge of my wing, had probably knocked on my door, and found my room empty. Would she call the police? Or would everyone assume I had simply left? To my knowledge no one had ever done such a thing. Was it a sin? Probably. Everything in the old country was a sin. But so was suicide, and one more day in that dungeon would have killed me.

My breathing calmed, and for the first time I was able to pay attention to the countryside. A duck stood on the steps of a white-washed cottage. A bend in the highway, and ahead of me was a roadside Rupintojelis. I slowed. Christ sat on a wooden stool, bent forward, His elbow on His knee, His chin resting in his hand. I almost braked, then thought of having to remount, so I wound up steering with one hand and crossing myself with the other. If I went back to the convent, explanations would be complicated. And there wasn't a lie big enough to accommodate my being out of the habit and riding an alien gender's bicycle alone on the highway. I had about five hundred dollars in traveler's checks and an American Express card. I could drive the ten more kilometers to Olecko where there might be a hotel, or at least a camp-site for the fishermen who came to the lakes in August. In the morning I could dump the bike and catch a ride to Olsztyn. Everyone hitchhiked in this country of few cars. Surely at the Olsztyn airport I could buy a through ticket to Warsaw, then New York. A crazy idea. But who could stop me?

The red sun finally sank behind a row of pines. The twi-light air was a swamp, and I felt I was pushing the bike through flat water that fought every turn of the wheels. Pumping hard, winded, I crested a hill and discov-ered I was on top of a ridge. In the valley below lay a vil-

lage of fifty, maybe seventy houses. A steeple like the peak
of a witch's hat centered the ring of rooftops. A cluster of
lights shone from what was probably the churchyard. I
coasted down the slope. As I approached the town, I
smelled food—pork broiling on charcoal —and I thought
of the untouched chicken soup. From a distance I heard of
strains of accordion music, a four-four polka beat.

The sooner I headed back to the convent, if that was
what I was going to do, the better. The longer I was gone
the more exercized everyone would be. If I was serious
about Olecko, I had better make tracks. I couldn't
decide. I was too hot to be hungry. But if I didn't eat soon
I would collapse.

The dirt road leading into the center of town was lined
with log cottages. Figures of snakes and eagles were
carved in the wooden lintels above the doors. Storks had
propped their nests like raggedy brooms against chimneys. Some front yards were surrounded by low picket
fences, others by crisscross rails that you might see in
West Virginia. Colored lights hung on the overhead wires
strung from one telephone pole to the next.

I wove through foot traffic of families, teenagers holding hands, and old women wearing babushkas despite the
heat. Everybody headed toward the churchyard, where
fragrant smoke rose straight up. A sign hung on a
gate. "Zabawa." I propped the bike against the fence near
a Militia Mercedes and headed towards the dance.

The drummer and clarinetist sat on a platform. The
accordion player, pouring sweat, swayed at the micro-
phone, his instrument strap blazing sequins, his gold satin
shirt tucked into tight jeans; shades of Johnny Broz-
houskas and the Shackle Valley Tomcats. For a minute I
worried that I might seem out of place. But no one paid
me any mind. The dance floor was a wooden deck inches
above the grass. Ten or twelve panting couples dipped and
stomped around the wobbly planks. The tune sounded
like Pops's favorite, "Drink, Drink, Don't Be Stingy." (My
gigs as accordionist with Johnny taught me there are only
five polka melodies in the world; the rest are variations of

a theme.) Old women fanning themselves with paper napkins and watching the dancers sat on folding chairs and talked, making feeble grabs at the little kids darting like beetles through the crowd. One child stumbled behind the rest. Her head was too big for her body, and her straight black hair was too short. Bright ribbons and embroidery covered the yoke of her linen pinafore. The hem hung to her high-topped shoes. Each time she toppled over, which was every few minutes, someone scooped her up, kissed each cheek, then set her down among the other kids.

I headed toward the food. Red-faced men leaned over a huge metal cattle-feeding trough filled with charcoal. Sausages and rolls of zrazai broiled on a grill. Oblivious to the heat from the red-hot coals, people milled around sweating, shouting, waving sandwiches and pint mugs of beer filled from kegs beside the troughs.

"Pozhalweista."

"Zharko."

Russian phrases blended into the Lithuanian and Polish. A girl with frizzy blonde hair walked by wearing an art deco T-shirt of Bruce Springsteen's profile above the word Nuremberg. I inched behind the line leading to the table where there were platters of boiled potatoes and broken cabbage rolls, the heavy red sauce soaking into barley pearls.

The woman behind the table caught my eye. One hand rested on her hip. In the other she held a wooden spoon and stirred the flies over the babka cake. Every few minutes she counted the vodka bottles grouped behind the kasha. Forty, maybe fifty years old, she had short blonde hair teased at the temples, round cheeks and kindly blue eyes. But the sharp lines around her smile meant this lady took no lip. A linen jacket covered her flowered dress. Her short fingers were knobby as carrots; the knuckles swollen red. Those hands could knead Boba dough to silk, raisins and all. I pictured her tuning a tractor or hoisting fifty pounds of grain. "Battle-axe," Pops would have called her. Gaspodina: the kind of woman who wrings a scrub rag and it's bone dry.

Just then a white dog with a smooth shiny head, tongue dripping, plunked its front paws on the table, grabbed a perogie and took off. Too late, Gaspodina lunged at it with the spoon, then leaned back and laughed. I laughed too, for the first time in months, and all at once I was starving. A girl at the end of the table was collecting zlotys and tucking them under a rock in a cigar box. I reached for my wallet, wondering what, if anything, my dollars were good for, when something wet hit my leg and I yanked back my foot. The cashier screamed, and I looked down at the black-haired child. Her warm mouth—goodness knows why—was covering my ankle. Maybe it was fascination with the Nikes, the only ones I had seen in Poland. Her breath was hot on my leg; her arms held onto my calf for dear life. I tried to ease out my foot. A shout, and I caught the Lithuanian word "kicking," then a fist slammed into my back. I struggled to turn and free my leg at the same time.

"Zydowka," someone yelled. The music stopped. A tug on my backpack and I grabbed it to my chest. "Zydowka, Zydowka." The burly man with a meat fork crossed himself and spit. Where did he get the idea I was Jewish? Suddenly I remembered the Hebrew letters stenciled across the pouch. It hit me that no one who could save me knew where I was. My knees buckled, and I grabbed the edge of the table. Two teenaged boys, one swinging a lasso like a cowboy, walked slowly toward me, grinning. The white dog shot past carrying a poppy-seed roll. Nyet Zydowka, I was about to yell. Probably not correct grammar, but the truth and easy enough to pronounce. Yet the words wouldn't come.

The vice on my leg tightened. The teenager twirled the end of the rope. The other boy stuck his index finger in the air. "God forgive you," I shouted in English. I jerked my leg, but the child clung like a terrier. A young woman rushed up and knelt beside her. Frantically I looked for a break in the solid wall of people. The man with the meat fork took a step closer. The mother raised her head. My heart raced, and I shut my eyes. There was nowhere to run. My shoulders gave in, and I quit trying to pull back my foot.

Suddenly the mother burst out laughing. Everyone, including me, watched her carefully pry the little fingers off my leg. The realization that the child had singled me out, not the other way around, must have hit everyone at once. There was a collective intake of breath, "Ah, so," and the mother scooped up the child and disappeared. I slumped against the back of a chair. My hands shook, and my dry lips tasted like chalk. My tongue seemed swollen, and I wondered if I would ever swallow again.

Across from me, the Gaspodina, standing straight as a Greek palace guard, folded her arms over the front of her jacket, the spoon erect in her fist. I wasn't sure my knees would support me a minute longer, and for one odd minute I wished she were on my side of the table. I could lean against her arm, bury my face in that shoulder, sturdy as a lumberjack's. Her eyes narrowed as she stared me down. Then she lowered the spoon and pointed it at my throat. I touched the Sudova Cross on the chain around my neck. "Leituva?" she called over the cabbage and dill pickles separating us.

"Da. Amerikanskas," I replied. A breeze cooled my wet anklebone. Throats cleared. The man rolled the handle of the meat fork back and forth between his hands and turned towards the grill. The old women drifted back to their seats. The line leading to the food straightened as if a comb had been slowly drawn through.

"Gerai." Gaspodina spun around and shouted, "Gerai, gerai," to what was left of the crowd. She turned and waved the spoon over the swarm circling the cake and without looking up she said in English, "You hungry?"

Before I could answer, someone slid the chair under me, and I was holding a beer in one hand and a sauerkraut sandwich in the other. Then I was bombarded with paper plates of pickled mushrooms and hard boiled eggs. Two swallows and my beer mug was empty, then magically refilled. The sausage stung my mouth with black pepper and caraway seeds, and I chased it down with a tumbler of vodka someone pushed into my hand. Was the crowd atoning for thinking I was a Jew? Or for assuming I went around kicking little kids. Instinct told me if the Gaspodina thought I was Jewish I would be on the road so fast my head would spin. Apparently I had been judged innocent in spite of the backpack: the Cross proved mightier than the word. But what if no one had spotted the chain around my neck? Would I have gone on keeping my mouth shut if the heat got worse? A housewife at my elbow slid another slice of kugelis onto my plate.

Three short blasts from the clarinet, the accordion broke into the "Dear Bartender" polka and I was pulled onto the dance floor. "Amerikanski," a few yelled, and I spun in the grip of a smiling guy who was a dead ringer for Eddy Broncheck, quarterback for the Shackle Rockdusters. At first I moved stiffly. Having seen the devil in these people, the minute the music stopped I wanted to get while the getting was good. Except "Dear Bartender" drifted into "Helen, Helen, Helen," next into "In Heaven There Is No Beer." The booming beat pounded down my resolve. I forgot the bike beside the fence. The moon got fuzzy and the lanterns flashed bright red and yellow on faces shining with sweat. At the end of each stanza Eddy and I yelled "Hey," and the next thing you know, I was standing aside and clapping, hands over my head, while a few couples practiced the suktinis. "Chardaz," Eddy shouted, and his hands went on top of my shoulders, mine on his. Croatian-style we shook the makeshift deck until I thought it would collapse in sticks.

The world throbbed, and I was back in the Shackle Teamsters Hall, strobe lights spinning over accordion keys and lavender eye shadow. I smelled the Butchers wax from the floor, the steam-trays of kielbasa, the carnations grouped around the Tomcats' stage. Eddy's truck, a jacked-up four by four with spotlights mounted on the cab, would be parked behind the dumpsters. For the first time in a long time I thought of Eddy grinding out his cigarette in the dashboard ashtray, then pulling my head against his chest.

I forced my thoughts back to what I would do when I left the churchyard. Would I turn west towards Olecko, or head back to Suvalki? All at once the choice didn't matter. After months of exile I seemed to have been brought back to earth, at least to this deck, maybe any earth wherever it was. And belonging somewhere meant I belonged anywhere. Somehow, during the past hour, movement had put me in my place.

A downbeat, a roll of the drums and the chardaz turned into a waltz. This Eddy pulled me close. His shoulder was hard. My hand slid to the back of his neck, under his collar-length blond hair curly and stiff.

Just then a floodlight over the church door snapped on. Eddy stepped back. It took me a second to realize the music had stopped. I caught my breath and wiped my forehead on my sleeve. Eddy lifted my hand, solemnly shook it, then turned and vanished behind the orchestra. The accordion player was unfastening his instrument strap. The dance floor was still. The night settled around the chirp of the crickets and the drone of a plane above a distant field. A few people started toward the church. I stepped down from the deck. Gaspodina came up beside me and said, "You coming or aren't you?"

"To where?"

"It's a sin to be late."

"Not if I don't know what I'm late to."

"Sin anyhow."

I patted the strap on my backpack. "I'd better be off," I said and smiled.

"Don't be an animal," she said.

I motioned to the bicycle and inched away.

Gaspodina's voice was suddenly gentle. "She comes here for a reason. But how many bother to come see?"

"Who?"

Gaspodina's voice was brusque again. "And another thing, it has to be paid for." She raised her hand and quickly moved her fingers up and down against her thumb in a chewing motion. "Some of them just eat, eat, eat, then not paying."

The bike's fender shone under a street light. I reached for the pouch on my backpack. "I'm happy to pay whetever the food costs," I said.

Her cheeks flamed, her hand curled into a ball and for a minute I thought she was going to swing her fist into my stomach. "Pay respects." Her fist loosened, and she nodded at the church. "Don't be an animal," she repeated.

I had no idea what she was talking about. But I wasn't about to argue. I nodded. Gaspodina's face softened. "Being nailed down is no laughs," she said.

All at once I thought of the Mother General back in West Virginia, the convent in Suvalki. "Tell me about it," I said.

She shrugged and held up her palm, as if baffled by what I said, then motioned for me to follow her. I squinted into the spotlight. August 15 was a day of obligation and I might as well go to Mass (if that was what was happening) here as anywhere else. I'd never heard of a midnight service for the Feast of the Assumption. But I was never in the old country either, so I trailed behind her across the damp flat grass.

The rectangular church was shingled in wood. An octagon bell tower formed one corner. Behind the main wing, half a brick wall stood in the weeds. At first I thought an addition must have been dismantled. Then I saw the charred bricks piled behind the tower, and I realized the annex had been bombed.

Inside, the church floors and walls were rough-hewn planks. The white ash altar shone by the light of three High Mass candles on each side. Two fir sticks, tied together, made the Crucifix over the apse.

At first I didn't notice the funny-looking statue sitting far right of the altar above a tier of votive candles. As I trailed the line down the aisle, I saw that instead of turning before a pew, everyone filed past the figure, quickly knelt then circled back.

Our Holy Mother, Queen of Heaven, unvarnished, stood in a tree. The light was too dim to see if the oak was real, trimmed and sanded, or if the limbs were dowels glued into a trunk. Mary's feet were nailed to a branch curving over the candles, Her skirt a stiff round cone. Chisled V's simulated ruffles or jewels, or maybe bark. Her narrow pointed crown tipped to one side above long wavy hair. A shawl covered Her shoulders. In one hand She held a scepter of twisted snakes. I stepped closer. Cat-faced snakes with flat whiskers and flat ears. Her other arm was stretched out, and She held an apple in Her palm.

I found end space in a pew near the front. An old man slid aside to make room. He fanned the sweltering air with his kerchief. There were no kneeling pads, and my knees felt every splinter of the grain. The Gaspodina, a few rows ahead, crossed herself, then stood. Automatically I rose too.

At the convent a decision must have been made on to how to cover questions the mother house in Shackle would pose about my leaving. Any Vatican bureaucrat worth her salt can cover anything. I would find out how Sister Jagellonia soft-soaped the bishop when I got back to the States. It occurred to me that as an American I had leverage. My complaints could make Sister Jagellonia look bad. Raise questions about Suvalki's compliance with Vatican II, about adherence to the concept of the exercise of free will among religious in the apostolic orders, about the convent's plumbing and low-fiber diet. Why should I lose credit for the course work I had almost finished? I shouldn't be afraid to go back to Suvalki. Other than order me to pray twenty Hail Marys to strengthen my commitment to obedience, there was nothing Sister Jagellonia could do.

A young blond priest swept down the aisle, then moved through the familiar motions. He read the Gospel in soft Polish. The Gaspodina knelt, her rosary dangling from her fingers. I reached for the marbles at my waist and realized they were gone, belt and all, and I felt naked. The Gaspodina's thumb slid the next bead along the chain. At the sign of peace, the man beside me patted the back of my hand. His face was small, round, and wrinkled as dried fruit.

All at once the congregation grew tense. The baby in the back pew stopped fussing. Not a cough, not a rustle. A strong chilly wind whipped through the vestibule, and the candles jumped. For the first time in days my skin cooled, and I took a deep breath. A whispering sound, and all heads turned to the statue. The hem of the Holy Mother lifted an inch, then settled. Father whirled to face the altar and dropped to his knees, prostrate, his forehead pressed on bare wood.

My knuckles whitened around the curved armrest. A stronger gust and Her skirt rose, billowed, twisted, then rested at Her ankles again. I grabbed the back of the pew in front of me. The man beside me leaned forward with a slight smile on his face like a proud grandfather "Zabawa,". he whispered.

And She could have been dancing, crown almost slipping off, balancing the apple in Her hand. My eyes burned. I touched the lashes that were still there. The third gust blew the coldest of all. A strand of wooden hair brushed Her shoulder. A votive candle died beneath her heel. My hands were too weak to grip the pew any longer. I was too tired to think, as if the breeze that lifted Her shawl had gathered up my will and turned it into air, and I was free.

Slowly the room grew warm again. A few bodies stirred. Without looking around, as if he knew what was happening behind him, Father rose, turned to the congregation and spread his arms wide. We stood. The Mass resumed.

It seemed everyone took Communion. I never could have made it to the altar. Then I thought of the sausage and realized I couldn't accept the Eucharist anyway. What about the others? That was the least important question going around in my mind. I rested on my knees. My breathing calmed. Peace, a feeling almost forgotten, settled inside me like a bird folding its wings. I would not have been brought here if God hadn't cared to set me free. And when you came right down to it, His caring was all that mattered. Not the Order, not the Rule, not ten thousand Mother Generals. What difference did it make if I left Suvalki, left the Order, my life was His wherever I was, wasn't it?

The service was over. Most walked up the aisle with downcast eyes, some smiled. A large man with a blond beard carried the black-haired child. She slept, arms dangling at her sides, mouth open, her heavy head on his shoulder.

Outside, a mist, not yet rain, slicked the church landing. Cicadas buzzed in the bushes along the bombed-out wall. The spotlight shone on the women wrapping leftover food and stuffing trash into garbage cans. The accordionist was unscrewing the tripod under the snare drum. I caught up with the Gaspodina, who was loaded down with two string bags and a paper sack. "Did you see?" I asked. "The wind, I mean?"

"Who's seeing wind?"

"I have the feeling it happened before."

She stopped to shift the sack to a better position under her arm. "Sure. Once a year, every year, for three, maybe four hundred." An old woman tapped her on the shoulder. She smiled, turned back to me.

"What does it mean?" I asked.

She nodded at a man who passed us pushing a baby carriage. "What does what mean? Zabawa."

"It means—" Gaspodina tightened the cord of a string bag around her wrist. "It means that today is August 15."

"Zdractyuite," a man shouted, and from the road I heard engines kicking over.

Near the entrance, she turned. "You living here?

I pointed to the bicycle a few feet away. "I came down from Suvalki."

"George," she yelled at a man heading towards a beat-up Moskvitch. George waved. "You know him?" she asked me.

"I'm afraid not."

"That's funny. He's from Suvalki, too." She walked over and touched the bike's tire with her toe. "Some beauty," she said. "Strong as ox."

"It's pretty old," I said.

She pointed to the rack over the rear bumper. "Was built for logs."

I drew my finger over the metal rungs. "It's not all that big."

"Has to be," she said sharply.

George was unlocking his car door. I looked up from the rack and on the spur of the moment shouted, "Hey, is there room for one more?"

He turned, shrugged and held up his hands. I pointed to his car, then to me and shouted, "Suvalki?" He nodded and motioned for me to come on. I pulled the bike from the fence and turned it to the Gaspodina. "Take it."

Her eyebrows rose.

"It's got a few years left."

Before she could answer, I ran to George's car and stuck my head in the passenger window. "Siluva convent?" I didn't have to shout. George smiled as if he knew where I was going.

Three false starts and the engine roared. George made a U-turn in the dirt road and we rattled past the churchyard gate. I looked back. The white dog was sniffing the tops of the Gaspodina's bags, which were on the ground. The last I saw of her, she was holding up the rear of the bike with one hand and squeezing the tire with the other, checking for air.

The convent was quiet when I got back. The next morning I told Sister Jagellonia I had gone out where it was cool and would probably do so again. Any difficulties this caused could be settled between the bishop and the mother house in Shackle. From that day on, I knew I was free. Free to come, free to go.

The village, I found out, is called Oblinsky. From time to time I trace the road from Suvalki to the dot on the map. Each time, my heart stops along the path. I hear the bike chain clanking, around and around. I smell chickens. Sometimes the accordion strap glitters behind my eyes. Sometimes the man with the meat fork stands like a czar, and the black-haired child rolls on the grass. Most of all I remember wood. Carved eagles, snakes, split-rail fences, pine crosses flayed of bark. A long spoon like a wand waves above the birches, straight in silver rows along the dusty road.

CHAPTER

4

I forced my thoughts from Oblinsky and back onto Father's reading from the lectionary. A gust of wind brushed my neck. I turned and saw Manny Giglianno lurching down the aisle and stepped aside to make room. His oily black hair was tied in a ponytail and his skin, pitted as an orange, shone from either rain or sweat. Tall, burly, he moved like a barge pushing lumber upstream, pews bobbing in his wake. I insisted that each Catholic resident at the Mission attend at least one week-day Mass a week; otherwise wild horses couldn't have dragged Manny to St. Stanislas. His job was to deliver lunch to the men's shelter on the other side of town. Afternoons he went to high school equivalency class. He valued his free mornings, telling me he went to the library, probably Gobetsky's video outlet.

"You're late."

"No shit," he said. In spite of his chronic rage, I believed down deep there was good in Manny. He was a hard worker, once you got him going. His only problem was he was simply a slave to whatever made him crazy to shoot up, blow, or wash down any fool substance he could get his hands on. Stella argued that my judgment of people was too generous—"all wet" were her exact words. Not true. Before assuming court-appointed cus-

tody of Manny, I had set conditions: school, work, no
dope. He didn't like it? He could serve the time in the
Monongahelia Correctional.

Father Kozakas lifted the chalice. Silver daylight,
lighter now, softened the rim. The air smelled of damp
wool. A cough echoed across the aisle, and Manny's
sleeve brushed my arm. The usher glided alongside the
pew. Manny's eyes were shut. "It's our turn," I said. He
shook his head, and I inched around him and into the
aisle. Father stared over my head as he placed the wafer in
my palms.

I had not confessed to Father Kozakas that I was leaving the Order: practical considerations. The bishop had
assigned the senior priest to minister to the older Ger-
mans, Polish, Czech, Slavish and Lithuanian members of
our congregation. Father himself had emigrated from
Kolensburg in the late seventies. Hard of hearing, his bat-
tle with English was a lost cause, and I preferred not to
shout my transgressions three or four times for the benefit
of the audience outside the confessional. The Jesuits in
Port Shirley came down once a month to help our under-
staffed parish. Last Saturday Father Morella, who wrote
liberal op-eds in "Faith-Style," was scheduled to hear rec-
onciliations, and I had joined the crowd in the front pews
and waited my turn.

"Bless me, Father, for I have sinned. My last confession
was two weeks ago." I proceeded with my dreary list of
shortcomings: three incidents of unfair anger at Stella, one
lie to Rabbi Finebaum as to why I missed his Interfaith
Workshop, twice I had been abrupt on the telephone with
Sister Silesia, once I thought an impure thought while
watching television.

"Did you turn it off?"

"It was near the end anyway."

"Anything else?"

"I'm a religious and am thinking about requesting dispensation from my vows."

The   shadow   behind   the   curtain   did   not
move. "Why?" Father's voice was calm.

My answer had been carefully rehearsed. "I feel isolated and alone. Miserable. I can't stand it anymore. I suppose that's included in what our Order calls incompatibility of temperament."

I paused, waiting for him to ask the name of the Order. He didn't.

"It's the worst of two worlds. The others share what they call a spirit of community. I feel miles apart, yet stuck with the same rules. In fact, being alone is less lonely than when I'm with them.

"Perhaps a transfer."

"It's over. It's over, that's all. But my commitment to God's mission for social action hasn't changed. I'll still work among the poor."

Somehow, I sensed his approval of my response, and I went on. "Looking back on it, I probably took vows for the wrong reasons. Maybe I wanted a family. And when I joined one, I found out I just wasn't suited for family life. Ordinary reasons, I guess. But I've been struggling with them for months."

"Have you discussed this with your superior?"

"Not yet."

"What will you do if you leave?"

"I've accepted a job—I'm a social worker—in another county."

I heard his sharp intake of breath. "So. You're not thinking about a request, you've already decided."

"I suppose, yes. Last year in Poland, the Holy Mother—I received a special grace—." Father coughed and a sixth sense told me he was suddenly impatient. "I know there's a line outside."

"Get to your superior. Handle the arrangements as best you can. Pray for guidance."

He gave me absolution, and I said my penance, two decades of the rosary, before I left the church. I was relieved by his matter-of-fact acceptance. Yet I felt cheated. As if my leaving made no difference to him, or to the world, one way or the other. And I could guess his thoughts about my reference to Poland. Just another hysterical nun; another fantasy of a Marianist revelation.

Father Kozakas worked his way down the last row of communicants standing before an invisible line where there should have been an altar rail. Back at my pew, I remained on my knees, my tongue pressed against the roof of my mouth until the floury, slightly vanilla taste of the wafer was gone. At this moment I was perfect; strong enough to avoid the next occasion of sin, as I had promised in the confessional. An illusion, I knew from experience that sacramental grace wore off as the day wore on. Within hours, venial offenses, chronic imperfections would breed like germs, and I would be reinfected. I stood and coiled my rosary back in its case.

Manny, zipping up his camouflage jacket, was waiting for me in the vestibule. Side by side we walked into the warm wind. "Better make Pavel put them new radials on the van," he said. Something in the tone of his voice led me to believe he was looking for trouble.

"Can't you?"

He tapped his chest with his thumb. "I drive, see?"

"Let's step on it. I have to check lunch trays, be at the mother house at one."

"I need to talk to you."

"Walk at the same time."

He strode a few feet ahead of me, hunched forward, hands jammed in his pockets, talking over his shoulder. "I drive the van, lug Stella's shit up and down the cellar steps—"

"Watch it."

"While Pavel don't do diddly-squat."

"As of this afternoon, he'll be a carpenter's trainee with Graziano Home Improvements."

"Beautiful." Manny kicked a Styrofoam cup into the gutter. "Like Jesus, man."

"Don't be irreverent."

The Mission had yet to civilize Manny. Meaning my idea of rehabilitating street people by simulating a family environment was turning out to be a colossal bust. In spite of my case-management plan, counseling, the Say

No Support Club—the essence of Manny hadn't changed one iota.

His voice changed to the falsetto whine I repeatedly told him I couldn't stand. "Ol' Pavel tells everyone he's this artist, and you go ape."

I started to defend myself, then realized it wasn't worth the effort. Besides, maybe it was true, as Stella said, that I wrapped Pavel in cotton. But she was as bad as I was about trying to make him eat and get more fresh air so he could go a night's sleep without pills. "I doubt if he could handle a jack."

Manny spit over a fire hydrant. "You never figured if I could work the chain saw on them dead pines. Or if I could—"

"I hear you." I hoped I didn't sound as defeated as I felt. I had probably betrayed Manny—in his eyes, anyway. "I'll ask Pavel to do the snow tires." A hint of light polished the red dogwood leaves, then the sky went darker than before.

Manny got to the kitchen door a few steps ahead of me. "Why's the ladder out here?" he asked. Whiffs of ammonia drifted across the back porch.

"Shut that before I'm an ice cube," Stella yelled from inside.

I closed the door behind me.

"Holy shit, look at the thing on the wall," Manny said, pointing to Stella's banner.

"Button the lip." Stella was filling a bucket in the sink, her face blurred by the steam billowing from the spigot. A barricade of chairs blocked the doorway between the kitchen and dining room. "My wax is turning to shine," she said. "Meanwhile, everyone in the kitchen."

Pavel, in the far corner of the room, was lifting the seed bowl from the canary's cage. The caterer had delivered on time, and Igloo chests piled on carts took up most of the room. Every morning Stella set aside fifteen for the congregate meal and fifty for Manny to load in the van. If Manny ran short, which rarely happened, Stella fixed box lunches of whatever we had on hand. Monday was a cold-food day. I opened a chest, took out a container, and lifted the plastic lid. A mound of chicken salad held down a lettuce leaf. Apple sauce that might have been homemade filled one section, the other contained a buttered roll. Not bad. Except the hard rolls would be difficult for the old people to chew. I would call the caterer.

"Any bacon left?" Manny shouted above the whine of the tap.

Stella turned off the water. "Breakfast is over." She followed my eyes to the skillet. "I fixed myself a few eggs, that's all. And Sister—"

"Domingo's not eating," Pavel interrupted, closing the cage door. "The seed was hardly touched."

Pavel's eyes seemed more swollen and bloodshot than usual. His dry blond hair, thin at the temples, feathered to his collar, and it seemed no amount of Stella's kugelis put color in his cheeks. His vocational counselor had lined him up a part-time job, and for his first half-day with Graziano Builders, Pavel had dressed to the teeth. The shoulder seams of his turtleneck hung to his elbows; pleated pants hung like overwashed drapes from his fake alligator-skin belt. The boy always seemed sickly although doctors said physically he was fine, stabilized on Haldol, schizophrenia having nothing to do with his not gaining weight. Reason told me the two were not related. Yet in my heart I felt if he could skip the drug for one day, swing a pick in the hot sun, come home sweating, and sit down to a rare steak and a cold beer everything inside him would shape up.

"Try lettuce," I said.

"No go." Pavel stuck his finger in the cage and moved it up and down. "Little guy's hungry."

Manny sat on a stool and rolled soft white bread around a slice of lunch meat. "So keep your flesh from his food."

"He likes me," Pavel said.

"Mr. Le Clair hasn't come down for his Sanka," Stella said.

"Go wake him," I said.

"I pounded and pounded on his door. No use. Something's wrong."

"The bird wants your Hartz Mountain," Manny said.

"Kiss off," Pavel replied.

"Take a minute," Stella said. "Open Vinnie's door, just a crack to check."

"Maybe he went out," Pavel said.

"Conked out on booze," Manny said. "He ripped me off for ten bucks last night."

"What's all this?" I asked.

Manny's singsong voice again. "What feeble-mind here means is Vinnie won a few rounds of poker."

"Knock it off," I said.

Orange-cat crept to his Nine-Lives beside the sink. Stella paced between the stove and the table, slamming down a salt shaker, the napkin holder she never filled.

"Hello in there." Viola Travis, the self-appointed leader of the Meet-and-Eat Club, stood on the dining room side of the barrier and held up a watering can. "I come early to wash the African violets." Mrs. Travis never set foot from the house without wearing a hat and shoes to match; a tall gray-haired woman with, Stella said, airs.

Stella hurried to the barricade.

"Your floor's bone dry," Mrs. Travis said. Stella lifted a chair and marched into the dining room.

Her head tipped back, Mrs. Travis pointed to the banner. "Imagine, all that fancywork."

Stella returned for another chair.

The room was closing in on me. I turned to Manny, "Let's load the van before the old people get here."

"Sister," Stella said quietly. "Vinnie, please."

If it wasn't one thing, it was another. Every day an aggravation; dissension in the self-help parenting group, weevils in the commodity flour, the Busy Bees ripping off Magic Markers. Not to mention the city inspectors prowling the basement for reasons to rescind our four-person board and care permit, finding new reasons to reject my application for a license to shelter twelve. "I'll get the key and go upstairs."

"Check the setup for the eaters on your way," Stella called after me.

In the dining room I paused beside the table, its center-piece of paper flowers and a Dixie Cup at each plastic knife. The kerosene-and-rubber smell of the vinyl table-cloth had never washed out. Newspaper covered the side-board. Paper bowls filled with sugar and coffee whitener flanked the twenty-cup urn. Somehow, the harder Stella worked, the more pathetic the room became.

The front door slammed. That would be Mr. Stotler's daughter dropping the old man off on her route to the IGA. She would pick him up after lunch. Sure enough Mr. Stotler, wearing a sweater with a golf club on the breast pocket and chino slacks pressed knife-sharp, leaned over his walker.

"Good morning," I shouted.

He smiled. His daughter knew one of us at the Mission would watch out for the old man whose mind was some-where else. Like the object thrown from hand to hand in the children's game Hot Potato, Mr. Stotler was tossed from his daughter to me, Stella, Mrs. Travis, then back to his daughter. I led him to a chair and wondered who would be holding his arm last.

He tugged at the sleeve of my blouse. "Bingo?"

It took me a second to catch on. "Not today, Mr. Stotler."

"Busy Bees?"

"Monday's Oldies But Goodies."

He shook his head sadly.

My office, a corner of the ballroom partitioned off, sported worn parquet floors and tall windows facing the parking lot. I rummaged for the key to Vinnie's room. The front door slammed. I looked outside and watched Pavel shuffle across the lawn toward the bus-stop. The driver of the Senior Overland van tapped his horn and inched the mud-streaked Volkswagen as close as possible to the front walk. The door slammed again, and I heard footsteps in the hall. Mrs. Travis's voice carried above the chatter of the noon crowd.

The shower-curtain key-ring wasn't in the desk. One of these days, I'd organize a key set-up, one like Pops's. He had hammered nails into a two-by-four, each key having its own nail and code number painted underneath. Funny thing, when it came to details, Pops tuned his days like a German mechanic. I paused at the open file cabinet drawer. Only he had been arrested. So when it came to his whole life, not just the details, he took chances, ground gears, had missed a downshift and blown his head.

The shower-curtain ring turned up in the accordion folder of Area Agency reports. I hurried to the stairs, not so much anxious about Vinnie as to avoid the opening ceremonies. Too late. The piano bench scraped linoleum and Mrs. Travis struck the first tinny chords of the "The Star-Spangled Banner." At least I would be on the second floor by the time she tackled "rocket's red glare."

I knocked on Vinnie's door. "Mr. Le Clair?" I jiggled the doorknob, then listened, hearing only the anthem. Reluctantly—I hated to invade his privacy—I shoved the key into the lock.

A warm breeze whipped through the window, the plastic curtains blew straight in. My shoulders tightened. Vinnie, there, stretched out on the bed. I stepped closer. "Mr. Le Clair?" I stepped back. Blood on his temple, over the stem of his aviator glasses, had dried on his cheek, the pillowcase, and on the Shackle *Star-Democrat* on the floor beside him. He must have fallen, maybe suffered a stroke. Then I looked around the room. Someone's rage had been left behind in the overturned nightstand drawers. Loose change, a Band-Aid, a Louie L'Amour paperback, lay scattered around a lamp on its side. The shade had rolled a few feet away.

"Put your arms around me honey, hold me tight."

The singing drifted from downstairs. I stared at the blood-stained gilt lamp. The bulb rested on a leather slipper. I went to the bed and touched Vinnie's wrist, then braced myself to pick it up. The skin felt cold and stiff, no pulse. I raised his glasses. Wide-open brown eyes stared straight ahead. I quickly dropped the glasses in place and walked backwards until I bumped into a chair.

"When you look at me my heart begins to float."

The voices came from the floor.

"Then it starts a'rockin' like a motorboat."

Vinnie's room was directly above the plywood table. Outside the dining room was the new fire escape, a ladder ending at a landing a foot from this room. Maybe someone had broken into the house and hurt—no. My mind struggled with the word—murdered Vinnie. But that's silly. People I know aren't murdered. A burglar? Maybe Vinnie had a what—cerebral hemorrhage? How would a criminal have broken in? Simple. My open door policy. The Mission was kept unlocked all day. Or anyone could crawl through a window. I couldn't even keep keys in one place, let alone remember to latch screens. I should have been more conscientious about security, had dead-bolts installed.

Fingers shaking, I leaned and for some reason felt the bulb. It was slightly warm. Then I jerked my hand away. On TV the police always say don't touch anything. I had to call them. And Father Kozakas. My mouth went dry. What on earth would Mother Silesia say? I went to the door, then looked back.

Vinnie was live dead, not dead dead the way they are in funeral homes. Just the same old Vinnie, straining at his clothes like a legume trying to burst its pod. My vision blurred and I almost saw, or did I see, him slowly shake his head, his frown darken behind those glasses? Then all at once I was seeing myself through his eyes.

Whatever got through to me, came in through you, Vida Zedonis. Through you and the flaw in your character.

CHAPTER
5

The police hauled Vinnie off bundled in a green plastic
bag zippered up the front, locked the door to his room
and sealed it with library tape. But only after they kept me
sitting in there beside the open window, answering the
same questions again and again, shivering. Lieutenant
Kalisky asked me three times, in a voice he would use on
a four-year-old, to describe the room as I had found
it. When I happened to refer to this as the first day of Vinnie's eternal life, Kalisky glanced at the ceiling, then at his
watch. I could tell he was thinking, spare me the Mother
Teresa types, saving the world to put themselves on the
map. So I wasn't about to give him the satisfaction of a
smart remark. Besides, I had his number. Judging from the
thickness and width of the bulge in his sports coat pocket,
the lieutenant was a Copenhagen man. Down the mines,
it was strictly no-smoking, so the men carried chew-
tobacco. Every kid in the Shackle Valley could guess the
brand from the outline of the can. Despite the Harris
tweed jacket, Kalisky was just another miner working his
way up.

It was going on one o'clock; I sat on the edge of my
bed. Kalisky had hinted that maybe Manny or Pavel had
had something to do with Vinnie; typical police reaction,
kids with records assumed guilty until proven

innocent. But when I asked him flat out, Kalisky said no one would know anything until the autopsy.

It would probably be a good idea for me to speak to Manny and Pavel, for that matter, Stella too, a gather-the-wagons-around-the circle talk. Control. It was crucial that I get a grip on what was going on and hang onto it. Meanwhile, how was I going to explain Vinnie to Mother Silesia? I had put off calling her until after the police left and I knew whether I could make our meeting on time. This wasn't the best day to spring my resignation, but even she would have enough common sense to reason that a decision like this had to have been a long time in the making. Pops busted. Vinnie in a Hefty bag. The day was only half over, and I was wiped out. Dealing with police, Father Kozakas (who reminded me I had to return the pickup I borrowed to visit Pops), Vinnie's niece in Port Shirley, and Bishop Crumrine's office. Everything in my day-at-a-glance calendar: the parents' group, the well-baby clinic, my talk at the Hadassah Roundtable, had had to be cancelled. I heard myself ordering Manny to empty the cat box and ordering the police technician to wipe the fingerprint dust from the footrail of Vinnie's bed. All this while the real me, the shadow, was curling over baseboards, climbing the walls. I took a deep breath and reached for the telephone to reschedule the meeting with Mother Silesia.

Sister Arnette, the secretary, answered, "Peace in Christ, Sister Vida." Sister, an Italian girl from Clarksburg, was quick to accommodate, impossible to please. Now her voice was tense with excitement. "A man from the *Star-Democrat* was here and talked to Mother Silesia. She said someone died upstairs at St. Michael's."

Tell me about it. "Apparently a breaking and entering," I said, slipping off my shoes. "Bishop Crumrine's been informed."

A sharp intake of her breath at the name Crumrine. What Sister didn't know was that I had merely left a message with Brother Dominec, the bishop's public relations secretary, saying there had been an accident, but that everything was under control.

"May I speak with Mother Silesia?" My stomach felt uneasy. I hadn't counted on anyone getting to her before I did. "I can't make our meeting at one."

"She's still to lunch with the Spirit of Renewal Committee."

"In our cafeteria?"

I could hear the smug smile in Sister's voice. "Their monthly meetings are always, always at the Holiday Inn." Sister was actually telling me that if I weren't living apart from the community, doing my own thing, I would know exactly where and when the Committee met. And yet her uncharitable attitude wasn't entirely her fault. She was expressing the resentment the Siluva clerical and housekeeper sisters felt toward the professionals. All Siluva work was supposed to be equal in dignity and in worth. Yet our Order had lost the spiritual glue that bonds a religious community together and helps it transcend petty differences.

"Please, Sister, look on her calendar if she's free at say, four." While I waited for Arnette to go into Mother Silesia's office I listened to Hank Williams, Jr., coming from the portable radio Sister Arnette kept beside her typewriter.

"There's the Diocesan Retreat Reorganization Seminar followed by a dinner."

"Three?"

I heard the rustle of paper. "I'll put you down. What's the meeting about?"

My mind went blank. "Catching up."

"If Mother General should need a background file?" Sister was pushing hard. "I mean, what if the Mother asks me why—"

"Tell her long-range planning for the Mission."

Sister sounded disappointed, said good-bye.

The room was getting warm, and I started to take off my sweater, changed my mind, leaned back against the headboard and swung my feet up onto the bed. Noon sun lit the pattern on the brittle silk wallcovering. Long before my time, this attic had been a nursery. Faded lambs, round and white against a pink field, jumped over pickets, each front hoof an arrow pointing to the tail ahead. Their eyes, black dots inside white dots, stared me down, hundreds of them, crazed. Vinnie's eyes wide open, black. I struggled to my feet—too fast—and steadied myself against the nightstand and focused on the pencil holder on the desk, a juice can painted red by a Busy Bee. Soup, maybe tea, something hot might settle my stomach. I waited until my head cleared and opened the bedroom door.

Downstairs, Manny sprawled on the living room sofa, his Walkman taking up most of the cushion beside him. The TV set in the corner was on, but his eyes were closed. He wore earphones and was banging his fist on the armrest. LaVerne Ray, the Mission's stay-in-school receptionist, leaned on the scarred library table reading a newspaper.

"Can you come into the kitchen?" I asked Manny.

"Why for?"

I nodded to LaVerne. "You too."

In the dining room a cop crept along the wall on his hands and knees. "I thought you people were gone," I said.

Sitting back on his heels, he rolled a tape measure around his fist. "I'm supposed to wrap things up."

I stepped over his clipboard on my way to the kitchen.

Stella was unloading the dishwasher. "You shouldn't have skipped lunch," she said. "You, on the verge of skin and bone. Let me fix your favorite cup of tea with canned milk."

"In a minute. First, please sit down." I pulled out a chair for her while Manny and LaVerne took seats at the table. I stood and rested my fist on the Formica.

"I wanted to get with all of you as soon as I could—"

"Pavel ain't here," Manny said.

"To fill you in on what's been going on. The police will be talking to each of you separately."

"He buttonholed me for a few minutes already," Stella

said.

I nodded. "We tell them the truth. Exactly what happened." I had mastered a firm, no-nonsense tone.

"So what did happen?" Manny asked.

"Vinnie passed away upstairs. He"—I crossed myself—"God bless his soul, liked to talk about his, let's say, accomplishments. It made him feel good to—" I searched for a tactful phrase.

"Shoot off his mouth about what a big shot he was," Manny said.

I winced. "Apparently someone, thinking there was cash, whatever, broke in. Vinnie woke up, there was a scuffle and—" I shrugged, tightened my shoulders and went on. "At any rate, a good part of this was my fault. I've been running this place on an open-door policy, not realizing the changes in the neighborhood or the increase, lately, of drug-related crime. This morning I called the Home Guardian people. They'll be out in a few days to do a security assessment and hook up an alarm system. Meanwhile—" I nodded to LaVerne. "every night after you leave, I'll lock up. I will be the only person here with a set of keys. Unless I'm out of town, in which case I'll leave them with Stella. If you're coming in late, ring the bell and the door will be opened from the inside."

Manny examined his thumbnail. LaVerne twisted the end of her permed ponytail around her finger.

"Got it?"

Stella nodded.

"I know what happened must have shaken up all of you. It certainly did me. But other than the locks, nothing has changed. We have duties; we have responsibilities." I felt like a football coach. The words sounded important, comforting, and I went on more for my own benefit than anyone else's.

"We must maintain self-control. Meaning no idle chit-chat about this. If anyone asks say what I just said. If you feel"—I groped for a non-threatening word—"troubled, I'm always available, as is Father Kozakas." I looked at each face. "Questions?"

LaVerne moved her chewing gum to one cheek. "Sister, you sure that's what went on with him? Like I was thinking it could a been a friend of Vinnie's, or—"

"Absolutely positive."

I was reasonably sure. But for purposes of control, it was best that everyone in the house grasp the party line and stick to it.

Chair legs scraped the linoleum. Manny, thumbs hooked in his belt, sauntered by. LaVerne skirted the table and shot out the door. My fist loosened, and I took a deep breath.

Stella resumed unloading the dishwasher, then looked up. "Now for tea?"

I took the kettle to the sink. "You have enough to do."

"You know that guy's thinking one of our boys hit Vinnie on the head."

"What guy?"

"The Polock cop with the pocket full of Red Man."

"Kalisky's no judge." I turned on the spigot. The kettle overflowed, the water glazing the sides. I closed my eyes. Horses slept standing up. Grackles slept gripping a wire.

"Sister, you okay?" Stella paused midway between the cupboard and the table.

I turned off the faucet.

"What could I say? Mention how everyone fought over card games? How—"

"Someone broke in. It happens."

Stella shrugged and shut the dishwasher door. "Another thing, I changed the Knights' meeting like you asked for. A problem. With one Knight it was no phone, another one was out. But we're on for tomorrow night."

"Any Little Debbies left?" I asked. "From the Busy Bees birthday party?"

"Cleaned out."

I set the kettle on the range and held the handle to gauge the instant the water boiled, knowing the whistle on the spout had the potential to shatter every bone in my skull. While I waited, I noticed the burners could use a scouring with Zud. The skillet on the back grid was up to the brim with soft white bacon fat.

Stella reached in the cabinet and rummaged through the cans. "Your Twinings' in here somewhere." She shoved aside a stack of IGA canned tomatoes. "Oh, brother."

"What's wrong?"

She held up a jar of Sanka with adhesive tape across the lid saying, "Vinnie's—Mitts Off."

The kettle whined, and I slid it onto the asbestos pad. "He swore by that stuff."

Stella shook her head sadly. "Now who's going to drink it?"

The orange frilly lid atop the brown jar seemed out of place, a cap on a dead circus bear. Stella studied the label, opened the jar and sniffed the coffee, then slowly screwed the lid back on. "Caffeine wouldn't hurt him."

Sometime this morning worry had become a substitute for reason. I could think only about what might be coming at me next. The jar of coffee for instance, reminded me that someone had better worry about the disposition of Vinnie's estate, lottery ticket stubs, old letters on mossy paper, and his Adidas bag filled with dusty shoes, no two alike.

Vinnie had been at the Mission three weeks, referred by the victims' assistance worker at the police station where he had been brought in sick and broke after his wallet had been ripped off. Vinnie, en route from Port Shirley to the Charlestown track, had decided to hole up in Shackle until he could shake his head cold. It turned out to be walking pneumonia complicated by a bad heart; a rocky liver aggravated by Sunrise gin.

"His niece, Cindy Le Clair, is coming down from Port Shirley to help sort his stuff," I said. "Although when you come right down to it, maybe it's easier if I just pack things in a box. The funeral will be up there. Cindy's shooting for Thursday morning." (Instantly I regretted the word). Shooting, a slip of the tongue.

Stella set the jar on the shelf, then brushed past me and

lifted the skillet. "Le Clair. Typical, those French. And where was this Miss Cindy," she asked on her way to the sink, "when her own flesh and blood shows up on our door, down-and-out, lungs full of cholesterol?" A flip of her wrist and the grease slid to the drain.

"Hold it," I said.

Stella, scraping the skillet, did not look up. "French, Schmench, I'm telling you the way it—"

"Grease!"

At least once a month the kitchen sink clogged, bologna rinds and tomato seeds treading water beneath the tap. A plumber's helper only sucked more coffee grounds into the mainstream.

Stella dropped the pan on the drainboard. "My mind was keeping off—" Her eyes reddened.

"Pour in dish stuff, quick," I said. The fat had already cleared the strainer. Bacon crumbs stuck to the chrome. I dashed from the stove and emptied the kettle into the pool of green detergent Stella squeezed from the bottle. "More." I turned on the hot water full force.

Stella stared into the soapsuds. "It's all my fault."

"I should have warned you sooner."

"It's everything that's my fault." Her voice shook.

"What are you talking about?"

"I mean my calling him Le Big-Shot, my kugelis without no-salt. Yesterday I broke up his poker game."

Her voice trembled. I noticed all at once her round cheeks sagged, squaring off her jaw. The lines around her thin lips were deep and shadowed blue. It occurred to me she was probably about the same age as Vinnie—as Vinnie had been. And anyone's death reminds us of our own. Only she wouldn't let herself think that way. Or would she? I had believed nothing could bring Stella, nerves-of-steel Stella, to her knees. My throat tightened. If Stella cracked, it was the end of the world.

"Hey, miss." The policeman sauntered across the room. "Got any chalk?"

"Not now."

He looked over my shoulder into the stainless steel

bowl. "What's happening, man?"

I spun around. He held his hands an inch apart. "This much to mark off with."

"There is no chalk."

He shrugged, then turned and pointed to the Knights' banner. "What's that a pitcher of?"

Stella started to say something, and I interrupted, "I'm sure you're in a hurry to go home."

He frowned. "I got them rooms to mark off."

"Those rooms," I shouted. "Say, those rooms, those rooms."

"Just what I said," he muttered, backing out of the kitchen.

Stella looked at me strangely. "I'll get your Twinings."

"You get off your feet." I put the kettle back on the burner.

"Frankly, I'm best off with you sitting down."

Truth be known, my knees were a bit shaky. I walked to the table, pulled out a chair and looked up at the wall clock that was always impossible to read. Chrome rockets swept through milky galaxies surrounding silver Roman numerals. Enrico, Vinnie's predecessor at the Mission, currently serving time for armed robbery, chose it from the Green Stamp catalogue. Enrico, Vinnie—now the front bedroom was vacant again. Which meant that tomorrow I'd better call the referral agencies. Another worry, "Would you say the big rocket's on the one?" I asked.

Stella nodded.

"I have to be at the mother house at three." When, I wondered, would this day be over.

"Sister?"

Something in her voice made me ask, "Now what?"

"Where there's Knights, there's vodka."

Wrong. Nothing would ever be over. Here I would sit a hundred years from now, old, older than Stella, older than Vinnie, while cocaine recidivists, Board and Care inspectors, well-babies, Mr. Stotler screamed, jumped over my head, tore down the walls and bashed each other over the head with the pieces.

"Vito's a big spender," Stella said.

"No alcohol in this house."

Stella poured my tea, then stepped back. "Listen."

"No way," I said. "Because you have to understand that abuse of a substance—"

"Stolnichnaya."

"—is exactly what the Mission's trying to wipe out. We can't say one thing and do another."

"We can shut the door."

"No."

Stella squinted down the spout of the kettle as if it were the barrel of a gun. "Then tell me how Knights are supposed to toast the Grand Master, the sacred oaks—"

"It's no model for the boys."

Stella looked up. "People aren't models. People are old men."

I stirred my tea with my fingertip. Was it possible for anyone to be this tired and live? "For heaven's sake, can't you have one meeting without liquor?"

Stella turned off the stove, then faced me and folded her arms across her chest. "You know what your problem is?"

I dropped the tea bag on a napkin and rolled it up.

"There's no play in your system," she said.

CHAPTER

6

I had a few minutes before leaving for the mother house. In my room, I opened the closet and pulled out the last vestige of the traditional habit, the black cloak for special occasions. I laid it on the bed, then went to the desk and opened the file drawer. One of the hanging pockets held a copy of the Order's Constitution, and I wanted to check the paragraph on what we sisters called an annulment. Under the regulations, vows made without full understanding of the commitment were void *ab initio* and a superior was under a high degree of responsibility to release a religious without undue question. I drew out the heavy leather folder embossed with the Siluva emblem—St. Michael and the dragon surrounded by three chains, obedience, poverty, chastity, linked together with hearts. The binder was empty. Where had I put the Code? I rummaged through the desk, then suddenly remembered the box of file stuff I had had sent to Suvalki last year, and that had never arrived. No big deal, Sister Silesia would have a copy. I swung the cape over my shoulders and looked around the room for the last time. The last time, that is, as Sister Vida Zedonis, SLS.

Afternoon light shimmered through the yellow blades of the walnut tree. A black spider was splayed in the center of a fantastic web stretched between a branch and a

telly pole. The ground was soggy from the morning drizzle, and I stepped over the maple roots swelling through
the sparse grass. I opened the door of the pickup, and
dried my hand on my hip. The convent was only a twenty-
minute drive. But being early never hurt.

Other than the regular Friday afternoon staff meetings
for our professional sisters serving in schools and nursing
homes (I was the one social worker), I went to the moth-
erhouse only on those rare occasions when Sister called
me in for what she referred to as a one-on-one. While the
motor warmed, I wiped the windshield with a napkin
from Hardee's. Sister would want to know the details of
Vinnie's death, then would pick my brain for how, exactly
how, Bishop Crumrine would twist the issue to fit his
agenda. And it would indeed be interesting to watch the
Bishop use Vinnie to augment his war against the Siluvas. I was almost sorry I wouldn't be around to see it.

Conflict between an Order and its diocese wasn't
unusual, but ours had a particularly nasty edge. The bishop was trying to kick our teaching sisters out of St. Elmo's
Academy, his fancy prep school. The diocese owned the
magnificent stone pre-Civil War facility. But the Siluvas
weren't about to give up their teaching rights in the institution our Mother Jadwiga founded a hundred years
ago. Crumrine needed big money, fast, to crank out *Faith-
Style*, his slick monthly magazine, stake his high visibility
"Missionaries in Place" program to convert the local Baptists, and to break ground on his cathedral which, to hear
him describe it, was to be one of the seven wonders of the
world. The bishop from California was blue-eyed, square-
jawed, and bald—the afflicted area being deeply
tanned. Nautalis Spas had perfected the muscles rippling
under his Italian-cut black suits. Just old enough to have
rubbed elbows with the brass of Vatican II, he was still
young enough to make cardinal if he played it right. All
he needed to triple St. Elmo's tuition, he said, were big-
name instructors to lure parents into choosing his school
over Choate or Philips Exeter. Our sisters made students
conjugate irregular Latin verbs and would flunk anyone's

kid at the drop of a hat.

Sister Silesia was no pushover. The bishop was no fool. He converted the teachers' lounge into library space. Sister partitioned the health room and put in a sofa, a vending machine and a microwave. Sister's financial backing had to come from somewhere, and since Crumrine had cut her overhead to bare bones, her only source was my federal money that ran the Mission. She had asked me to factor her hourly rate into the negotiated indirect cost agreement between the Order and the Department of Health and Human Services. Perfectly legal, providing she did indeed devote the percentage of her time to Mission affairs that I said she did. I never counted.

She would probably be discouraged about my leaving, another professional gone. And since I was the source of her leverage, my resignation would have a double impact. I could train someone else to work up the budget, except the Order's procurator had retired and I was the only one around who understood grantsmanship. My stomach tightened. There I was, doing it again, taking responsibility that wasn't mine. Not to be hard-nosed, but the Crumrine wars were Mother Silesia's problem, I had enough of my own.

Downtown traffic was backed up three lights at PAW's gate and didn't thin out until Old Cheat Furnace Road. The hot sun drew steam from the asphalt. On my right was the line of shoulder-to-shoulder six-limbed poles connected by snarls and loops of gleaming transformers enclosed by a twelve-foot-high Cyclone fence. A few yards away sprawled a new subdivision of modular starter homes. Why would anyone live next door to a city of wires, risk electrocution, cancer? Siluva Estates was written on the gatepost at the entrance. Twenty-five years ago the Order had sold the original mother house and the two hundred acres around it to Graziano Developers.

The old mother house was a mile down the road, and I slowed as I drove by. The long two-story wooden building, a replica of a convent near Warsaw, had been built around 1840, then auctioned off in the sixties when the repair bills were wiping out the Order's allowance for food. Once there had been ornate carving around the windows. But Graziano had sided the oak planks with canyon stone and replaced the window frames with Anderson inserts. Tubs of dead canna lilies sat at each end of the row of rain-streaked plate-glass doors. A square sign framed in naked bulbs—like a theater marquee—in the parking lot spelled out the names of the tenants in movable black letters: Century 21, Ramona Saharajee, D.D.S., Dairy-Mart.

Probably the sisters had done the best they could to hang onto the building. But after the Second Vatican Council ended in 1965, diocesan revenue to all religious communities started drying up. Instead of allowances adjusted for inflation, we were sent self-help technical assistance manuals: "Mobilizing State and Local Resources" and "Innovative Strategies for Garnering Support."

The new mother house, the only place we could afford, was the Ramada Inn that had been put on the market after plans for a mining theme park went defunct when a contractor in Charleston pocketed the Economic Development funds. The sisters bought the building for a song. By the time I came on board as a postulant, the ballroom had been converted into a cafeteria, and the lobby into a chapel. The bedrooms had been lowered to Siluva standards, meaning the motel's mediterranean-style dressers, mirrors and draperies had been shipped to St. Vincent de Paul. Stripped to the concrete block walls and cement floors, the rooms now captured the ambiance of an Alcatraz built by HUD. There was still conference space that could be turned into a library. But somewhere along the line we had run out of steam. I pictured a mother house that would always look like a motel. Then I remembered the softly weathered wood of the pre-Graziano convent. All at once it came to me that the transformation of the old building symbolized the transformation of the Order itself: both converted to another, shabbier use.

I pulled up beside Mother Silesia's Chevette. The gravel sparkled in the warm sun, and crackled underfoot. A soft wind swelled the hem of my cloak, and for one instant I was back in Suvalki. I walked to the edge of the clearing. Below me three counties spread over the mountains draped in mist. The Shackle sliced a chrome S between the hills, and two turkey vultures crisscrossed in lazy circles above the ridge. High on the bank over Number Six Lock sat St. Elmo's Academy, its chimneys on either side jutting above the gray metal roof like the sharp ears of a wolf.

I turned to the mother house. A tattered canopy flapped over the entrance to the lobby. The indoor-outdoor carpet covering the concrete walk had rotted into spongy islands of gray-green moss. I lifted a shred with my toe, and instantly the air smelled of a dishrag left wadded in the sink, galoshes forgotten behind a cellar door, of irresponsibility and neglect. I fought down a burst of irritation. All it would take was a putty knife, a hose, and a stiff dose of muriatic acid to clean up this mess. Where was Mother Silesia's mind?

The glass doors slid apart automatically—Ramada lives—and I found myself face-to-face with Sister Cleo tacking notices on the bulletin board.

"It's not three yet. So early for you," she said.

Once, only once, I had been late for a meeting. That had been the Liturgical Workshop Debriefing when I was a novice eleven years ago. I studied Sister's clear-skinned shiny face, her round silvery eyes empty as Christmas tree ornaments. Teachers and supervisors loved her. The best I could muster up was tolerance. To think of her as God's messenger, to show us the difference between blind obedience and commitment. She held up a notice. I walked over and read the dot-matrixed print aloud, "Autumn Renewal. A time to reap, to join in prayer and fellowship. Friday night cookout."

"In the cafeteria," Sister added.

I smiled and nodded, then all at once remembered the Knights' picnic. I had promised Pops I would be there. "I have another engagement."

Sister pushed a tack-pin into the corkboard. "You won't come?"

"It's not that I won't—"

"You have to."

I brushed past her towards the door to the administrative offices.

"Are you going to tell Mother General you won't come?"

"Why bother? You will."

I knocked on the knotty pine panel.

"I thought I heard your cute little truck," Sister Arnette called from behind the wall. The flimsy partition was about five feet high, yet every night the door was locked tight and double checked. I turned the tiny brass ball, the doorknob for a doll house. The whole place was a doll house.

Sister Arnette spun her swivel chair to face me and smiled. "You're too early."

"Was that Sister Vida's truck?" Mother Silesia called from the inner office.

"Go on in," Sister Arnette said.

Mother Silesia's office was labeled the Morgantown Room, another reminder of Ramada's occupation. She leaned over the windowsill and pumped the bulb of a plant atomizer. "I appreciate your coming early. Have a seat," she said without turning. I pulled an orange canvas director's chair closer to her desk.

On my left hung a framed poster of swirling African art commemorating the International Year of Women. Behind Sister's desk, another poster depicted a toad and was captioned, "I am an endangered species." An IBM-PC sat on Sister's desk. Manuscripts, presumably drafts of her revision of Butler's *Lives of the Saints*, were neatly stacked beside bookends, replicas of The Thinker, that held the Bible, Butler's of course, *Webster's*, and Volume "K" of the *Catholic Encyclopedia*. Sister aimed the nozzle at the underside of a leaf. "I heard about Mr. Le Clair," she said. "From Barry Grecco at the *Star*. What did Bishop Crumrine say?"

Sister Arnette worked fast. "I just told the PR secretary, you know, Father O'Reilly—"

"What?"

"That everything was under control."

I wondered if I should announce my leaving quickly, before we got into Vinnie, but decided not to risk starting off on the wrong foot. According to the protocol of the Order, a subordinate could not introduce a change in a subject being discussed with a superior until the superior indicated it was appropriate. Sister set the atomizer on the sill and faced me. She was slight and brisk. I had never seen her hair but imagined it to be blond, short and swept back Washington-style. Like most New Englanders, she had a sharp-featured, pointy face. "Why didn't I hear about Mr. Le Clair from you?"

"I was going to tell you as soon as I got away from the police and the Meet-and-Eat crowd."

She sat behind her desk and slowly pivoted her chair back and forth. "No one should have to run an outreach center single-handed. None of this would have happened if you had staff."

Maybe, maybe not, but I nodded.

She lifted a pen from a brass holder. "That is, if we had had staff to spare. Once we were hundreds spread from Pittsburgh to Buchannon, nurses, teachers." She looked straight at me. "Social workers. Now what? Twenty-nine. And that's counting myself."

"Perhaps our recruitment ads in *Faith-Style*."

She turned the pen slowly and said, "Relevance. I'm almost finished editing my video of our second Congress on Women Religious Empowered. When prospective applicants see us in action, they'll see relevance." She tapped the pen on the manuscript. "And even more relevance in this."

Sister always spoke of relevance as a cumulative phenomenon, like an antibody level.

"By the way, I'm calling my book *Saints Alive*."

"Terrific," I said. "How's it coming?" For years she had been working on Butler, an interpretation of the lives of the saints in contemporary terms, as she put it. Redeeming Word Press in Boston had given her an advance.

"Bad trouble with St. Katherine," she said.

"Of Sienna?"

"Alexandria."

I tried to remember my novice's course on virtuous paths. "I recall the wheel she was being tortured on blew to smithereens."

Sister waved her hand impatiently. "That's irrelevant. What's important is the basis of her unresolved frigidity. Also, why she converted those soldiers and why they got their heads cut off. Sublimated rage against authority? Or an ordinary castration fantasy?"

Her face tensed, waiting for my response. My first thought was, who cares? Then I wanted to shout, why are you trashing Saint Katherine? And our faith and our Order in the process, you idiot.

"I know what you're thinking," she said. "The tie-in with the emergence of the lesbian cultism that ravaged the Eastern Church."

I kept my face as expressionless as I could, reminding myself no one would read this nonsense anyway. All at once I recalled Pops saying, "If God was alive today, they'd break his windows."

"Why are you smiling?" Sister asked.

"It sounds like the work is coming along nicely."

Her shoulders straightened. "Do you think the movie should show the actual heads? I mean, them coming off?"

"No," I said. "But Hollywood will show it anyway."

For a minute she seemed pleased. Then she cleared her throat and shoved the pen back into its holder. "Now about Mr. Le Clair."

I downplayed Kalisky's probing. Sister asked if the newspaperman knew about the funeral arrangements. I said no, then told her about Vinnie's niece. "It was a day and a half," I concluded.

"The ramifications come next. The bishop's going to say that Mr. Le Clair's death proves conclusively that places like the Mission don't work."

Something in her voice made me wonder if she was the one who believed the Mission wouldn't work. She had a master's in public adminstration from Fordham. But I had assumed her interest in psychology meant she got the gist of our program.

She smoothed the top of her paperweight, a Lucite ball divided inside into sections of yin and yang. My mind groped for a transition, a few words to ease into my resignation, but she was only warming up. "The bishop won't hesitate to throw us to the dogs. The Bible-Belt types he's after will fall all over him when he says only family prayer and women staying out of the workforce will stop drug addiction. Not you handing out free room and board."

You? The strip of canvas bit into my back. Wasn't the Mission hers too?

Sister had just been elected Mother General when the bishop bought St. Michael's House from the United Way for one dollar. Probably the contingent of homeless who were threatening to picket the Archdiocese had something to do with why he took on the white elephant. He had immediately passed it to the Siluvas.

"The bishop is buying into the right-wing rhetoric," I said with a tone of finality, hopeful a clue for her to drop the subject.

"Except—" She outlined circles on the yin and launched into a complicated scenario. With Vinnie, the bishop had fodder, she explained. He could use it to stir up the department of licensing and inspection. Which would mean kissing my board-and-care permit goodbye along with my restaurant waiver for Meet-and-Eat.

What was she driving at?

She wound up saying, "He knows that means no more HUD, Eduation, or HHS money."

"The indirect costs you need," I said sharply.

She turned the plastic ball. "That's why damage control is critical. I'm going to contact all the media people I know, cash in my chips. You Sister, play up our success rate, the number of residents who've returned to the community and stayed clean. By the way, how many are there?"

I held up two fingers.

"How many passed through, all told?"

"About twenty."

"Ten percent. Play that up." Her eyes narrowed. "You're an effective spokeswoman. I want high visibility projecting the old Siluva standards: competence, stability and loyalty."

The timing for my announcement was getting worse.

She looked directly at me and spoke quietly. "Meanwhile, what can we do, Sister Vida, ourselves to improve our situation?"

Her tone was my cue to grovel, Siluva-style. Just as Stella and I had one litany, Sister and I had another. At this point in our dialogue I was supposed to name a shortcoming and vow to correct it. It could be anything—my management technique, failure to lock doors, lack of moral fiber—so long as my admission left me weak and humiliated, giving her license to do whatever it was she had in mind. I crossed my arms across my vest and said, "Why not throw the bishop a crumb?"

"You mean lower his level of aggression?"

I had changed the game, but to her credit she didn't miss a beat.

"Worth a try," I said. "Maybe you could get Sister Angela to agree to, say, giving that course he wants on the sociology of soaps."

I watched her drum her fingers on the blotter and pretend to entertain the idea. "Except soaps are so noninterpretive," she said. "Children—especially boys—must learn to interpret."

"You could tie each episode to a spiritual theme."

She nodded. "Make them relevant."

"They're ecumenical."

"Themes like the emptiness of materialism." Her voice was polite. "Retention of cultural values in a pluralistic society. Good thinking." She pushed the paperweight toward me and said shrewdly, "You know you're wasted in direct services. The procurator position is vacant. It would take maybe two days a week. Here at the mother house."

I sat back stunned with admiration. The perfect opening to get me under her thumb and she had grasped it. I was aware everyone in the Order thought of me as a loose canon. And Vinnie's death had reminded her how much autonomy I had. She could have been heavy-handed. But I was the only sister who understood funding, so she had to tailgate me without my minding.

All at once it struck me, how conditioned I was to the Order. Why was I bothering to observe protocol? I was on my way out. "I appreciate your confidence in me," I said. I took a deep breath. "I came this afternoon to request an indult of exclaustration."

The overhead light dimmed. The plants behind Sister seemed to wilt as if all the energy in the world had been gathered into my words.

"Oh?"

I folded my hands on my lap and looked her straight in the eye. "Incompatibility of temperament. I took vows not fully understanding the nature of a contemporary religious community. I made a mistake."

"Is there some, rather, a significant relationship with a person of another gender?" She asked quietly.

"No." Funny, I hadn't heard the word gender since the old country.

"A crisis of faith?"

"I'm at peace with my faith. I simply took vows not realizing I would be working in the present, but living in the past."

"What's that supposed to mean?"

She stared at me coolly while I delivered what I remembered of my speech. I had rehearsed an explanation for my leaving expressly for her. An organizational, impersonal, rational statement, protecting my feelings. The church was in a temporary period of reassessment and, for the time anyway, religious communities had been set aside. The Second Vatican Council was supposed to have brought about Christian renewal. Unfortunately, new had been constructed as glitzy public relations campaigns and high-powered lobbyists. Sister looked impatient when I reminded her how the homeless, the helpless went on suffering, and how apostolic communities—those of us ministering to the poor—went begging. From her expression I gathered I was saying what she did not want to hear, that the new church had no use for monasticism. I paused for breath, then said, "If the church no longer has a commitment to its own religious, how can we? How can I?"

Her face was granite. I knew I was talking too fast, but couldn't stop, which was probably why, at that point, I blew it. "We're irrelevant," I said. "Absolutely, totally irrelevant."

All at once she smiled and shifted a book on her desk. "Stress. A month or two at St. William's."

Her remedy for spiritual malaise was our retreat center in the Alleghenies run by a burned-out Jesuit, his love-beads hanging over his crock of macrobiotic soup.

"No."

The angrier a Siluva gets, the softer her voice. "Sister, I did not hear that *no*. I understand however, the strain of Mr. Le Clair."

"I had made up my mind before—"

"No one," she whispered, "could make a decision now."

I stood. "I know you'll want me to leave quietly. I have four weeks of vacation coming. I would appreciate your dating the papers to include them in the thirty-six months."

"What papers?"

It took me a minute to catch on. "You can't do that."

Her voice was calm. "Of course I can." She smoothed the blotter with her palms.

"The Constitution says those requesting release from their vows must be afforded consideration and justice."

"It also says if a religious leaves against the will and concurrence of her superiors the religious is excommunicated."

Everything in the room seemed to be melting, the green of the rubber plant oozing down the plastic-walnut sides of the assemble-it-yourself Montgomery Ward's credenza. The Thinker's elbow dripping over his knee. Excommunicated. I heard the word but could not believe she had said it.

"That means, Sister Vida, you will be denied the Holy Sacrament."

As if I didn't know.

"The Sacrament of the Dying," she continued. "You will not enter eternal life in a state of grace." She leaned back. "That means you will spend your eternal days in Hell." Her lower lip quivered. Was she suppressing a look of compassion? Or a smile. It occurred to me that she might be enjoying this, milking her power for all it was worth. I had never heard of a Siluva being banned from the church for leaving the Order. If it had ever happened, it would have been in the Dark Ages. I struggled to recall the wording in the Rule of the Order.

"Whatever language of excommunication there might have been in the old regulations was dropped in the early seventies when we revised the Constitution." I was bluffing.

"It was not dropped."

"Look, my copy was lost last year in the mail to Poland. May I see yours?"

Sister swung her chair around to face the plants, then back to me. "Having declared your intent, I cannot allow you access to the Code of the Order of Our Lady of Siluva."

She was right about no one outside the Order being allowed to see the Constitution. "But I'm still here."

"You could turn on your heel this minute and walk out for good." She tapped her chest. "I am the keeper of the word. And furthermore, Sister, you will make an appointment with Sister Rosemary in Charleston.

"I don't need a psychiatrist."

Her tone was patronizing. "She can prescribe something."

My face burned, and my knees shook. I wanted to sit
down but was afraid it would look weak. My forehead
itched, and I ran my finger around the cuff.

"Stop that."

I dropped my hand. "This is crazy. I can't be held pris-
oner so you can keep up a good front during the crisis
over Mr. Le Clair. And keep me pumping money into the
Crumrine wars—"

"The what?"

"St. Elmo's. I'll train a replacement. If we can agree on
a date."

She stood. "God speaks through your superiors."

I had marshaled all of my rational thinking into con-
trolling panic and desperation. Which was why I fell back
on intimidation. I stepped forward. "You're trying to play
it both ways, Sister, and it won't work. One minute it's
pop psychology and psychiatrists, the next it's medieval
dogma." I waited for her breathing to slow, then I spoke
carefully, my voice coming down hard on each
word. "You can't have it all."

She held up her hand. "This discussion is over. You will
see Sister Rosemary." She lowered her hand, reached into
her out-box, and pretended to study whatever was on
top. "Furthermore, I'm sending someone to St. Michael's
to assist you."

"Who?"

"Our Sister Cleo," she said without looking up.

I closed my eyes. Shit happens.

I opened them and studied the poster toad, enlarged
two hundred times, the endangered one. I forced myself to
smile slightly and to execute a civilized Siluva departure. I
asked for Sister's blessing. She gave it, we agreed to pray
for each other, and I left the room.

Sister Arnette leaned over the carriage of her Selec-
tric. "Have a good one," she said.

My hand was on the knob of the make-believe door
when Mother Silesia called out. "Sister Vida."

"Yes?"

"Why are you wearing the Siluva cape?"

I looked down at the soft black wool as if I had never seen it before. "I don't know," I said. "I honestly don't know."

I didn't stagger through the glass doors, but I felt as if I had. It took me a minute to adjust to the sunny afternoon. My mind was numb. Thoughts shot like the pins and needles when your foot, having been asleep, stirs. Excommunication. Unless I stayed in the Order, I would be out of the church.

The parking lot seemed enormous, and I wondered if I had the strength to make it across the vast plain of blazing stone. I had never known anyone who had been excommunicated. Do you get a letter? All I knew was that you did not get absolution. "Forgive me, Father, for I have sinned, I left my Order without sanction. You're telling me to go back? And if I don't?" I saw myself turning from the confessional without stopping at the altar to say the ten Hail Marys, or whatever penance. Saw myself at Mass the next morning, kneeling alone while everybody else filed down the Communion line. Who would take me in? Episcopalians? Surely Baptists. Only I believed in the Holy Spirit, the Holy Catholic Church, the Communion of Saints. People not knowing these words, say, Kalahari bushmen, can spend eternity in Limbo. But for those knowing, then deliberately rejecting the Creed, it was Hell.

The cape was soaking up the weight of the sun. I took it off and draped it over my arm, the whole time fighting the panic pounding in my chest. Someone to talk to. Sister Angela, the councillor and my spiritual advisor. I returned to the shade of the canopy and slipped between the sliding doors. Sister Cleo was emptying a wastebasket into a bigger wastebasket on wheels parked in the lobby. Suddenly I couldn't stand the mother house, not one more second of it. I spun on my heel and shot through the entrance, then forced myself to walk slowly to the edge of the clearing. A chain to stop cars from going over the hill was strung between cement blocks. A strong mild wind swung the links back and forth, one minute flashing silver in the sun, the next minute falling dull as old rope. I stared at the wild shadows and lights zigzagging over the red-dog chips.

CHAPTER

7

Back at the Mission I sat at my desk. "Hail, Mary, full of grace—" The prayer sounded like a poem recited by a third grader. What was I talking about? What was I asking for? Once it had seemed so simple. Was it unreasonable to want only to go on my own way? To be left alone; to serve God through good work and to live by myself in peace? It seemed such a modest want, sensible, unobtrusive. Mother Silesia had no right to block my leaving. The Magisterium of the Church was infallible, but administrative decisions made by mid-level clerics certainly were not. "She's wrong, I'm not. I control my own life. I'm not a slave to her mistakes." My heart pounded. "I'm walking out." Jesus overturning the tables of the moneylenders. "Send me a letter, anything you want. I can pray anywhere. God knows I'm right." I stood and swept a pile of paperclips, a few pens, and a box of unused bank checks into a folder. Then I went to the closet, pulled a suitcase from the top shelf and flung it on the bed. Trembling, I unlatched the locks, then suddenly realized this was a child running away from home. I shouldn't panic. Not yet, anyway. I would work this out step by step, go to the bishop, follow the paths of appeal. If there were any. But, above all, I had to keep a grip on myself. I was responsible for the Mission. The residents, the staff, so many depended on my judgment. I closed the suitcase and turned toward the closet, changed my mind and slipped the bag under the bed, knowing full well this was an act of blind faith. I had to believe that the day to pack would come—in its own good time, but soon.

Downstairs in the foyer, I stood beside LaVerne's desk while she pulled my messages off a spindle. A frail seventeen-year-old, she was well-intentioned but none too bright. Maroon-framed glasses and earrings the shape and color of apples did not compliment the acne spread across her cheeks. She received academic credit for her time at the Mission, thanks to Shackle High's Stay-in-School program. "I typed the budget revision format. It's five. Can I go home?"

"Yes, but leave the format on my desk." I sorted through my messages. Calls from agencies about referrals and meetings, a reminder from Father Kozakas to return the truck, an ex-resident wanting a job reference, I held up a yellow slip. "What time did this one come in?"

"About ten minutes ago. Sister Cleo said it was urgent." A pink bubble-gum balloon swelled from La Verne's lips. It burst, and she quickly resumed chewing.

I handed her the message. "Wrap that gum in this paper and put it in the wastebasket. Now."

LaVerne pitched the gum, and I turned her calendar and checked my schedule. "Tomorrow morning I'll be at my grandfather's who doesn't have a phone. The Mission will be closed Thursday for the funeral. The van's leaving for Port Shirley at seven, and I expect you to be with us. I have a visit at Chafin State Hospital Wednesday morning. Oh, and, LaVerne, tomorrow please call Mountain Greenery and have a plant sent to Mrs. Clotilda Grappo. You know her, she's in for surgery at Shackle General. Call for the room number."

"What kind of a plant?"

"Try to keep it under fifteen dollars. Have the card read from us at St. Michael's Mission."

"Yes, Sister," LaVerne said, inching towards the door.

"If you get calls, Meet-and-Eat as usual on Friday. I've

arranged for Meals-on-Wheels to cover emergencies. The well-baby clinic will be held Wednesday afternoon as usual.

LaVerne's attention span had been stretched beyond its limits, and I waved as she hurried into the vestibule. I lifted the stack of mail and started to sort the ads from the bills. But when I tried to read, the print blurred. Mother Silesia's words crept back. I took the letters to my office, dropped them on top of the budget, and went upstairs to lie down before dinner.

An hour later, Manny, Pavel, Stella, and I sat around the table in the residents' dining room, what used to be the breakfast room of the old house. Stella had changed the seating arrangement. Vinnie used to sit at the end of the table. Now his place was against the wall, and I was seated by the window where Manny used to be. Another spin-off of death, the filling of the space the person left behind, a spiritual vacuum causing subtle shifts in relationships to fill it.

"So Kalisky gives me the same question a million times." Manny affected his singsong voice. "Who can swear you never left your room Sunday night?"

"Stop that," I said.

His mouth full of bread, Manny looked up at me. "I ain't lying."

"That whiny tone."

"The cop's a trip," Pavel said. "He asks me how long I had it in for Vinnie? I go, 'You setting me up or something?' "

Stella stacked the empty serving dishes. "Better not talk smart to Mr. Kalisky. They have a mean streak, those Polocks." She pushed a platter holding two pork steaks towards Pavel. "Finish, please."

He shook his head.

"Ask me," Manny said.

Stella handed him the dish.

Pavel's face flushed. "What's Kalisky think I would have totaled Vinnie for? His bowling ball bag? What he calls his red-hot collector's item, a Lyndon LaRouche button?"

"Who's Linton LaRouche?" Manny asked.

I finished my helping of canned peas. Vinnie's death, the police, were taking their toll on the residents, too. Let Manny and Pavel gripe, get it out of their systems.

Manny looked at Pavel and raised his eyebrows. "Don't give me the dumb routine. Everybody knows Vinnie had more cash than he let on."

"That," I said, drawn into the conversation despite myself, "simply is not true. He was on the streets when he came to us."

"You never heard about the track?" Manny asked.

"Don't listen to idle talk."

Manny dug at the marrow from the pork bone with his index finger.

"Use your fork," I said. "You mean Shackle Downs?"

"Like the Preakness. He figured to parlay his win, see, into knocking down his next million at Shackle. Then buy a stake in Eager Beaver, the yearling that's going to win the Kentucky Derby."

I remembered the night I met Vinnie, drove him from the police station to the Mission. He could hardly catch his breath. I wanted to take him straight to the emergency room, but he insisted his asthma attack would blow over. He told me he had been the president of a tool-and-dye company in Jersey City that went bankrupt. Temporarily down on his luck, he explained. The next day when he was admitted to Shackle General with pneumonia, he produced a New York State Medicaid card. The floor nurse mentioned that Vinnie told her he had been a heart surgeon in Florida—that was before he took to drink.

"The guy was a genius," Manny said. He held his fork by its tines and scraped out the marrow with the handle.

"A swindler, 100 percent," Stella said.

Manny dropped the bone and rubbed his hand flat against the napkin beside his plate. "A man on his way up."

"Why not?" Stella said. "From the gutter there's no

place to fall."

I stood and piled my silverware on my plate. "Just as Jesus forgives our failings, we forgive Mr. Le Clair his. Pray for him. And be ready to leave for the funeral Thursday morning, seven o'clock sharp."

"Sister," Stella said as I moved towards the door. "The Knights are coming tomorrow after supper."

"Fine, remind me again tomorrow."

A mug of coffee in one hand, an Oreo in the other, I went into my office. Work would help control my thoughts, the budget revision on my area agency grant. Sixty thousand of projected carry-over had to be obligated before the end of the fiscal year, three weeks away. I pulled the chain on the brass lamp, sat at my desk and studied the draft line items. I wondered if I would be around to use what we bought, tires for the Senior Citizens' van, a Radio Shack PC, a kiln, furniture for the bedrooms in case the city increased the number on our board-and-care permit, a new Kitchen Aide for Stella.

A few hours later I had just finished the three-year projection and was about to start the narrative when beams from headlights swept over the credenza and around the wall. A motor cut off, a car door slammed. Who on earth? It was almost eleven—I heard the music for the news coming from the living room where Stella was watching TV. I looked out at the dark parking lot. But the driver must have pulled around to the basketball court. I rose just as the doorbell rang.

I met Stella coming down the hall. "I'll get it, you go back to your show," I said.

I studied the oval insert of stained glass in the front door. Whoever was behind it was tall. I unfastened the latch.

"Vida." Hunting Sun said softly. "Sister."

The warm wind shot slim grainy clouds across the moon. Hunt held a trench coat over his shoulder, its collar hooked on his middle finger. "You're looking good," he said. A gust lifted my veil; silver light danced in his hair. I opened the door wide, and he brushed past me on his way into the hall. Fifteen years, and that same smell of juniper and Tiparillos. "I tried to call, but no one answered," he said.

Slippage, my trademark these days. After Buccalotta's visit I had forgotten to turn up the volume on the extension phone after Stella had turned it down.

"I'm here for the Maternal and Child Health conference and thought someone should explain Matewan County, ease you down into it. When do you start the job?"

"Monday after next. How on earth did you find St. Michael's?"

"You give good directions."

I did recall inviting him to stop should he ever be in Shackle. Now he was here, and the forty watt overhead deepened the hollows in his cheeks. He was thinner than I remembered, too thin. "Have you had dinner?" I asked.

"At a truck stop off the Weston exit." He looked down at me, his eyes far-away and warm, and I pictured those farmhouse windows shining in the middle of nowhere that you see from the window of a plane. A slant of dark hair fell across his eyes, and he pushed it back. What would it feel like twisted around a finger? I jammed my hands in my skirt pocket and nodded at my office door. "Come sit down."

"It's late, and I still have to check in at the motel. I only came by to let you know I was here." He glanced at his Levis and brushed at his knees. "Besides, I'm a mess, had to change a flat."

"Blowout?"

"Not mine. A guy going white-water rafting. Driving a Volvo wagon full of L.L. Bean camping gear along with three kids and two setters. Why would someone who can't work a tire iron think he can pitch a tent? They should stay in their condos in Washington." He raised his head. "What drives them on?"

"Dreams. And after Labor Day, their time's running out."

Hunt straightened, and I glanced from his tight jeans to his belt buckle, a winged turquoise stone centered in a silver square. He crossed his arms, the coat over his elbow. "We could do dinner after my Wednesday sessions. I mean, the sisters in Cherokee—they man, rather, run, the Fransiscan Day Care Center—seem to come and go. Sort of."

I slowly drew the veil over my shoulder as if it were hair. "It isn't that Siluvas can't go places with—" I almost said another gender. "Of course Shackle's a small town." My face went hot. To him that slip of the tongue could mean I was suggesting that onlookers might think there was something between us, which might make him think I was thinking there might be. I twisted my gold ring. "No big deal. I'd like to hear about Matewan. Sure, all about it."

We settled on meeting at the Mission at six, he slipped out the door, and I quietly closed it behind him. But for the faint smell of pine, it was hard to imagine he had ever been there.

Later, in bed, unconnected thoughts floated slowly

through my mind. Sister Silesia. Pops. What if the old
man was indicted? Again I picked through the numbers as
if I hadn't done it one hundred times. To leave the
Order—if not in style, at least without going too deeply
into debt, I needed, say, fifty thousand. That would get
me five acres of so-so mountain land and a
doublewide. The housing part of my plan could be mort-
gaged. (What was the prime interest rate these days, anyway?) Twenty percent down would leave me forty thousand in cash. A used car, a few clothes, a few sticks of furniture. I should be able to set money aside for Pops, just
in case. On the other hand, maybe I should put the whole
idea of leaving on hold. But I wasn't getting any
younger. Negotiating the job in Matewan had been a
colossal pain, what with interviewing, explaining myself
to the director of social services, a woman ten years my
junior. Come to think of it, she couldn't be that
young. She just looked it.

I sat up, slightly dizzy, and smoothed the pillows back
into shape. Then I lay flat on my back and stared at the
circle of streetlight reflected on the ceiling. Hunt's long
lean thighs in tight jeans. I ran my hands over my stomach
and along my ribs. Not exactly Jane Fonda, but the muscles seemed to be holding. When laying down,
anyhow. They say the throat's the first to go. I stroked my
neck with the back of my hand. Some looseness there
under the chin, like the softness in the paraffin sealing
jelly, where the mold sneaks through. I tipped back my
head and checked the skin again—tight as drum. How
had I held my head when talking to Hunt? How had I
come across in his eyes?

He looked the same to me—the same as when we were
at Mountain State. Of course being the only Cherokee
there, he stood out. Everyone on campus knew his Tribal
Council paid for him to study medicine and to run track. I
remember those bright September mornings, him rounding the dirt road, a flash of yellow satin shorts, long
sinewy legs sweat-slick with black hairs, a headband tied
at the nape of his neck, the ends trailing down his

back. Then, same as now, up close his eyes were solid brown, with no centers of light. At least that I ever saw. Taut skin stretched over his fine-boned nose like leather drawn across a pommel. A few pitted scars dotted his forehead. Acne I thought, until he told me smallpox.

Despite its name, Mountain State is no spit-and-whittle place. The campus spreads over one hundred acres on the outskirts of Confluence, where the Ocawah River flows into the Shackle. Confluence is the only town in West Virginia I know of where you can buy Perrier in the Krogers and where a Mercedes dealer stocks parts. At the turn of the century, coal and railroad magnates endowed university chairs. Low admission standards, meant to encourage the locals to apply, instead drew rich people rejected by big-name schools. Pops wangled me a scholarship from the United Mine Workers, Sleaze Gobetsky having greased the wheels. At any rate, my stipend was more than I needed, but certainly not enough to board a horse, or to wear Irish sweaters like most girls there. A sensible poor person would have felt left out. But at twenty-one I was more interested in martyrdom than greed. Childhood scars, flesh wounds from Tillie and Ralph, were still soft. Looking back, it was no wonder I was high-strung, wary, and feeling dangerously close to death.

For starters, I never ate at drive-ins. Always expecting my tin-bucket VW to be crushed by an eighteen-wheeler, I didn't want the coroner to see what I'd eaten last. I bought funeral insurance. Sometimes I pictured myself dying in the electric chair, then years later being vindicated, beatified, canonized. A mile out of town, the Sisters of Siluva had opened their mountain convent to public retreats. For twenty dollars a weekend, I slept in a mossy cell, said the rosary kneeling on damp stone, and ate three meals a day without meat. Most women visited for the peace and serenity. I was drawn to the boxy pews hacked, not planed, from splintery wood, to the hard narrow cot and the mushroom-smelling sheets. After Mass, I would kneel at the altar rail, a row of marble lyres topped by a granite slab. On the western wall, leaded glass panels divided the

Stations of the Cross. Light softened the chiseled edge of the
stone altar rail. Me, Mary Magdala at the rock beside the
empty tomb. I felt the hot Jeruselum sun raising the veins
of the olive leaves, lifting the mist, pulling song birds right
up through the clouds. The sisters urged me to pray for a
calling. I did, but in the convent nothing came of it.

Then in my junior year I took up with Scott Adams—
although he wasn't the type who would ordinarily fool
with someone like me. Blond, blue-eyed, you would swear
Scott had been born in his navy blazer and brought up
crisp on iceburg lettuce and percale. He was captain of the
debating team and editor of the *Sorry Dog News*. I would
spot his black Porsche around campus, each time a different girl in the passenger seat.

The night we met I was sitting in a booth at the Mountaineer Bar and Grille with my roommate, Penny, and Ron,
her steady of the month. It had been her birthday, and Ron
was footing the bill. The restaurant, a hole-in-the-wall
along Confluence Avenue, had two things going for it—the
food wasn't bad and the bartenders didn't ask for IDs.
Brown vinyl booths flanked one wall, a bar of oak-grained
Formica flanked the other. Grass-colored indoor-outdoor
carpet carried out the simulated forest motif, perfect
except for the shelves holding tall chrome trophies, each
sporting a bowler soldered onto a silver globe.

Penny slipped a quarter into the jukebox mounted on
the wall, and a second later Elvis moaned above the hum
of blenders coming from behind the bar. Ron, his stomach
wedged against the table, drummed his fingers on the
paper placemat in time to "Heartbreak Hotel." Penny
wrapped a strand of long red hair around her ear and
nodded at the doorway. I turned just as Scott ushered a
tall lanky blonde past the planter filled with plastic
ivy. "Do you know her?" Penny asked.

I shook my head.

Ron waved, "Over here."

Scott moved around our waitress, who was pouring
beer into mugs, and rested his hand on his date's shoulder. "Stacy Ravenal."

Ron introduced Penny, then me.

"Vida Za'who?" Scott laughed.

"—Donis," I said primly. Smartface. He'd heard it the first time. I reached for my drink while Ron launched into one of his restaurant reviews. Scott, his arm around Stacy, inched her toward the bar.

"She ought to do something with that hair," Penny whispered.

"Looks good to me," I said.

Stacy's page boy might have been dated, but she was a dead ringer for the models who posed for the Lord and Taylor's ads. I had never been in a Lord andTaylor's. Mainly because there wasn't a single one in the entire state of West Virginia. But the University library subscribed to the Sunday New York *Times* and I pored over the pictures. I watched Scott lean and light Stacy's cigarette, Stacy throw back her head and inhale. A wave of depression crept into me, then settled into a fog inside. There were too many things that I knew about but had never seen. Tiffany's, oriental rugs, a real Rembrandt. "Material things," the Sisters would point out. Things Pops would call "shit baggage." I turned away from Scott and Stacy and stared at the chrome bowlers. The waitress brought our chicken wings and I bit into the breading, only half listening to Penny and Ron go on about their weekend at Lake Ocawah.

Suddenly Stacy jerked her hand from Scott's arm. He grabbed her wrist. Why was she wearing riding pants? Then in one motion she swept up her cigarette case and spun around, and without a never-you-mind, sailed past our table and out the door. Scott's body seemed to stiffen. Then it occurred to me he could see my face in the mirror behind the bar. I lowered my head. When I looked up, Scott, carrying his mug, was making his way to our booth.

An hour later Ron paid the check. When I moved to follow him and Penny, Scott touched my sleeve and motioned to the pitcher of beer which was still half full. "Help me kill it?"

I sat back down. Penny waved to me, then disappeared out the door. Scott's knee brushed mine. "Like I was saying, three generations of chairmanships of PAW's board. I'll inherit it from my old man."

Was he always this smug? Or was it for my benefit. "Isn't the board supposed to vote or something?"

Scott ran his finger around his collar. "You don't understand how the world works. What does your dad do anyway?"

A good question. My last weekend home, Pops said Ralph had been fired as an outside salesman for Shannahin Products. Scott leaned closer. I smelled his aftershave, and I pictured the ad in the *Times*, the sketch of a man in a tweed jacket holding a bridle of a racehorse. "He's in business."

"For himself?"

For right now, I almost said. "No. I mean, yes, sort of."

"What kind?"

"Computers."

Scott raised his eyebrows.

"IBM."

Scott nodded.

I studied his face to see if he could tell I was lying. It had worked. Furthermore, being this someone else was interesting. It hardly mattered who, I had nowhere to go but up. "He does consulting for corporations, ALCOA."

On a roll, I expanded on Ralph's expertise in software technology. Then I branched out to my mother's charitable activities. "She's so conventional," I complained. "The League of Women Voters, hanging geraniums, Williamsburg placemats." All the while a voice inside me shouted I was out of my mind. There were places to put people like me—hospitals. What would the sisters say? Of course they would never find out. On the other hand, Scott could find out about me easily enough by asking around. If he took the trouble. But why would he bother? He would never see me again anyway. Not when he could tap the Stacy Ravenals of the world.

Scott waited until I finished my description of my

mother's garden, then said quietly, "Your skin is perfect, porcelain, the skin of a beautiful doll."

Was he serious? "You're drunk," I said finally.

He ran his finger up and down the pitcher drawing ladders in the condensation. "What are you afraid of?"

"Don't be silly." I laughed. Yet what an odd thing to say. He must have sensed I was—afraid might not be the exact word. But I was certainly acting weird, behaving like a cross between a con artist and a psychopath. Maybe it wasn't me—him, Scott, bringing something out I never knew was there. Envy? Social climbing?

Blaming someone else was dirty pool. One bit of attention from a son-of-a-big-shot and I had abandoned every spiritual value I had ever owned. I reached for my bookbag.

"Now you're angry."

"It's late."

He held my arm, and I sank back onto the upholstery. "Vida—whoever you are—let's take you home."

Not that night, but a few weeks later I did go with Scott to his apartment. Off-campus housing was hard to come by. He and Hunting Sun, his roommate, had been lucky to find a third-floor walk-up near the stadium. The landlord, Ari Aristophanas, lived on the second floor above his gyros takeout and bar.

"You can smell oregano clear up here," I laughed. I walked around the living room admiring the woven rugs hanging on the walls. "They say Hunting Sun's a Cherokee,"

"He goes home to the reservation in North Carolina every weekend. He and I run track. Funny, never in my life did I think I'd meet an Indian, let alone live with one. Of course, Hunt's different."

"From what?"

Scott moved to the efficiency kitchen. "Let's get these egg rolls in the oven."

I had thought it would be easier for Scott to make love in his waterbed rather than in the Porsche. I was wrong. We started off all right. Then, as always, it was

over in a second with him mumbling—a cold, too hard a
workout in the gym. I would change the subject. Everyone
knew about performance anxiety. My theory was that
Scott, more insecure than he appeared, would work out
the problem inside himself in time. Of course he claimed
with other women it had been all right. One time he
blamed me straight out, "I can't get a rise out of you."

I resisted a play on words. "I'm a misanthrope. So
shoot me."

Scott's voice had softened. "No, you're just reflec-
tive. Deep. Awkward with men."

"But I've always been interested in you people. Not
that I've had many as friends. But I'm touched by your
vulnerability—combat, football, hemophilia, and
impressed by the way you manage to work around it,
curious about your mind's eye that sees only shades of
red. The world seen through rose petals, sunsets, Soviet
flags."

"Listen to yourself. You act like you're so far above
everybody else."

Our relationship muddled along. We spent Thanksgiv-
ing with his parents. This was two months after we
met. They lived in Port Shirley Estates, the Adams estate
being a six-bedroom tract mansion on five acres of what
had been mountain land with first-rate timber. Scott's
father had pulled up the oaks and planted designer trees,
saplings trailing wispy Laura Ashley leaves. As we settled
around the massive dining room table, a style
Mrs. Adams called Medici, Mr. Adams asked if Zedonis
was a Greek name.

"Lithuanian."

"Oh?"

So I told him where the country was and how our village was now governed by Warsaw. This was while he
passed me a brandy snifter half-filled with Del Monte
fruit salad. Suddenly I thought of Tillie and of Ralph's
family, the Protestant Bowsers. I had only visited there
once or twice when a toddler. Tillie refused to go. "Goody
two-shoes, the whole pack of them," she had said. What-

ever that meant.

Mrs. Adams started passing other dishes from her end of the table, and I wondered if I had enough hands to channel the onrushing traffic of condiments, sauces, and pitchers of a pink sweet punch. Scott's mother was a burly woman with a pad of coarse reddish hair atop her head. She stared at the circle of fake pearls on my navy suit, frowned, and asked about my parents, then handed me a platter piled with crusty dark meat.

How on earth could I explain my past? I handed Scott a gravy boat heavy with shiny gray sauce. Talking fast, smiling, I described a composite father, a mixture of Ralph the computer expert and Pops, and a childhood that almost made sense.

"You don't look Polish," Mr. Adams said. "You know, a lot of Polocks—"

He caught my eye.

"Poles aren't as . . ." He picked through his Waldorf salad as if looking for the right word. "Limited, that's right, as limited as folks think. There are, of course, exceptions," he added quickly.

To remind him I wasn't Polish would sound as if I wanted to be sure I wasn't counted as one. And it wouldn't be diplomatic to argue. It was important for Scott's people to like me. So I kept quiet and handed him a divided dish, one side filled with green olives, the other, mint jelly. Mrs. Adams handed me a china basket of rolls, and all at once I turned clumsy, a peasant not knowing how to act in the big house. My hands felt stiff and puffy, the way they felt after a day reshingling the barn, or digging beets. "Hands swoll to fit the job," Pops always said. They were big now. A gorilla's. Rake tines. Mickey Mouse paws. I was terrified I would drop the saucer of butter pats. I broke off a section of cloverleaf roll and weighed it in my palm. Suddenly an illusion hit me, like when you see a postcard of Mt. Fujiyama and think how climbing it would be a snap. If I wanted to, I could scoop up the table and balance it over our heads on the fingertips of one hand. A flip of my wrist and the plates would whirl to the ceiling, hover, then spin—a Wedgewood galaxy forever orbiting the crystal chandelier.

Mrs. Adams was cutting into what she called a tipsy cake, apparently flavored with bourbon. A Zedonis respects good whiskey. I smiled at a sudden picture of Pops sniffing the yellow spongy slice and asking, "What's this shit?"

"Just a little piece for Vida." Mr. Adams said, then winked at me. "Myrtle uses the real McCoy."

Mr. Adams should have been at the Shackle Teamsters Hall last summer, when to earn pocket money I played the accordion with Johnny Bruzouskas and his Polka Tomcats, the guys standing me to rounds of boilermakers between sets. Mrs. Adams looked at me, then scored a smaller wedge of cake than the one she had cut for Scott. It was then I realized my future with his parents would be downhill all the way.

As was my relationship with Scott. Yet for some reason we kept trying. Maybe simply because neither of us knew how to break it off. By winter, our time together had disintegrated into an odd arrangement of comings and goings. Scott and I fought Monday through Thursday. Fridays we made up and went to his apartment—unless Hunting Sun stayed in town, in which case I went to the convent. The stone floor and altar rail took me back without a word of my defection. The sisters welcomed me, no questions asked. But the confessional loomed like an erect coffin beside the sacristy. I wasn't ready for reconciliation, to swear off my alternate weekends of half-baked sin.

One snowy Saturday night in his bedroom, Scott shouted at me, "You're like some life-doll for sale at Doc's Marital Aids. Sure their thing feels real. But it's rubber."

I pulled the sheet up to my chin. The cool slick spots of vaseline stuck to my thigh. The play in me was all wrung out. Only to be alone, with a Ritz cracker and a warm beer. "Don't blame me."

"It's been weeks since I've made it," he said.

Weeks for me too, I could have added. He ran his hands through his blond hair. I wondered if I really was the first time his smile failed, and his thick curls had gone limp.

"Talk about dolls."

He leaped out of bed. His skin shone skimmed-milk blue in the pale light from the street. "I feel like a fucking pervert."

"Perverts don't fuck," I said primly. "By definition they—"

"Smart ass." He shook his finger at me. "That's exactly what I mean about you." He grabbed his shorts from the rung of a ladder-backed chair.

I could hardly breathe. I watched him pull on his jeans, then, forgetting his t-shirt, jam his arm into his shetland sweater, the one that itched. He ran his finger around his watchband. I was careful to keep my voice calm. "Going somewhere?"

"I want out."

My fingers shook while I undid my braid. "You forget you live here."

Scott scooped his wallet from the dresser. "Only after you're gone." He opened the closet and groped around the floor.

I sectioned my hair into threes and methodically, so not to show panic, I started to plait. Scott was leaving. There must be something I should do.

I used to listen to Tillie and Ralph yell at each other. I would lie in bed staring at the snail's track of silver light under the door. When I couldn't stand it any longer, I would get up and head down the hall to the kitchen. Their door would be open. Tillie would be in her slip and sitting on the edge of the bed. I don't remember seeing Ralph— just hearing his lisp from a far corner of the room. The kitchen would be lit by the stove's flourescent fixture that slid back and forth when you raised or lowered the lid that covered the burners. Tillie lived on junk food washed down with junk drink. She stashed her peanut butter cups in the breadbox. Shaking, I would rip open the orange cellophane wrappers. How I hated those prim pleated skirts, the mealy hearts. But they would make me strong. One after another, I forced them down until my tongue was caulked to the roof of my mouth and I gagged.

I said to Scott, "Your boots are under the couch."

He walked closer and spoke through clenched teeth. "You're not human. You don't feel anything, do you?"

"Don't talk in my face."

He leaned over me. "Bitch," he whispered. "Dumb, Polock, hunky bitch."

Hunky. I knew it—that had been it all along. I was too low-class for Mr. Chairman of the Board. White slave owners did it with the black help. But Scott doing it with a hunky couldn't be done at all. Hunkys, untouchables. Something inside me uncoiled and lashed back and forth. I flipped the sheet on the floor and jumped out of bed. I pulled on Scott's t-shirt, then ran into the living room. Hunting Sun, who wasn't due back until Monday, was stomping snow off his boots in the hallway. I paid him no mind and flew on by. The island in the kitchen blocked my path, and I paused to catch my breath and to remember why I was there. The meat cleaver hung over the wok. It took a minute to unwind the leather thong from the hook, then I dashed towards the bedroom.

"Jesus Christ Almighty," Scott flattened himself against the wall as I shot past.

I stood over the bed, raised the cleaver and swung it down on the mattress full force. Nothing happened.

"Six hundred dollars," Scott shouted from the door-way. "You'll pay, hear me?"

I spun around and pointed the cleaver at his throat.

"She's crazy," Scott yelled over his shoulder. "I'm getting out."

I turned back to the bed, and a second later the front door slammed. I yanked off the bottom sheet and struck. But the cleaver hardly dented the puckered vinyl seam. I raised it to try again, when suddenly a turquoise ring, then lean amber fingers grabbed my wrist. Hunting Sun tightened his grip, and the blade clattered on the floor.

"Let me be," I shouted. Something hard hit my palm,

and I found myself holding a tool like Pops used to flay deer, the short pointed blade razor sharp on each side. I bent forward and plunged the knife into the mattress up to the hilt. Water gushed over the pillows and soaked the lace trim of the slips. "Dead doll," I whispered. I drove the blade deep into the bed's center, slicing the vinyl like butter all the way down to the foot. A stream smelling faintly of chlorine bubbled over my hand and stained the scatter rug dark.

The hardwood floor was cool and strangely dry beneath my feet. I stood back and stared at the murdered bed. The tundra of glistening sheets seemed to stretch to the end of the world. I rubbed my arms from the cold of it. Something moved. I stepped closer. The lips of the incision, flecked with plastic shreds, quivered, parted, smiled, exposing pools of black water, bigger and bigger clots of black sponge. I sank to my knees just as my shaking started, first a ripple down the spine, soon my whole body shivering without stop. My teeth chattered. More than anything I wanted to be on my slim cot at the Sisters, moonlight slanting on the terra-cotta floor. "Please."

Just then the longing to be safe behind the convent's walls swelled inside me and thickened, hardened, grew diamond sharp, slipped from my body and soared, pulling the rest of me behind. "Rise up and follow." Wind filling a sail.

"Here," Hunting Sun said.

I opened my eyes. Hunt stood on the rug, his weight causing water to seep from the fringe. He shook out a soft cotton blanket. I struggled to my feet. The living room light polished his hair, loose to his shoulders. All at once I realized the tee-shirt I wore was paper thin, and I looked up. Those eyes of his with no centers reflected nothing. Gently, he draped the blanket over my shoulders, crossed the ends under my chin and slowly drew me against him. His chest was solid, warm, and his sweater smelled of tobacco and pine needles. I felt his ornate silver belt buckle hard against me. I pictured the turquoise stone set in the hammered rim. In a minute my shaking stopped and my muscles moved freely, as if I had frozen almost to death and was gathering heat against a stone in the sun.

Suddenly, there was pounding on the front door. "We got a dripper in there," Ari yelled.

I jumped away. "Coming," Hunt called, putting his finger on his lips. He slipped from the bedroom and closed the door behind him.

My jeans and sweater hung on the rim of the wastebasket. I dressed quickly while listening to Ari stomp into the bathroom, into the kitchen. "Busted pipe," he shouted. "Ceiling's raining dogs and cats." I couldn't hear Hunt's reply. The panel of the cabinet under the sink clicked shut, then the front door slammed.

Hunt's knife lay on the floor. The embossed leather handle felt brittle and damp. I straightened and turned to the living room. Every few minutes the pipes banged, and downstairs water taps hummed on and off.

Hunt sat on a high three-legged stool at the drawing table he used as a desk. The air in his room was cool and smelled of crushed juniper. A scarlet and yellow kelim, bold stripes, arrows, and jagged stars hung above his single bed. Animals carved of smooth bright-grained wood stood on his bookcase. They were positioned as if alive in the North Carolina Smokies. Stalkers, cats with tails at least a foot long. The stalked: herons posed to take off, snakes coiled to strike back. A shallow basket beside a wicker chair held a pile of AMA Journals. Hunt ground out his slim cigar and nodded. I walked over and handed him the knife. "Thank you," he said.

He held it to the light and ran his thumb along the edge.

"I'm going with the Sisters," I added, "Of our Lady of Siluva."

Hunt slowly wiped the blade on his knee.

"You take good care of it."

"I'd better," he replied, then laid it on the desk. He smiled, strong white teeth, faint tracks curling up from the edges of his eyes. "You might be needing it again."

Pops rubbed the roof of his four by four with a soapy rag. "If you're finished with the tailgate, bring that bucket around," he shouted.

It was ten in the morning and already seventy degrees. A warm breeze stirred the dogwood leaves, scarlet against a bright blue sky. I had gone to seven o'clock Mass, and right afterward taken off for the farm. By the time I got there, Vinnie, Mother Silesia, Hunt had been relegated to the back of my mind; Tillie and Ralph loomed up front. If just once, once, one of our visits could end without my having diarrhea, a migraine, or both. Pops and I sat at the kitchen table speculating on when they would show up. Then he talked me into helping him wash the truck while we waited. Never waste good weather, he said.

I came up beside him and set the pail filled with diluted Zip by the front tire. He turned toward the barn. "I need a hard rag for the windows, I'll be back."

I strolled to the edge of the driveway bordered with Queen Anne's lace. A yellow-tailed hawk sat on a branch midway up a sycamore. Off in the distance Geezer's Ridge was a layer of blue fur beyond the crisp fall leaves bordering Pops's land. Sure as anything, driving to the farm just to see the Bowsers was pointless. But I came anyway: even though they had never once visited me at the mother house or the Mission. And Pops took it upon himself to invite me. I knew they never asked him to.

Everything was wrong between Tillie and Ralph and me. But when wrongness fills the sky, it's hard to put your finger on the specifics. As far as those two went, they fought like animals, Ralph beating up on her, she, back-biting just to get even. Yet, enemies to each other, they hung together against everyone else. And another thing, in spite of Ralph's job changes and their irresponsible spend-ing, they never went broke, never got sick. As if the devil knew better than to mess with them. They were co-con-spirators, allies, more than husband and wife: ferrets sealed in a bottle that had washed up on some strange shore.

I pulled a tentacle of crabgrass from the gravel. Tille and Ralph, solidarity against the world, against me in particular. But—and I had given this some thought—when you came down to it, it wasn't being left out by both of them that bothered me. No, it was Tillie: Tillie and me. I couldn't recall her ever being around. But she had never had a job, or done community-minded things. Then where had she been? Not there for me, that's for sure. Hadn't she heard of Mothers Against Drunk Dri-ving, of mothers marching against birth defects? I tried to drown the badness between us and resurrect the good, the way you soak the mud off kale, then lift the clean leaves from the water. It didn't work.

Take the lockouts.

When we were a threesome, that is, before Tillie and Ralph gave me to Pops, Tillie would lock me out of our apartment as punishment for childhood crimes. We moved so often there must have been a dozen doorstops and hallways. Yet my strongest recollection is of one par-ticular stairwell, of me sitting on the landing alongside a pale green wall strung with cobwebs like hairs growing from the paint. Over my head hung a chandelier with rosebud bulbs trapped in a glass box edged with solid gold. An old man dragging a grocery-bag carrier on wheels trudged up the stairs, then stepped around me. "Hello there, little person."

I cringed against the rail. He leaned, and diamonds of short white hairs sparkled around his jaw. Slowly he drew a key chain from his hip pocket, one key dangling from brass beads, a tiny brass book beside it.

"Look it here," he said.

It wasn't a book at all. He pressed a snap, and the pages spread apart. The picture inside showed a naked girl, one about my age, and a man standing in front of her who I could tell was naked too because the picture showed him from the back.

"I'm going to tell my mother." He pocketed the chain, reached for his grocery cart, then vanished to the second floor, the thump-thump of the wheels against the stairs growing softer, softer, like a dying heart.

Black rubber treads led to the bottom of the steps, the bristly doormat lay at an angle as if creeping toward the blade of light beneath the front door. Dusty footprints trailed across the foyer. My eyes tracked the marks. All at once I was struck with an urge—no—more than an urge, a drive to throw myself down the steps. I grabbed the bannister and pulled my knees tight to my chest, keeping my feet from the edge. Any minute I would be bumping over the polished brass strips on the treads, crash through the white wooden doorpanels, and roll onto the sidewalk, face up.

I would wake up dead. Dead people couldn't talk, but they could hear. The school crossing guard would be leaning over me, saying how I had never stood a chance.

I jumped to my feet, ran, and banged on our apartment door.

"I don't care," Tillie yelled from inside. I pressed my forehead against the cool wood; she was alive, thank God. That night she let me in minutes before Ralph came home. Later, they talked about me as if I wasn't there.

"She had to be put out again."

"Why this time?"

"Spilling a whole box of cereal. I had to wipe it up."

"Does it to show off."

Then I hit upon preventive diligence. Make my own breakfast before Tillie got up. Sign my report card when they forgot. Iron my own blouses. Celebrate my own birthday (they usually remembered it a few days afterward, and Tillie would say, "We'll get you something later"). Wipe up my own spills. They never knew I started going to daily Mass when I was ten. They never mentioned the dog-eared copy of *A Child's Imitation of Christ* beside my bed. When I graduated from Mountain State, I sent them an announcement and a note saying I would be entering the Siluvas as a postulant. They sent me a compact with a comb and lipstick case attached.

As a novice I concentrated on the Sixth Commandment. Then I gave up and didn't call for a few years, but no one seemed to notice. You would think by then I would have simply written them off. But it seemed the farther I tried to pull away, the larger they became: figures on the horizen growing bigger, not smaller as I drew away. In spite of all common sense, I suppose I believed that someday everything could be different. Which was why each time they came to visit Pops, I managed to be there. And so the three of us muddled along in a balance of low-level tolerance.

Footsteps crackled through the raspberry bushes, and I turned just as a crowd of wild turkeys crashed into the field, each bird turning its head back and forth as if talking to the one beside it. Pops rounded the corner of the shed, and the flock shot into the woods. "You want me to use this soap on the chrome?" I asked.

He held a rag in one hand and sprayed the windshield with Glass-Brite with the other. "Sure."

"Tillie's late," I said.

"You shouldn't call her by her name."

"We've been all through that."

"Use Mother."

"She doesn't understand the word."

And she probably didn't. She had never been a mother

to me, and sometimes I wondered if I was roaming the world looking for one.

Pops licked his thumb and rubbed a spot on the glass. "She can't help herself. Just remember the person who was your mother's mother died when she was a baby."

Pops always blamed Tillie's irresponsibility on her childhood. "Give me a break," I said.

"Don't be mean on her. What with mine layoffs, strikes, I couldn't even afford her a Scout uniform or Camp Kanahwa. I couldn't give her nothing."

"Except yourself."

Pops lowered the windshield wiper blades back in place. "Only she wanted a uniform."

We worked in silence for a while, until I said, "At any rate, how about not mentioning my leaving the Order. It's too soon, and I'm not sure how it's going to fall out."

Pops aimed the bottle of Glass-Brite at the rearview mirror. "Look, you're ready to go, go and be done with it."

I had told him the gist of yesterday's meeting at the mother house. "You forget leaving without Sister's sign off's a mortal sin. You said so yourself." I struggled to keep my voice light. "No Sacraments. Unless," I added, "I make a good confession." I knelt and scrubbed the slats of the grill. "Meaning Father gives me absolution. But he's only going to do that after I promise to go back and work out quitting properly no matter how long it takes."

"What if he don't send you back and says everything's okay?"

"Highly unlikely as long as I'm AWOL. Which puts me between a rock and a hard place. Leaving the Order is a sin." I tested a joke. "So is killing Mother Silesia. Or myself. Or both of us."

Pops didn't laugh and my hands shook as I draped the rag over the pail. "But I can't live in the Order forever."

"Who lives forever?"

"Which is why I can't leave the Church."

Pops pushed up his cap, the one with 'Nothing runs

like a Deere' printed over the bill. "Are you sure Sister's right?"

"No. And there's one hope. The Bishop might be able to waive the requirement for her concurrence. I'm making an appointment with him."

"If he won't?"

"Or can't."

"Big shots can do anything."

"Then I'm back where I started."

"Only if you think the Mother General's right."

"Do I have a choice?"

Pops reached into the oil drum where he stored the hose and started to haul it out, hand over hand. "You bet. To do what you feel is okay and stop thinking."

"I thought of that." I walked over and helped him unsnarl a loop in the green rubber. "And I think faith means trust even when the going gets bad. Besides," I said, trying to keep the catch from my voice, to lighten up, "the church is my life." It was so much more than that, and I studied Pops's face to see if he knew what I meant. He nodded, then bent to lift the piled-up hose, straightened, then bent again and hoisted the coil over his arm. I saw how the shoulders of his plaid shirt hung limp, no longer muscle-filled. "The church is your life, too," I said softly.

"That's why I make my Easter duty." He pointed the nozzle at the door and turned on the water. Soapsuds rolled down the paint and frosted the gravel with white foam.

I brushed off my vest. My skirt was damp, and I could have kicked myself for not having more sense than to wear slacks out to the farm. Slippage again. "After last Sunday, you'd better not wait until Easter," I said.

He circled the truck and turned the spray full force on the hood. I waited until he was finished. "The Jesuits are hearing confessions this Saturday."

"So?"

"Should I spell it out?"

"What did I do wrong?"

"For starters, you were arrested."

Pops shrugged.

"Don't give me that. You grow dope, kids smoke a cigarette, then they want more and their lives are ruined."

Pops turned off the valve and faced me. "You believe
that shit?"

I emptied the pail and set the cleanser and Zip in
it. "Just get yourself on down there."

"Not if there's no sin."

"That's for Father to decide."

Pops drew back. "How come you, a nun, don't know
how it works? You're not supposed to say every single
thing you did, so he can pick and sort. No sir, you just
have to say sins." Pops's back was to the sun, and I
couldn't see his face. "You know why you think you're in
trouble? Because you don't know how it works. If your
heart says the Mother General's all wet, then go to confession where they don't recognize you. Some big city. Go to
Port Shirley and tell Father easy things like I lied three
times, kicked my old cat, had too many Four Roses. Next
day go to Mass clean as a whistle." He sprayed the tailgate, then up under the back wheels.

Pops's way, the old country way. The way women had
reconciled abortion in Sicily, adultery in France. "You're
only cheating yourself," I shouted above the hissing
water. "Cheating the church doesn't work."

"The hell it don't." He shut off the hose and laid it on
the grass. "Them mini-skirters married ten years with one
kid marching up the Communion line like brides. Old
Sleaze right there behind them smiling like a monk." Pops
moved around the driveway gathering the soap, pail, and
rags. "I'm taking this stuff to the barn before someone
steals it."

Suddenly I heard the clack of wooden planks knocking
together and an engine race. Ralph's Thunderbird crawled
over the rickety bridge.

"I forgot, he's scared of the boards," Pops shouted. He
ran to the center of the yard, and, motioning with his
hands, coaxed Ralph forward an inch, then an inch to the

right, a foot to the left. Tillie's arm shot out of the window, the sun catching her gold bracelets. I waved back.

The Thunderbird—Ralph always drove the latest model, thanks to his uncle now running the family Ford dealership—lumbered up the drive, stopped in front of the barn, and sat silently rocking back and forth, a plane at the landing gate, passengers scrambling into the aisles and groping for luggage overhead. Tillie's door swung open, and she struggled from the bucket seat. She half-stood, brushing off her lap. The jacket of her green pantsuit hung open showing a beige jersey, which, I suspected, had no sleeves, a garment Gabe's discount house calls a shell. Her dull red hair was cropped too close on the sides and neck. Spikes, stiffened with gel, circled her temple, like the Statute of Liberty's. "We didn't stop but once. On the Interstate."

"You eat in there?" Pops asked.

Ralph rounded the front of the car and slammed the door on Tillie's side. A small flabby man, today he was taller than her—those special shoes he ordered by mail. His brown felt hat matched his suit, the jacket hanging loose over a yellow polo shirt buttoned to the neck.

"You lost weight," Tillie said, kissing my cheek. "Is that a new veil, cut fuller? It softens your face."

Tillie probably believed Liz Claibourne designed habits, only I was too cheap to buy one. Each time she saw me she asked the same sort of question. "Nothing's changed," I said before I could control my voice. Jesus, Mary and Joseph, help me stop snapping.

Ralph walked toward me and wound off his tinted aviator glasses. His round face seemed pudgier than usual along the jaw. I had never once seen a trace of a beard on him, and I often wondered if he shaved that soft pink skin, aging baby-doll skin. He wiped his lips, gave me a peck on the forehead, then stepped back and wiped his mouth again. He pointed to Tillie but turned to Pops. "This one gets herself a cheeseburger with peanut butter on it, like at nine in the morning. Jiminy Christmas, out front of everybody."

Not that I approve of profanity, but Ralph's character might climb a notch in his own mind if he could talk and act like a real man. He was prissy, nervous, afraid to use Pops's bathroom in the cellar. Yet, in spite of the Sunday school affect, there was something unwholesome about him, a keeper of dirty little secrets.

"I always tell you, don't eat garbage," Pops said to Tillie. "I got everything inside."

She touched his arm and smiled. "You're looking younger every day."

What brought this on? She usually greeted Pops griping about his house being too far from Weirton. We followed Pops through the back door and into the kitchen while Ralph described the wide-load trailer he had been stuck behind. "A monster," he repeated. When he was especially nervous, his lisp was more pronounced, a slight "th" sound to the "s." "I was too scared to path. Pass."

Tillie put her hand on his arm and said in a stage whisper, "Let's unload his present."

"Now. Now you say something." Ralph looked at me and pointed at Tillie. "She could have tol' me at the car." He turned and a few minutes later was back, kicking open the screen door and carrying a metal-cornered glass box higher than his head and about six feet wide. Pops swept a row of Mason jars off the top of a cabinet and shouted, "Sit whatever it is over here."

Ralph craned his neck. "I can't see."

"Along the cellar wall."

Ralph lowered one end while Pops steadied the other.

"There ought be a plug behind this-here stand," Ralph said.

Pops stepped back from the cabinet and scratched his head.

"They got to have them lights," Ralph added. "An electric filter, or they croak." He disappeared onto the back porch.

Tillie turned to Pops, who stared at the tank. "Our new apartment Ralph picked out looks over the river." She glanced at the window. "The Tug, maybe it's the Ohio. I forget. Anyway, the rooms are teeney, so Ralph's been bugging me, 'Sell the fish, sell the fish.'"

"Fish," Pops said.

"We could have got a fortune, but I said, no way, that you would get a big kick out of the mollies. See, I'm thinking someday we might move to where we can have them back."

Pops pushed up the bill of his cap. "I'm to baby-sit your fish?"

My stomach muscles tightened. What had Pops said when they gave me to him?

"They're no trouble," Tillie said.

"I have enough to do."

Tillie's lower lip trembled. "You can use them for free. I wouldn't give them up, but Ralph says we don't have the room."

The words came at me like bullets. 'Don't have the room,' the same reason she had dumped me. How long ago? Twenty-five years? Then why were my insides in knots? My skin went clammy, and for some reason I felt ashamed although by rights the shame was their's. I looked around the kitchen as if there could be a place to hide.

"I thought you'd love them to death." Tillie sounded hurt.

"The whole shebang," Ralph said, jockeying a cardboard box through the doorway. He dropped it beside the tank. "Flakes, gravel, nets, light bulbs, aerators, you name it." He tossed a book on the table, *Happiness is Fish*. "Owner's manual."

I had brought my *Child's Imitation of Christ* when I moved in with Pops. That, jeans, a few blouses, and two or three pair of ragged panties. "No point in buying you stuff that don't show," Tillie had said. Pops had done the laundry that week, then had taken me straight to Gabe's. I came out with seven pairs of what he called seat covers and the first slip I ever owned.

"He don't like the mollies," Tillie said to Ralph.

His jaw tensed, and I wondered if the time had come

for him to pick a fight. Whenever we all were together, he would find something to get ticked off about and torment Tillie until she cried and me until I ran to my room.

"I told her I had enough work," Pops said.

Tillie reached into the box and lifted a Tupperware bowl filled with what looked like whirling black hairpins. "See how cute? Once you get to know them, you won't mind."

Enough was enough. I slipped around Pops and headed downstairs to the bathroom.

Instead of toilet paper, Pops cut newspaper into squares and impaled them on a bolt in the wall. Waste not, want not. I flushed, waited to see if the tank filled, jiggled the handle, then washed the newsprint off my hands in the stationary tub. When I opened the door to the outer basement I saw Pops rummaging through a box of extension cords. He handed me a four-way plug. "Don't lose this."

"Did you mind me?"

He smiled as he sorted through piles of tangled wire. "You bet your ass. When you bossed, I listened. Remember the night I was all tanked up and wanted to go to the Knights, and you took my keys and gave me hell? Saved my life."

"I didn't mean it that way."

He stood and carefully wrapped a cord around his wrist. "I know."

Upstairs, Tillie sat at the table. A saucer holding a smoldering Virginia Slim rested at her elbow. Lyda crouched on the table in front of her, lapping milk from a coffee cup. "Don't they feed you," Tillie crooned.

Ralph, standing by the outlet on the cellar wall, monkeyed with the aerator's motor, using a kitchen knife as screwdriver. "We decided to let you set up the fish yourself," Tillie said to Pops. "You know exactly how you'll want it." Meaning she and Ralph had no intention of hauling fifty gallons of water from the sink to the tank. Pops's lips were white, a sign his patience was stretched to the limit. I picked up the coffee cup and poured the milk into the cat's bowl. One smack from me and she jumped from the table.

"So," I said, sitting across from Tillie, "how have you been?"

She flicked on her lighter and described how the girl next door (a forty-year-old housewife) had bought a Chrysler right off the showroom floor the same week the men delivered a Magnavox forty-inch color set. "GE," Ralph corrected.

I leaned toward her. "I mean, how are you? You."

"Me? I'd never go Chrysler, what with the discount we get on Fords."

She propped her elbow on the table and lit another cigarette, and I rose to help with lunch. Ralph carried a chair to the corner beside the tank and sat down while Pops and I crossed paths carrying pots and dishes between the stove and the refrigerator, then to the table to set out pickles, horseradish, and bowls of hard-boiled eggs. I ladled cabbage rolls onto the turkey serving platter. Finally Pops brought out the juice container of whiskey, shot glasses, a six-pack of Bud, and his football-helmet tumblers. "None for me," I said.

"Have to have one shot for luck," Pops said, filling the tiny glass.

He poured beer into three tumblers.

"Got any Tom Collins mix?" Ralph asked. He must have caught Pops's expression. "Anything's okay." He dragged his chair midway between the wall and the table.

Pops lifted his drink. "To your new—" He paused.

"Place," I said clinking glasses with Tillie and Pops.

"Sveikas," Pops shouted. He downed the whiskey, the tumbler of beer, then slammed the glass on the table.

Ralph sipped and made a face. Tillie lowered her shot glass, a smile of orange lipstick curved below the rim.

Pops started passing roast pork, cabbage, kohlrabi crowns boiled soft as old tennis balls, kohlrabi greens garnished with short strips of white bacon. Ralph brought his chair to the table, surveyed the platters, and helped himself to the mashed potatoes. Light slanted through the window. The air, white with Tillie's cigarette smoke, seemed dusted with flour. Lyda slept on her side in a circle of sun.

I leaned back and idly watched Ralph holding his fork as if it was a trowel, smashing potatoes into a flat circle, dragging the tines across the top to make ridges, and I wondered why I hated him so much. True, he slapped Tillie around. But it was more, more than any one thing. The way he rubbed the front of his pants, looking slantways to see if anyone was watching. The way he hid in the bedroom when a neighbor stopped by to chat with Tillie, probably in there studying the lash and lust magazines buried in his closet. The way he paraded around in his terry-cloth bathrobe, hinting he wore nothing underneath, propping his feet up on the coffee table and allowing the robe to fall open—just for a second. As if anyone cared. Yes, my hatred was bigger than the sum of the parts—the climate, you might say, to his weather of day-by-day habits. As a novice I tried to get over it. Then I gave up and learned to live with the low maintenance feeling that lay there untouchable, like a cobweb under the bed just beyond reach of the broom.

He swallowed a mouthful and frowned. "Pasty."

Pops passed him the butter. "Where's the new job?"

"Air-Tek," Ralph replied. "This Williamson company bought out by PAW." He dug into the butter with his fork. "Me? I'll be designing software for the EPA." He lowered his head and said with his mouth full, "And selling." Ralph always tried to pass himself off as a computer expert.

"Which more than the other?" Pops asked.

"Thelling. Selling."

"You get a regular paycheck?" Pops asked.

"A draw, for now. But only at first," Ralph added quickly. "There's big money in this, man, real big."

Tillie broke in, "Ralph says since we're right on a river we can have a—"

Ralph's lips puckered, and he shot her a warning look,

then asked Pops, "Still in the rabbit business?"

"Meat or fur?"

"Meat, I guess it was. You had them bunnies penned up in boxes in that old bus."

"That old bus is empty now," I said, looking straight at Pops. "Isn't it."

He tipped his glass to me, then drank. "I sold it to Bayloukas."

Bayloukas was Pops's crony who lived a few miles down the road. I sat back and folded my napkin in my lap. "Mirabile dictu."

"But it didn't have no motor," Ralph said.

"Bayloukas don't drive," Pops replied.

"Why—" I began.

"He don't read either," Pops said. "That's why they won't give him a license."

"I mean, why did he buy it?"

"Snakes," Pops said, as if that explained everything.

"Sorry I asked."

"Smart mouth." Pops loosened a cabbage roll with his fork. "He needs a place for the biggest bunch in West Virginia. Which reminds me, can you do me a favor? Someday this week, come with me when I take the bus to Bayloukas—it's up on his kid's flatbed. Then you can drive me home."

Pops, knowing the Order's attitude about family ties, would never have asked before. Which meant in his eyes I must have been already free. Thursday was Vinnie's funeral, Friday was the staff meeting at the mother house. "Tomorrow morning I go to Chafin State for a sick call. How about after work?"

"Sure."

Then I remembered Hunt. "And I might be bringing a friend."

The whiskey eased the knots in my shoulders. Ralph and Pops drifted into their usual discussion about horsepower and gas guzzlers. Lyda sat under the table gnawing at pork fat that had been dropped on a napkin. Empty beer cans surrounded each plate except mine. The kitchen grew warmer, and I felt drowsy, almost safe. Then Ralph leaned back, rubbed his stomach, and nodded at Tillie.

She looked at Pops, then at her plate and said, "We're in a bind, sort of."

I straightened, and Pops lowered his glass.

She spoke softly, the words coming out fast and flat. "We need a loan. We'll pay back with interest," she added quickly. "It's not the money see, it's a credit rating thing, this judgment against—"

"What for?" Pops sounded wary.

Ralph said, "This creep says I owe him—."

"The money," Pops said irritably. "What's the money for?"

Ralph smiled, his dentures sparkling white. "A Chris-Craft cabin cruiser, flying deck, the works." He pointed to me. "She can tell you we been needing one for years."

True. Dusty issues of *Yachting* magazine had always lain on Tillie's maple cobbler's bench, fanned out like a hand of cards slapped on a table.

Ralph turned to her, and they spoke as if they were alone. "A good investment."

"They don't depreciate."

"Collateral."

"How much?" Pops asked.

Tillie answered, "Dealer financing. Twenty percent down, that's twelve thousand. Not much."

Pops lay his fork across the top of his dish and said quietly. "That could buy a whole fucking house."

Tillie's eyes filled. "We want a boat."

He laid his knife alongside the fork. "Where you could keep your fucking fish."

My mouth went dry.

Tillie turned to Ralph. "I told you he didn't want the mollies."

"I don't have to listen to his kind a obscene language. No way." Ralph said, pushing aside his plate. He stood and adjusted his belt. "I'm going out to get me some gas."

Pops reached under the table for the juice jar. "Funny,

you're too good to shit in my cellar."

Ralph headed toward the door.

"But not on yourself," Pops said calmly. "Want to hear about my money? Go sit down." He leaned back and watched Ralph slink back to his seat, then poured himself a shot. "I don't have it. When I retired, I paid off the house. There's two, maybe three hundred in the bank for emergencies." He added thoughtfully, "That is, I don't have it unless I borrow on this place."

Was he out of his mind? How could he dream of giving these people anything? Then I recalled Camp Kanahwa, the Scout uniform apparently following him around like a police record. Except Tillie was grown up now.

"Why a boat?" I asked her.

The question seemed to hit her by surprise. She thought for a minute and said, "To help me lose weight."

"Six people can sleep on it at once," Ralph said.

I thought of Hunt's story about the fellow with the flat tire and of his question: "What drives them on?"

Ralph leaned toward Pops. "You don't have to borrow nothing. As I recollect, my dad's last will and testament—" He shrugged as if it wasn't important. "It left cash to her here, instead of lawful to me, that must be clocking down interest in your name because she had to, what is it they say, Til? Take the vow of poverty?"

Pops shook his head. "I'm keeping that money for her."

Except I had it now and Pops was buffering me from having to say no. That would be his way.

"Not exactly," I said. "The account had been owned jointly, perfectly acceptable under the Rule. It's been signed over to me because I need it."

"What for?" Tillie asked.

There was no way to get around it. "I'm leaving the Order."

Her eyes widened.

"So I'll need a place to live." For a minute I forgot it wasn't people who cared sitting across from me, but Tillie and Ralph. My mind's eye saw me looking out a picture window at my garden; corn, tomatoes staked knee high. My books and lithographs arranged just the way I wanted them around a wood-burning stove. "A small trailer, but on a lot big enough for a garden." My voice was dreamy. "Some furniture, that Scandanavian stuff, teak and bright reds and blues. I'll have a dog and—"

"Why are you splitting?" Ralph asked.

Everyone's question these days, and by now my answer should have been down pat. But this time it had to be one Tillie and Ralph could grasp. Then I recalled the reason he had used for every job he had ever quit. "There's no future in it."

"Bet you get good bennies. Blue Cross."

Suddenly Tillie choked, and tears ran down her face.

"Why on earth are you crying?" I asked.

"How could you do this to us?"

"Do what?"

She blew her nose in a napkin. "Leave. How will I explain it to people?"

I didn't know whether to laugh or scream. "You didn't care two cents when I entered. You never even took me to church. Pops bought my First Communion dress." I touched the collar of my blouse. "Remember the one with white roses on the yoke?" Tillie stared as if she had never seen me, and I dropped my arm. "Oh, what's the use?"

She reached in her purse for a tissue and dried her eyes. "There's only one of you. There's two of us. You won't need all of it."

Ralph said quickly. "That's an idea there, Til. It must be what, over thirty grand by now." He and his calculator had been busy. "Take some off the top, buy your trailer on time, and we'll better the interest rate, whatever it is."

"That's the least you could do," Tillie said.

"What I don't spend, I have to save."

Ralph turned to Tillie. "You hear that selfishness?"

"Convents train them that way."

I glanced at Pops sitting quietly, as if lost in thought. It was possible, just possible, that he might be planning to take out that loan. Against the house he risked forty years in the mines to pay off. For a boat? For Tillie? I turned to her, "You don't even know what river you're on."

She crumpled the tissue and dropped it in an ashtray.

This time Pops needed protection, not me. From himself.

"I'm saving that money for my grandfather."

Pops looked at me, startled.

I spoke deliberately, so he would get the message. "Just last Sunday night I was thinking the next few months could bring anything. Anything."

He avoided my eyes.

"Convents train them to worry about old people," Tillie said. "Only he looks younger every day."

"I'm not giving you money for a boat."

The room was quiet.

"It's the convent," Tillie repeated.

"You're making excuses," Ralph said. "Because she's just like you and your old man."

"I'm not like—"

"Look at you, all whiny-eyed."

Usually his fight came earlier, but I suppose hoping to get something he had been on good behavior. He watched Tillie dig for another tissue. "You're too sensitive, can't say anything around any of you. Too sensitive."

When Ralph got ugly, Pops would find something to do in the barn, I would sit with clenched teeth, Tillie would cry, Ralph would shout, march out the door and slam it behind him, then a minute later be back, calm. Then he would start in all over again—as if we were reading from scripts.

Only it didn't have to be this way. Time was running out for each of us. On Pops for sure. Who could say when God would give us another chance to make up for the bad years. Getting old was a high-wire act without the net.

I reached to touch Ralph's arm, thought better of it, and rested my hand near his. "I know you're disappointed," I said quietly. "It's not that no one wants you to have"—a boat would be too precise a lie—"what you want."

Ralph shrugged and wiped his mouth on his sleeve.

"But Pops has a point." I went on. "For that money you could buy a house. You can come visit me when I'm settled, and when I see my way clear, we might work something out." My words amazed me. An out-and-out bribe to keep, or to get, a relationship with them—how on earth had I stooped to this?

Ralph moved his hand away.

Tillie poured herself a second cup of coffee and said thoughtfully, "It's silly, a house. Most of the time we eat out." She held the sugar spoon over her cup and watched the stream of white grains, and if I didn't know her better, I would have sworn her eyes had a look of shrewdness. "Of course, you could always ride in the boat with us."

I drew back. So she had understood my bribe and was countering with one of her own. And if she sensed what I wanted and was holding out for better terms, it meant she wasn't so dumb after all: food for thought. The skin on my forehead pulled together, a sure sign of migraine.

Ralph said, "The old writing on the wall, Til. She's not going to work out anything." He stood and stretched. "Even if she did want to, she can't. She can't even hold a job." He lifted his jacket from the back of his chair. Tillie glanced at his face, drained her cup and pushed it away.

"You don't know anything about me," I said.

He slid the chair under the table. I fought panic. They couldn't walk out, not just like that. There were still things to say. They didn't know about me going to Matewan. They hadn't asked about Pops. Not even about his high blood pressure. My eyes felt grainy and wouldn't focus, but I struggled to my feet.

Ralph nodded at Pops. "We got the rest of I-79 to tackle."

"Don't go," I said. "We've got to stop hurting each other."

His eyes seemed to grow larger, those watery turquiose pupils too shallow to retain any image inside his brain. "Me? Hurting you? You the one's sitting on my lawful money."

We were pulling further apart, and minutes were slipping away. "Don't you understand that you are dying?"

Ralph pointed to his chest. "Who, me?"

"I mean, we all are, and today will be a part of our judgment."

He reached into his jacket and pulled out his car keys. "Time we hit the road, Til."

"Sit, while I fix you a little bite for in the car," Pops said.

Tillie looked at Ralph, then at me, swept her cigarettes into her purse, and rose.

I stepped aside as they filed past me on their way out the door. "I'll pray for you," I said.

I followed them to the porch and watched them trail across the yard. Ralph handed Tillie his coat, then climbed into the driver's seat. She slammed the passenger door. A minute later, the window came down and a strip of cellophane from a pack of Virginia Slims glinted in the sun, then whirled to the grass. The car backed onto the driveway, turned, and clattered across the bridge. No one had said good-bye.

I felt empty, spent. A knife hacked at the nerves behind my eyes. I rested my arms on the banister and stared into the trees. Migraines always gave me fever and chills, and I shivered despite the hot sun. Pops came up from behind and said, "Someone just walked over your grave."

"You can see the fire tower on Geezer's Ridge."

He put his elbows beside mine on the railing, and we stared at the scarlet and gold leaves dancing in the wind. "Don't save no money for me," he said finally.

"Somebody had better."

"It's for you."

"I have more than I'll ever need." I nodded at the driveway where Ralph's car had been. "But never enough for them."

"They're over," he said firmly. "For today, anyway." He picked his teeth with a matchstick. "You know what?"

"What?"

"I been down to the Apache place. They got a special on doublewides with cathedral ceilings." His voice grew excited. "Free set-up and skirt. Plunk that baby in the middle of twenty acres. Nobody bothers you."

"A bit much."

"Baloney. Down Matewan that's nothing. One hundred, one thousand, twenty acres. Level if you can find it. You know what else?"

I turned to face him.

"It was to be a surprise, but what the hell." He pitched the matchstick into the weeds, and pulled a tin of Chattanooga from his breast pocket. "Bayloukas's dog."

"The mongrel with the big head?"

Pops wadded the tobacco between his fingers. "Lump's smart as a whip." He slipped the ball into his mouth and worked it along his jaw. "She had ten puppies, and yesterday, no shit, I bought you a black one with white spots."

I smiled, and the knife cut deep. "How big is its head?"

"Tomorrow night when we go out to Bayloukas's—" He stopped and studied my face. "You look like hell."

"Just a headache." By now it was short, sharp blows.

He put his hand on my forehead. "It's a blazer. Go upstairs, take a nap."

"I wish I could. But the teenager manning the door at the Mission expects me back. If you had a phone."

"I'll run over to Gigliano's. Mafalda can call for you."

I sat on the end of my narrow single bed. The same trough in the middle of the mattress, the same squeak in the box springs. I eased off my shoes and lay down. By now Ralph and Tillie were on the interstate. And unless I put them out of my mind, my head would get worse. Before coming upstairs I had taken half a Percodan. The prescription said one every four hours, but a whole tablet knocked me out. Tillie's mouth, caked with orange lipstick, Ralph's face, half-hidden behind aviator glasses, floated behind my eyes.

I tried to pray. Help us, the people of God. The words stopped me flat. No one is born to the devil, I reminded myself, not even Tillie and Ralph. But, Dear God, there's nothing inside them, they're animals born without souls. Look how I reached out, and Jesus says every single person in the world can be reached. A counterthought rolled beneath a wave of pain. If the reacher is good enough.

The knife bore down on my optic nerve. I held my breath until the throb settled into a steady beat. My mind was inching toward danger, the way I approached the garbage cans behind the Mission at night, always on the lookout for rats. I was blaming Tillie and Ralph when the failure was mine, wasn't it? It had to be. After all, whom had I not failed? God knew. I betrayed Him, my vocation. I had not helped—really helped—one single person who had passed through St. Michael's House. Vinnie—I held my breath again while the knife scraped bone—I had destroyed Vinnie. Who else? Who had been the first?

I had failed Scott, for sure.

My palms sweat from the rush of the drug; my heart pounded and I struggled to catch my breath.

Could I change? Not unless I relived every second of my life and this time got it right. Here all along I had acted as if someday I could start over and correct the mistakes, like practicing music. I had buried myself in a convent. Not getting along, I buried myself in the Mission. Now I would bury myself in the Matewan hills.

My face was on fire, and my thoughts softened as if melting. Somehow I would have to redo my time with everyone I had ever touched. Where was Scott now, so I could unzip his jeans and slip my fingers into the hot pocket, stroke his smooth dry skin, the stiff hairs I knew were blond.

I sat up and stared at my hand. The gold ring of the Blood of the Lamb, wire closing tighter around my finger. I was trapped in a corridor so narrow there was no room to turn. I couldn't breathe, couldn't retreat. There was only the struggle forward, and forward was just one more place to be buried.

I might as well go downstairs and finish off the Percodan. It wouldn't make any difference. Eternity would be Hell, of course. But it would be Hell anyway if I left the Order.

I lay back and covered my eyes with my arm. And if I didn't leave the Order, life would be Hell on earth.

10

That evening right after dinner, Sister Cleo showed up at the Mission. Just what I needed considering the morning at the farm. The Percodan had done the trick on the headache, but the dizziness and queasy stomach hung on. One good thing about migraines: they're a distraction, a proxy for other problems, like digging your nails into your palm when you're in the dentist's chair.

The minute I walked in the door, LaVerne hit me with a pile of telephone messages and the Shackle *Star-Democrat* folded to a front-page article about Vinnie. Then she pointed to Mr. Stotler, whose daughter had stood him up. The poor soul had been sitting in the hallway since noon waiting to go home. Manny was on his way out the door to return an ice chest to the caterer, and I asked him to drop the old man off. I took care of the phone calls and scanned the newspaper at the same time. The article was short and to the point: "Cause of death to be determined."

I went through the afternoon routine, but what with preoccupation over funeral arrangements (I had another long talk with Cindy Le Clair) and what I would say to the bishop (I made an appointment for the following Monday), my every move was forced—pick up the telephone, open the mail—one half of me a robot taking

orders from the other half. Stella had fixed an early dinner; the Knights were meeting at seven, she reminded
me. After Pops's cabbage rolls I needed food like a hole in
the head, but I went to the table anyway. Control, structure, the whole point of the Mission: model self-control,
impose structure onto the resident's lives, set limits. I
blessed the meal, then passed the gravy.

"How's the job going?" I asked Pavel. His eyes seemed
brighter, and his cheeks were slightly pink, the first hint of
sunburn his skin had ever seen.

"I'm beat. Sanding floors is like work." He bent over
his plate and finished his slice of meat loaf. The job
seemed to be doing his appetite as much good as it was
his bank account. "Tomorrow we varnish if the weather
holds."

"A stupid waste," Manny said. He wiped his hand on
the front of his sweatshirt. Someone—or maybe he had
done it himself—had whacked off his ponytail, and his
kinky hair now stood in spools. I noticed his arms seemed
loose-jointed, floppy, and I wondered if he was doing
drugs again. I tried to see if his pupils were dilated, but he
avoided my eyes.

"Let's work on being more supportive of each other," I
said.

Manny tore a slice of bread in half.

"And chew with your mouth closed," I said.

"So tomorrow I might get time and a half after
five," Pavel said. "Varnish has to go on all at once."

Stella held her fork midair. "What about my bingo
club?"

Every Wednesday she volunteered at the potluck supper
and bingo at the firemen's hall. Pavel ran his fingers
through his thin brown hair. "I could be until eight or
nine."

"Can you run Stella over?" I asked Manny.

He tipped back his chair and tossed his napkin beside
his plate. "I got plans." He brought his knee up against
the table. I pointed to it, and he swung the chair forward.

"Such as?"

"A social engagement, you might say."

Hanging out in Gobetsky's is what he meant. "Pavel's on a new job, and they count on Stella to call numbers. How about you and Pavel working this out?" I leaned towards Manny. "Sometimes we have to do for one another."

Manny launched into a complicated lie about his study group meeting at the Dairy Queen. Pavel pointed out that he had to empty the trash cans; Manny said he was being dumped on. I reached in my pocket and felt for the Percodan tablet, broke it along the scored line, then swallowed it while they went on haggling. What was I doing here anyway? Trying to make a dent in these kids was banging my head against one more stone wall. I picked at a wedge of IGA cake. Maybe Pops had been right, that people do what they're going to, no matter what do-gooders do. On and off I had been thinking about Pops's snake story; it was beginning to take on a new meaning.

One afternoon at the farm I had tried to explain the concept of social work to Pops.

"What do you do it for?" he had asked.

"To help people."

"Help them what?"

I thought for a minute, then said, "Whatever they want to do."

"What if they want to do bad?"

"You help them see right is better."

"You ever hear a snake bark?"

I shook my head, and he went on. "One day Dog felt sorry for an adder—copperheads, the hillbillies call them. Anyway, Adder couldn't bark. Bark, Dog said, and you chase the owls and hawks that want to do you in. Try it. You'll be a better person. You won't bite anymore. Adder thought it was a terrific idea. So Dog rolled up his sleeves. It took them all day and all night, but finally Adder yapped, then growled, and pretty soon he was howling to beat the band. Satisfied, Dog went home. Next thing you know all the adders in the village growled, snapped, and howled. Before long they got so good they started getting barking jobs. Herding sheep—they were lightning fast. They guarded houses like nobody's business. Soon there were no dog jobs left. Something had to be done. Dog went back to Adder and apologized. Said he had wanted to do good, but overdid it. He asked Adder to forget the whole thing. Sure, Adder said. Except help me, please, to give back the bark. Just move your neck down to here where I can reach it."

Pops had laughed and leaned back in his kitchen chair.

"Then what?" I asked.

"Figure it out."

"He put the bark back?"

Pops looked at me strangely. "What's wrong with you?"

I was about to slice another piece of cake when Stella glanced at the doorway, then struggled to her feet. Sister Cleo, briefcase under her arm, stood on the threshold. "The front door was unlocked," she said. "The little girl at the desk in the foyer said you'd be in here. Don't you lock the door?" Sister's voice was sharp, but she was smiling.

I nodded to the residents. "This is Sister Cleo Maria." A good name for a clipper ship, I was tempted to add. "She's the assistant coordinator for recreational activities at the mother house. She's coming to help us."

Stella moved a folding chair to the table. "Sit," she said.

Ignoring her, Sister turned to me. "Is the door always unlocked?"

"How else could people drop in at a drop-in center?"

"Someone's going to— Did the police decide what happened to the man upstairs? The *Star-Democrat* said—"

"What happened was that someone, perhaps on drugs, broke in. There was a scuffle, our resident was killed."

"That's your theory. When will you know for sure?"

"The lead detective is hard to reach." Technically true. But I didn't tell her that I had spoken to Kalisky this afternoon. The autopsy report would be released tomorrow after the commissioner reviewed it. Meanwhile,

Kalisky had added, in a rare burst of candor, that I was not to worry. I took it to mean that the police had a lead on the burglar, and it was someone who would not be returning to the Mission.

"How will this affect the Mission? Does Bishop Crumrine know?" Sister asked.

Questions, questions, Sister Cleo could drive you nuts with them, always trying to get more than she gave, a perverse form of aggression. I rose. "It's time we put up the dishes," I said to Manny and Pavel. We circled the table, crumpling napkins and stacking plates, Sister one step behind me. "Did you know I'm moving in Monday?" she said. "Could I see my room?"

One side of me said let her come, let them all come. Would anything make a difference? Yet I instinctively moved to protect the Mission from her no-mind interference. "The police will tell us when the room can be used again. For now it's sealed shut."

Manny shoved a chair in place under the table. "She's to be in Vinnie's old room? The same bed and everything?"

Sister raised her eyebrows. "But this house must have at least ten bedrooms."

"Six," I said. "But we're certified for only four residents because of fire escapes, sprinkler systems, stainless steel—never mind."

"What's that got to do with me?" she asked. "I'm staff, not a"—it took her a minute to remember—"resident."

Pavel had disappeared into the kitchen. Stella was brushing crumbs from the tablecloth, and Manny was staring out the window and, I suspect, taking in every word. "The building needs major work, and there's no point applying for HUD money until the city certifies us for more occupants."

Sister shrugged. "It doesn't have to be fancy. I can make do."

"The west wing was wiped out by fire years ago. The windows are boarded up, there's no heat, and powderpost beetles are chewing through the baseboards."

She stared at the centerpiece of plastic flowers, then raised her head. "What about bunking in with you?"

"Forget it."

Manmy snorted. Sister glanced at him, then back at me. "We'll talk later."

"After you line up Mother Silesia," I said.

She shifted her briefcase to her other hand. "May I see the rest of the place before I leave?" she asked politely. "I hardly remember it from open house four years ago."

Stella called out, "Is that all the dishes?" Manny, balancing three glasses in one hand, kicked open the kitchen door.

I made a show of looking at my watch. My head hurt, and I wasn't about to act as a guide. Also, limiting her time with me would prevent a slip-up, her weaseling herself a corner somewhere. "Excuse me," I said and went into the kitchen. Manny was tapping the door of the bird cage and whistling. "Can you give Sister a tour of the Mission, then see her to her car? I have things to attend to."

"She seen the best of it on her way in."

"Just show her the lounge, dining room, the Busy Bees' workshop—don't forget the kiln and the well-baby clinic." As an afterthought, I said, "Skip my attic, Stella's sewing room, and the storage center."

"I got you," Manny said. "How be I show her the cellar? The coal bin wall the rat bit through?"

"Overkill," I said, swinging open the kitchen door.

Sister was inspecting Stella's rubber plant staked to a pencil.

"Manny will show you around. Be sure to send the notes you take to the Bishop. He should know what shape this place is in."

In the attic, I slipped on my bathrobe, snapped on the news, sat, and lowered the back of the chair to where the stiffness in my shoulders let up. My body fit precisely into the worn lumps and hollows of the upholstery. It had taken me awhile to get used to the green-and-purple Barca Lounger thrown in with the 1950s bedroom suite, the bishop's largess. The day the delivery truck came from St. Vincent de Paul's Thrift Shop, I had been on a home visit, and Stella, whom I had just hired, had the monstrosity hauled to my room. I meant to have it moved downstairs. But after catnapping in it every night during MacNeil-Lehrer, the chair was starting to grow on me.

I felt drowsy and regretted not bringing a second cup of coffee upstairs. But slipping it past Sister Cleo would have been tricky. Besides, Stella was all wound up over her meeting, and I gathered she wanted the kitchen to herself. It was just as well. I had come around on the issue of the Knights having whiskey but didn't want anyone to see me see it in the house. I closed my eyes, my thoughts sharper than the noise from the TV set. In retrospect, my no-liquor policy might have been a bit arbitrary. After all, the Knights were adults and had a right to serve what they wanted at their club. Not arbitrary, I reminded myself. Dogmatic. I could be so rigid I made myself sick. I should have gone along with the liquor in the first place, spared Stella my pontificating. Besides the Knights were Baltic Sea giants, as Pops called them, and he was probably right when he said Baltic Sea giants couldn't be pushed around. Especially old ones. And most of the Knights were as old or older than Pops unless the lodge had mustered up new blood. I recalled the photographs in his Streikas, their tabloid filled with sandy snapshots of men with their hands flat on their knees, sitting in folding chairs against a backdrop of knotty pine. I never knew what the captions said; I couldn't read the language until my residence in Suvalki, and I hadn't come across a Streikas since I returned.

Were the Knights' parties as wild as they used to be? When I was a kid, Pops always took me to the Barley Festival at Shackle Run, five hundred yards of muddy beach and a splintery platform of railroad ties on pontoons in the middle of the river. Three solid days of boilermakers, polkas, sweat, and potato salad curdling in the hot sun usually ended with some Knight being dragged out of the water fully dressed and half-drowned.

Then there was December 8, commemorated by the Knights sitting around tables in the Teamsters' Hall and singing Lithuanian drinking songs (which sound like hymns) accompanied by Charlie Antonaitas on the accordion—until Charlie passed out and the Knights went a cappella. During novice's training, I discovered the date marked the conclusion of Vatican II. I had asked Pops about this and about the crusade business that I had gotten wind of through Stella.

"This Grand Master's a snake in the grass," was all Pops would say.

The Grand Master I remembered was a huge back-slapping Suvalkian, who, whenever he saw me, yelled, "Here comes the little Miss Marlene Dietrich." He could play "Red Sails in the Sunset" on the mandolin and read tarot cards.

Apparently Vito's style of Grand Mastership was more restrained. Stella told me he dropped out of Jesuit training in the old country to come to Shackle to be a millionaire. He settled for steady work as a long-wall operator and a pension from PAW.

The West Virginia news covered Governor Caperton's budget crisis and the miners' strike in Rum Creek. Then it seemed only a minute later Stella was knocking and "Having it All" was almost over. Half-asleep, I opened the door. One look, and she spun to face the hall. Then I realized my head was bare, the veil draped over the lampshade.

"It's all right," I said.

She didn't turn around. "Remember yesterday when that grease got mixed up in the drain?" she asked.

"What now?"

"It's no go." She continued to look away. Her black smock, of some slithery material, was cut along the lines of her housedresses. Earrings matched her rope of jet beads.

"How much standing water?"

"A foot. Give or take."

"I must have fallen asleep. What time is it?"

"After seven-thirty. The Knights are almost here. So far Joe's truck is in the parking lot. He brought Bayloukas." She started toward the stairs.

"By the way, is my grandfather coming? He didn't mention it this afternoon."

"Your old man pays dues, sure," Stella called over her shoulder. "But these days he's boycotting meetings." Her tone implied it was just as well.

"I'll be down in a minute."

"And, Sister," she said over her shoulder, "I warned Manny and Pavel, it's stay out of the meeting or else."

The kitchen table was extended to double-length and pulled to the center of the room. A white linen cloth covered the formica and hung to the floor. In the center a purple Czechoslovakian crystal candelabrum lorded over a circle of tiny paper flags glued on matchstick poles; Lithuania's red, white, and green alternating with our red, white, and blue. Off to the side, a tole tray held a silvery forest of vodka bottles and one fifth of Jack Daniel's, Green Label. Stella caught my glance and said, "In case Father Kozakas stops by." Tumblers decorated with geese sporting nooses of pink ribbons around their necks sat at the tip of silver knives.

I touched a brilliant armature. "Where did all this stuff come from?" I asked.

"The Knights' treasury."

I straightened. "Why do I smell onions?"

"Kugelis is all."

A scarlet cut-glass platter piled high with Crushiki sat on the countertop beside loaves of plutonium-dense Baltic bread. On the stove, a ring of kielbasi simmered in a casserole filled with sauerkraut. I suddenly remembered Stella was authorized to charge food to the Mission's account in stores around town. "Vito's footing the bill for everything?" I asked. "Quite a spread."

Stella bent and fiddled with the oven thermostat. "Not necessarily."

My jaw tightened, and I remembered the warning about gritting my teeth. "How am I supposed to do the

bookkeeping on this? Where's the line item for your parties? In the archdiocese overhead? Our Older Americans
grant, the state supplemental?" My voice rose. "The West
Virginia Coalition for the Homeless?"

Stella carefully closed the oven door, then clicked the
dial ahead one notch. "A problem," she said.

The back door slammed shut, and Bayloukas was
scraping his boots on the doormat. He was skinny, nervous; black lung seemed to fire his energy instead of
draining it, as the disease did with others. Fighting time,
he was everywhere at once, full of plans and ideas, most
of them half-baked. A burly black dog on a leash padded
up beside him, then shook. Bayloukas, polishing his heel
on the bristles, said, "Lump don't like it cooped up in the
truck alone, Sister. Stel said it was okay to bring 'er in."

Squinting, from panting too hard, Lump stared up at
me. I smiled, and her eyes, gray slits, narrowed smugly,
and her mouth widened an inch. Bayloukas slapped the
long-haired flank. "Solid Weimaraner." I looked at the
bushy tail. "Except the collie parts," he added. "Ten
babies too. Every one of them dead ringers for their old
lady."

"Why the chain?" asked Stella.

Bayloukas stooped, unsnapped the leash, and Lump
scrambled across the room, skidded to a stop at the cat's
dish and wolfed down the leftover Nine Lives. Bayloukas
clapped his hands. "Here girl." Lump swung to the next
bowl and water splashed over the linoleum. Then she was
licking the dish, clack-clacking it against the wall.

I went to the sink. Greasy ripples rubbed the steel
banks.

"Zedonis pick his apples yet?" Bayloukas asked.

"I was out to the farm this morning, but he didn't say."

Wilson's Plumbing and Heating, practically on retainer
to the Mission, used radio-dispatched vans. Except after
hours Harry Wilson would be coming out himself and
couldn't miss the whiskey on the table.

Bayloukas swung the lid off the pot of sauerkraut.
"You don't get them winter apples before now, you're a

goner."

I opened the lower cabinet and studied the pipes.
Harry, who was none too bright, simply took the trap
apart and cleaned it. "Where's that wrench with the red
handle?" I asked Stella.

Footsteps thumped on the back porch, voices, then
three men stood in the doorway. Stella rounded the stove
and said, "Sister, here's Joe Jaluski." I nodded at the man
in a camel hair jacket at least three sizes too big. A faded
button reading "I gave at the office" didn't cover the hole
in the lapel.

"Jake," Stella said. Then she stage-whispered, "A distant relation of Johnny Unitas." Jake smiled.

"And Ace." He held out a hairy calloused hand.

Bayloukas shouted in my ear, "Shot down over the
Burma Hump."

Not one of the three could have been under
seventy. They lived in the B and O Hotel, a firetrap
licensed for single-room occupancies. Most of the men
there were immigrant miners who had outgrown or out-
lived their families. During the day they congregated on
the benches in front of the Friendlies in the Mountaineer
Mall. Love or money couldn't lure them to Meet-and-Eat
or the Busy Bees. No question that the table-wiping,
hymn-singing, old-line West Virginia women who tyran-
nized the Mission's senior citizens' club scared the living
daylights out of the B and O crowd.

"Sit, sit," Stella said. "This is your home."

I rolled back my sleeve, dipped an arm in the water,
and jiggled the strainer. For half a second I considered
asking for a volunteer plumber. Except there wasn't a sensible or a steady eye in the room except for Stella's, and
she was dressed to the teeth.

Bayloukas dashed from the counter to the table setting
out napkins and fine-tuning the lineup of the silverware.

"Your dog's all head," Ace yelled.

Stella sidled up to me to me and said quietly, "The
wrench is down the cellar. Only no one can monkey with
it now. Our meeting's a secret."

"Exactly why I'm not calling Wilson's. I'm going to tackle that trap myself and you will just have to trust me."

"Head does load it down some," Jake said.

Stella considered the carrot top turning slowly in the pool. "I imagine," she said thoughtfully, "a sister's closed-mouth as a priest."

"Right on." I laughed, as I moved toward the basement.

The day I moved into the Mission I resolved to steer clear of the cellar, knowing I could spend the rest of my life down there pitching out junk without ever hitting bare concrete floor. Just as I remembered, the rider-mower, its bag spilling grass shredded fine as dill, sat among empty paint cans. Hacksaw blades bound in spider web cocoons hung from nails in the crumbling block walls. I lifted a rusty coffee can and a waterbug shot behind a gasoline engine. The corner of the coal bin was dark, and I wondered if Manny, after all, had shown Sister Cleo the black hole in the wall edged with rat teeth marks. A few more minutes of rummaging, and I found the wrench on top of a five-gallon drum of blacktop. I peeled off the shriveled balloon stuck on the handle. All the while, I had been vaguely aware of the constant growl of the furnace even though it was at least seventy degrees outside. It hit me halfway up the stairs—this would be Stella's old-time hospitality—whiskey and a house hot as a fire in the Sahara.

Vito's voice soared, "To the Republic for which it stands—" I waited on the landing for a break in the opening ceremonies.

All told, nine knights stood around the table, their hands over their hearts. Stella, the auxiliary and the only non-voting member, she had explained, stood between Ace and Serge Adamaikas. Serge's corduroy jacket flared like a tutu over his wide hips. Some years ago his daughter took over the family restaurant, and he retired to a brick rancher near Lake Louise. Beside him stood gentle white-bearded Magnanias, nicknamed Magus, The Wizard. Magus owned the Universe, the newspaper kiosk beside the courthouse. Stella told me he had cut back his hours to finish his memoirs. Across from him, Louie, the chiropractor, leaned on an aluminum cane.

"—justice for all."

Before I could take a step, Vito whipped a pitchpipe from his breast pocket, blew, hummed, and faced the paper Lithuanian flag closest to him. "Leituva, tevyne musu," the Knights joined in. Fortunately, the anthem had only four verses. Most of the knights' songs have at least a hundred, and the singers never cheat.

Vito marked time with stiff jerks of his wrist. Tonight he seemed less mousey than usual, despite the hound's tooth double-knit leisure suit, no doubt a yard-sale relic. Somehow the pinched waist and stitched-in belt gave him stature, military airs. Something else—glasses—I didn't know he wore them. The round gold wire-rims offset his delicate, almost effeminate nose and sharp, pointy chin. All at once a picture came back to me, a reproduction of a sepia photo Pops had hung on the living room wall. Czar Nicholas, emperor of all the Russias, held the bridle of his horse with one hand and saluted with the other. A row of shiny buttons held his belted tunic tight across his chest. His eyes stared with fierce concentration into nothing.

I waited until the part about the sun destroying the clouds over the forests, then started past the table.

"Put down that wrench," Bayloukas whispered. The last stanza closed, and the Knights turned to me.

"I can help Sister." Jake slid back his chair, bumping the wall.

Louie, moving slowly to keep his balance, reached for his cane hooked on the edge of the table. "I fixed my own hydrotherapy."

"Just a clogged drain." Inspired, I added, "Insurance won't let anyone but staff fool with fixtures."

Bayloukas nodded knowingly and backed off. The Knights, chatting among themselves, took their seats. I dropped the bucket on the floor beside the sink, then for a second wondered if I could handle the job, and what I should do first. Christ was a carpenter, I reminded myself. First off, I would tackle the standing water. I hadn't watched Harry Wilson for nothing. Lifting the coffee can, I started to bail. From the corner of my eye, I noticed Stella and Vito mumbling back and forth.

"Hey, Bayloukas," Jake yelled. "You get them snakes together for the museum?"

"I bought me Zedonis's bus. The tourists will pay up front like you're supposed to, circle round and out the side door."

Vito raised his head. "In case you're wondering, Sister Zedonis has privileged communications, like Father Kozakas. Her being around during the meeting will be strictly kosher." No one seemed to be listening.

Then Stella got up and snapped off the overhead switch. The only light came from the turrets on the candelabrum, and the shaded lamp hanging low over the sink. Vito stood and tapped his glass with a fork.

"Welcome to the 223rd meeting of the Knights of Puntuckas, St. Stanislas Parish chapter of the international society dedicated to the aggrandizement and restoration of the most apostolic Holy Church of Rome before She turned."

I spilled a can filled with water into the bucket. Rome didn't turn, it fell. I mopped my brow with my sleeve. Then I recalled Stella saying how the Church had turned Protestant. So it was Vito who had given her that peculiar idea.

Lump padded towards the bucket, and I swung it onto the counter.

"The benediction. Please stand." Coughs, the scraping of chairs. I bowed my head.

"Dear God." The Grand Master's voice was firm. "Help me promulgrate Your blessings on us, Your crusaders. Deliver our Church from Protestant captivity. Send us to Jerusalem with the will to victory and the wisdom to rule the world in Your place."

Holding his glass in both hands, as he would a chalice,

Vito raised it to the ceiling. "Sveikas," he shouted.

"I Sveikata." The Knights clinked tumblers.

Captivity? I resumed bailing. Then I recalled Stella also telling me she believed Catholics were in a slump and that someday soon, thanks to the newly freed Eastern Europeans coming into the mainstream of the church, it would reemerge as a world power.

The sink was empty now. At this point Harry always turned off the water supply. I tried to recall where the valve was.

Vito snapped his fingers. "Minutes."

I took a flashlight from the drawer, knelt and opened the cabinet, then inched a mousetrap baited with Velveeta from under the sink to under the stove. Something warm brushed my arm, then blasts of hot dog-breath smelling of Nine Lives. I checked to see that Bayloukas wasn't watching and gave Lump a swift punch in the ribs. She ambled back to the radiator and flopped down.

Louie adjusted his glasses. "Our Grand Master called the meeting to order. First item was to finalize the Barley picnic at the Teamsters' pavilion this coming Friday with or without their folding chairs that come extra. Jake said he'd ask Hoffenburger's Funeral Parlor. Same's last year, it's BYOB, with Bayloukas tending bar for beer and setups, and he said he'd buy ahead so long as he's covered up front by ticket sales. Everyone went yay on Broderick's, them giving the best price anyway on cabbage roll and spaghetti party trays."

"You call?" Vito asked.

"We're all squared away," Louie replied. "It was an eight-to-one vote for the Polka Punks on the music."

"It's the name what gets to me," Jake interrupted.

"Next item of business, the Grand Master asked the secretary, meaning me, if we heard back yet from Mr. Arafat."

My hand froze on the valve.

"Talking it over, we said wait. The next item—"

"He's stalling," Vito said.

The room became still. Lump yipped in her sleep; her

paws twitched, her tail pounded the linoleum.

"Arafat travels," Ace finally said.

"Islams have a whole month Christmas, only it comes at different times," Joe said hopefully. "I bet that's where he is."

Serge sounded confident. "You know what I think?"

Vito passed the vodka to Stella. She leaned and filled his drink to the top, then handed the bottle back.

"I think he's working on it," Serge continued. "Look at it this way. Suppose Yasir says, right off the bat, sure we'll swing with this cartel. Anybody could use Jerusalem. He's still got to check with his legal-eagles."

"Makes sense," Jake said.

"You sure you got the right address?" Vito asked.

Louie set down his drink. "You keep asking and I keep telling you, the letter would of come back."

"Rag-head," Vito muttered. He pushed the bottle towards Stella and pointed to Ace's empty glass. "Don't he realize a PLO-Vatican cartel can't lose?"

"We don't have a cartel yet," Magus said.

The wire rims of Vito's glasses flashed. "The PLO's leverage for the Vatican and visie-versa. How many times do I have to drum it in?"

"That you work both sides of the street, I get," Magus said. "What I don't get is how you think no one else can catch up."

Bayloukas intervened. "Sure as shooting Yasir's on that Christmas thing." He shouted at me. "Sister, what's that called?"

I struggled to my feet. Maybe I should I just say flat out, "Look, all of you, don't write to terrorists and don't listen to Vito Pucas, who's obviously lost his marbles." On the other hand, most likely their crackpot mail was lying in a dead letter pile. It wasn't going anywhere. And neither were these sorry old men.

"Ramadan."

Bayloukas turned to Vito. "Ramadan."

Then I remembered Jim Vichanno in Chafin State Hospital. Jim's body had come back from Vietnam, his mind

had not. Posttraumatic shock syndrome. "I can't go to the
snack bar with you, Sister," he said. "I gotta wait on the
supply chopper."

"No sweat," said the aide. "I'll keep a watch out and
you two go on down."

Later, in the superintendent's office, I had slammed my
fist on the desk. "Every attendant must be trained to
never, never enter a patient's delusional system."

I stepped toward the table. "Might I say something?"

Magus tapped the Grand Master's elbow, and they
went into a huddle. Bayloukas folded his napkin into
thirds. Harry picked at his sleeve. Louie, his lips moving,
turned a page in his notebook. "We still have to go
refreshments," Stella said irritably.

Vito straightened. "Just don't ask about our bylaws,"
he said to me.

"Writing terrorists won't resolve anything. I think
you're misunderstanding the changes in the Church and I
think you should invite Sister Jo Ann from our educational outreach office at the diocese to speak at one of your
meetings."

The candlelight softened Vito's face. It glowed from an
inner light, or maybe from the heat. He must not have
heard me. "Mr. Arafat will pay for our crusade. The crusade that will unite us with our Eastern European brothers
who for fifty-eight years have been locked up behind the
Iron Curtain and who will help us create the new world,
mobilize with us against the Vatican II sham." He closed
his eyes. "The second world is over. The new Jerusalem
will be Vatican East, the third world."

"The second is over," Joe repeated softly.

"Did you know Vatican II recaptured the spirit of the
early Christians in the catacombs?" My voice sounded
prim even to me.

"Bull feathers," Vito snapped.

"What the Grand Master means is, Sister," Magus said,
"with all respect, the changes aren't so hot.

"What changes?" I asked.

"For instance, why doesn't our new St. Stanislas have

an altar rail?" Magus allowed a few minutes for the question to sink in.

I forced a smile, but suddenly recalled an incident I hadn't thought of in years, a story involving Sister Cordelia's brother, a Jesuit. One night shortly after the wrap-up of Vatican Two, he and a few others were ordered to gather jackhammers, picks, and wheelbarrows and load them into the monastery's van. In the dead of night (presumably to avoid a run-in with a devout parishioner) they drove to Saint Ignatius. The altar rail was the first to go, the marble stanchions chopped clean out from the foundation. Then statues were hacked from plaster niches: Stations of the Cross, cornices, icons ripped from the walls. While this was going on, I wondered, did the monks sing? Above the rat-a-tat-tat of the jackhammers? Did they shout, "*Ad majorem Dei gloriam,*" with each swing of the pick? Sister Cordelia didn't say.

"Why don't we have real candles anymore?" Magus asked.

I avoided his eyes. "The Women's Aglow Society—."

"Iconoclasts," he said sadly. "Like flies."

"Oh come on, Mr. Maganias." The cuff of my veil had become steel wool, and I desperately needed to scratch, but, somehow, in front of Magus it would be obscene.

His beard quivered. "They took our sacred language."

Every single Knight seemed to stop breathing. The radiator clanged. Lump stood, circled, then collapsed a few feet further from the heat.

"You mean the Latin Mass?" I asked, knowing perfectly well what he meant.

His voice seemed to come from a hundred miles away. "The First World was the World of Our Father. The Second is the Son. It's over now. The Third will be the World of the Holy Ghost."

The candles burned straight up. Each Knight stared ahead. For one minute hearing the old man's words, not thinking them, but hearing them, they made sense—the way music makes sense.

Stella pressed her palms on the table and stood.

"Meanwhile, your refreshments are cementing."

The room stirred. Vito straightened his jacket with a shift of the lapels. "Thank you, Sister, for your interest," he said. He pointed to Stella, the vodka, then to Joe. "The minutes, go on," he said to Louie.

I picked up the wrench.

"Not much left." Louie said. "Our Grand Master gave a special commendation to George Bayloukas, who says he'll donate one half of his proceeds from the West Virginia Great Snakes Museum to us Knights. The meeting closed at eleven, Daylight Savings Time."

While the treasurer's report dragged on, I managed to get the trap apart. Using the wrench handle, I inched a slimy ball of what seemed to be wet bread into my palm. A few long black hairs and something pink—it could have been bubble gum—stuck to what probably had been a hard roll from Meet-and-Eat. I studied the wad and thought of the clogged toilet on the second floor, of how plumbers earned a living. Best that Jesus had been a carpenter. I dropped the roll into the garbage, tightened the fitting best I could, then turned on the tap and stared at the joint under the sink.

Dry as a bone. I turned the spigot on again full force, then off. Still dry. I dropped the wrench in the bucket and brushed my hands together. Who said we needed Wilson's Plumbing? And tomorrow I would take a look at that upstairs commode. I stepped back and admired my work, suddenly feeling capable and strong. Pops always said jobs with your hands were bigger than jobs with your brain. Now I knew how Jesus must have felt after a day in the woodshop. Most pictures of Him show a frail, effeminate Englishman's face. I think He was a huge burly man—strong enough to carry a lamb under one arm and a lost little kid under the other. He had a full black beard and flashing white teeth, sang as He built things like sturdy ash tables sanded velvet smooth, oak doors, walnut dressers and nightstands. My head felt light and clear; the cloud over the awful day had lifted and life became possible once more. I polished the sink with a paper towel, then turned on the tap one last time and stood back to reflect on the importance of having faith in oneself, the meaning of work, and the symbolism of the pipe curved gracefully as a child's arm reaching up to hold a parent's hand.

A glint of light caught my eye. I leaned forward, then dropped to my knees, and ran my finger along the joint. I drew back my wet palm and stared at the slim silver drop sliding around the curve.

Then I lifted the wrench from the bucket, slammed the cabinet shut, and picked up the coffee can. First thing tomorrow, before I left for the hospital to visit Angie, I'd call Wilson's. Meanwhile, the pail I had left under the sink would catch the slow, steady drip.

CHAPTER

11

The next morning I stood in the lobby of Chafin State Hospital. The watery light leaking through the barred windows, the cinder-block walls, this seventy-year-old building had to be the world's newest dungeon. I fastened the loop on my umbrella while my eyes adjusted to the light, and looked up at the life-sized photos of statesmen hanging above the mix-matched vinyl sofas, chairs, and standing ashtrays. There was ex-Governor Jay Rockefeller, gripping the bridle of an Appaloosa. Arch Moore hung beside him, a sheaf of papers in one hand, a gavel in the other. Don Chafin himself, ex-sheriff of Logan County, sat in a wicker rocker on what looked to be a verandah. A "No Loitering" sign was tacked beneath the gilt frame. That moldy smell of fresh-turned earth—where was it coming from? The cement walls festered, gray pocks erupting through thin green paint.

Some time ago I had decided when I got old, really old, or if they told me I had something incurable, I would make myself crazy. Not ranting and raving, just dotty, live in a cabin filled with old newspapers and cats somewhere in the middle of the woods. Going nuts was one thing, I reminded myself. But calling attention to it and winding up in here was another.

I tucked the umbrella under my arm and headed

toward the guard.

"Hep you?" He swung his feet from the desk. His stiff black pompadour narrowed into sideburns at his ears and fanned across his jaw. He laid the *Star-Democrat* on the blotter and smoothed it with his palm.

"I'm here to see Mrs. Hawkins, she's on Chafin Five."

He nodded to a corridor, and I moved toward the bank of elevators.

"Hold on."

I waited while he pulled his can of Red Man from his breast pocket, wiped the blade of his penknife back and forth on his knee, and slowly cut a wedge of tobacco. "I got to ring for someone to come get you." He lay down his knife and reached for the phone. "Why maximum security?" I asked. "She isn't the least bit dangerous."

After mumbling a few words into the mouthpiece he dropped the receiver. "Hawkins is new here." He lifted the empty Hardee's cup sitting on his desk. "She's got to earn the right to come down the lounge, same's you and me." Discretely he turned his head and spit into the Styrofoam.

Had he any idea of what he had said? I was on the verge of asking, then figured why waste the energy. "Rules without reason," I said.

He wiped his mouth on his sleeve. "Ain't it the truth."

I crossed the room to a chair mounted on an octagonal iron pedestal bolted to the floor, propped my umbrella against the armrest, then quickly stepped back. A pendant of dried yellow phlegm hung from the edge of the seat. Holding my breath, I knocked the crust onto the linoleum with the umbrella tip. The sofa on the other side of the room had a torn plastic cover, but I went over and sat on it anyway. Why on earth had I promised Clotilda I would come here? One simple excuse, and the whole thing could have been scotched.

Chafin was a dump, a landfill for every offender a judge decided was too crazy to clutter up the jails: old mountain men paying little girls to lift their dresses; street people from Parkersburg, their teeth rotting out of their heads, brains blown by PCB. Not one of them competent to be tried, or to live on their own either, floating in limbo like unbaptized babies, carriers of original sin. Officially Chafin was a mental rehabilitation center. Meaning every weekend Anapsine was passed out to the patients like afterdinner mints to quiet the halls when the place was short-staffed. The wards held six beds in hardly enough space for two. The one time I had tried to get a patient weekend leave, I found out assessments for therapeutic outings were running two years behind. The part-time psychiatrist—moonlighting from his Charleston practice—dropped in once a week to sign the prescriptions that the nurses wrote.

I glanced at my watch. The truth was the only reason I came was that I hadn't the heart to tell Clotilda I wouldn't. For months she had kept me posted on how Angie was getting on, and somehow that made me involved. But never, in spite of my prompting, would Clotilda talk about the girl's trial: I only knew what I had read in the *Star-Democrat*. That was two years ago, when Angie was seventeen with three kids, the twins still in diapers, Dwayne, her husband, ran out on her. A week later Angie gave birth to Kevin. Home from the hospital, she took to her bed and stayed put. Dwayne's sister kept the older kids, and Clotilda managed the baby during the day. One morning when Kevin was two weeks old, Clotilda found the infant face down in the toilet bowl, dead.

An aide with pale skin, blue eyes and dark curls tumbling to her shoulders, the hair of a country-western singer, twirled a key ring and called out, "You for Hawkins?" I joined her at the elevator. A few minutes later I was in the day room adjoining the ward. Someone had tried to make the place homey: a lampshade decorated with faded colonial soldiers, a picture of St. Mark's Square in Day-Glo. Folding chairs flanked two long Samsonite tables butted together end-to-end. Another visitor, a miner, judging from his black fingernails, sat across from a woman who was probably his mother. She wore a terry-cloth robe and was digging at a wart on her neck. The man didn't seem to notice her bloody fingers and lapel. A guard in a khaki skirt, a pistol in a leather case strapped to her belt, strolled between the tables and a coffee machine with cardboard wedged in the coin slot. I was just about to flag her to point out the wart business, when a door slammed and the aide led Angie in.

She was thinner than she was before being locked up. Plastic barrettes held her limp brown hair behind her ears. Her washed-out dress sagged like a rag on a broomstick. Wrinkles at the waist had been mangled flat, and I pictured her in a laundry somewhere in the bowels of the building, cauldrons of boiling blue starch, steam sharp with Clorox. One good thing, those sores on her cheeks seemed to be healing; they were pale pink and crusty, like the tail end of a bad case of poison ivy. The rash, Clotilda explained, came from reactions to Haldol, Mellaril—goodness knows what all they were pumping into her. Parchment skin cupped her dark eyes. Her face was calm, but her body quivered like a branch stirred by a breeze no one else could feel. She carried a gold beaded evening bag.

The aide motioned for Angie to sit, then knelt to snap a leg iron around her ankle, chaining the girl to the folding chair.

"When Mrs. Hawkins escapes, you'll lose your furniture," I said.

The aide stood and rubbed the small of her back. "Rules, honey. Rules." She ran her fingers through her curls, then sauntered to the sofa and lit a cigarette.

Angie moved and the chain clattered. "It don't bother me none," she said quietly.

"Are they treating you okay?"

Angie stroked the glittering bag.

"Do you remember me?" I asked. Before Angie's trouble, she and Clotilda had sat behind me every Sunday at Mass.

Angie shrugged. "You look like that nun runs the community center."

"I'm with the Mission."

Angie shifted and the chain clinked. Her voice sounded weary, as if tired from explaining the same thing again and again. "No you're not. You're dressed up to look like the nun what was in the first bunch of world people, but you're from the second bunch."

"What are you talking about?"

Her eyes narrowed, and her breath grew harsh. "You second bunchers lie. You got to pretend you never kilt the first bunchers." She struggled to her feet, and I put my hand on her arm. Her voice rose, "You running things now, but just you wait—"

The guard rounded the corner of the table. "Hawkins, you asking for the seclusion room?"

The man in the plaid jacket rose, leaned and kissed his mother's cheek.

Angie, her eyes on the miner, slid slowly back into her seat.

"Does your sister-in-law bring your children to see you?" I asked, trying to get the girl's attention.

Her breath quieted, and she nodded at the window. "They let me wave."

"Time's up," the guard said. The man patted his mother's hand.

Angie lowered her head and smiled a secret smile. Then she blew on the metallic purse strap and polished it with her elbow. "I got one in the oven you know."

It took me a minute to catch on. Then I stared into her yellow eyes, bright, too bright, not one single ray of common sense shining out. The person inside Angie would be born in this building. I looked away, to St. Mark's Square.

"Say 'Hi' to Benjy," the mother called to her son, now in the doorway. The aide took the woman's arm, and she resumed picking the wart with her other hand.

I faced Angie, searching for a sign that she understood what was going on inside her. No one could raise a child in Chafin. Clotilda was pushing seventy, and Dwayne's sister had a full house. A foster home? Another throwaway kid, a runaway soon enough. Running-tos, I called them, looking for someone, someplace, a home. They found one all right: jail or an institution as bad, or worse, than this warehouse.

I had been thrown away too. But for Pops.

Angie resumed rubbing the bag. "My mom was mad. You should have saw."

"You told her?"

Angie nodded, then yawned. "I'm sleepy most of the time. Only there's a rule says we can't lay down till four-fifteen." She yawned again.

But for Pops, I could have wound up in a place like this, with barred windows and rules crazier than the victims. I pictured the flimsy panelled walls of the convent, the tiny brass doorknobs. There was no connection between Chafin and the mother house, I told myself firmly. Absolutely no connection at all.

Angie dangled the purse above her head, opened her mouth and nipped at the beaded trim along the bottom. How easy it must have been for some guy to take advantage of her. I guessed at the number of weeks she had been locked up and figured whoever it had been hadn't been Dwayne. Jesus, Mary and Joseph, there should be something I could do for Angie. There wasn't much, except look out for her rights. The man who abused this kid should pay and pay through the nose. Chafin crawled with creepy attendants. The guy in the lobby. I checked to see that no one was listening. "Which one? I'll get a lawyer."

Angie dropped the bag in her lap. "Weren't like that, no sir. New bunch is way different." She leaned over the table. Her breath smelled of bacon. "New bunch does it with a bitty sunbeam of dirty light. Dirty, dirty." She made a circle with her thumb and third finger. "It comes down on me no better than that big around." She bent and started to pull up her dress.

"Stop that."

The girl cringed.

"It's all right, Angie. It's all right."

"Not yet," Angie said, drawing back. "The doctor's fixing me. Be later on today."

Fixing. The word blocked the idea. What had been broken? An addict fixed his delusion. Races, juries, elections were fixed. "Today?"

"Doc Ray don't come but once a week."

The skin on the back of my neck tightened. "Abortion is murder," I said stiffly. Then I remembered Kevin who would be—what?—one year old now? What did abortion, or murder, mean to Angie? Time was about all. The baby would be dead at ten weeks instead of ten months. Or ten years. Twenty years. "Do you understand what you are doing?"

"I'm supposed to sign a paper, says 'yes.' They been working on me."

The diagnosis, it seemed, was that the girl was crazy enough to be chained, but sane enough to decide life and death.

"That's too much for you to handle right now."

Angie gazed at the ceiling, and lowered her head and pointed. "Got you!"

I looked around for the guard.

Angie smiled smugly. "If you really was a Sister from the first bunch, you'd holler at me."

Is that what I was supposed to do? It occurred to me that Clotilda might have set me up, that I was here to read a script.

I touched the Siluva pin on my collar. The tail on the dragon pricked my finger. In any event, Angie was right. I was being paid—in a sense—to affirm the sacredness of life, the existential authority of the fetus.

"Wrap it up, Hawkins," the guard called.

"Sister?"

There was no time for existential authority.

The aide seated on the couch struggled to her feet, walked over to the table, and crouched beside the chair. "Lift the footsie." Angie's face was blank as she watched the woman struggle with the lock.

I couldn't look anywhere except at the floor. I should be reminding Angie about Hell, warning her not to sign anything. She was putty in the hands of authority, and I was it, wasn't I? This veil and black skirt a delegation of God's power. Big deal. The power to scare a crazy kid into having a baby in jail.

"Hold still," the aide grumbled.

A gritty red octagon on the linoleum caught my eye. The shape of the stain seemed familiar. I bent to examine it more closely, and pushed aside the chair next to my own. Another stain; a row of octagons. Apparently at one time chairs like the ones bolted to the floor in the lobby had been bolted into this floor. At one time ankles had been chained to iron pedestals. The manacles, perhaps even the rules, at one time had made their own kind of sense.

The guard in khaki spotted me and hurried from the coffee machine. She lifted the folding chair that I had moved, held it midair, then lowered it precisely over the octagon and firmly set it down. She shook her finger at me, and strolled away.

I was afraid I would laugh and wind up chained to a rust stain. Then I fought a stronger urge to run outside, through the parking lot and up the slope of Sorry Dog Mountain and never look back.

The aide was slipping the key onto the huge ring. "Sister?" Angie gripped the edge of the table. "Should I sign?"

I had seen it in other patients. The split second the cloud of crazy lifts, then reason sinks back behind the gray. The aide reached in her pocket.

Suddenly I was standing outside listening and looking through the bars at me, at Angie, and at the aide who was unwinding the seal of a cigarette pack. The cellophane crackled like fire. How many times had I grappled with the idea of abortion, life's wrongs destroyed by will? How many times had I wondered about Tillie's choice? But those had been the days of coat hangers and ergotamine poisoning and my mother was no hero. Or maybe—the thought that had dawned on me yesterday at the farm occurred to me again. That maybe Tillie wasn't so dumb. Hadn't I been aborted anyway? When I was nine, or eight, or six? A thought, just a thought, but if, at the age of Angie's baby, I had had the choice what would I have said?

"Should I, Sister?" Angie repeated.

I held my breath to hear how I would answer: watched myself lean and lift a strand of Angie's soft hair and tuck it behind the barrette. "Yes, my dear. Yes."

The words echoed as my heels pounded down the corridor. I paused in the lobby. The guard was picking burdock crowns from the cuff of his pants. I pushed down on the brass bar and opened the door. "Have a nice day," he called.

The wind from the mountain whispered through the trees, one branch stroking another. I bent into a gust and unlocked the door to the pickup. Three false starts and the engine kicked over. Neither my mind or my fingers could move. Like the time I realized my car skidding on wet leaves was about to plow straight into a guardrail.

An hour later I sat in my office thinking how easily that "yes" had slippd out. From me, who had suffered through at least a dozen Right to Life rallies, who had helped The Women Aglow Society rent buses for their march on Capitol Hill. Yet I had wormed out of actually going. Too queasy, perhaps, to face the jars held aloft by schoolchildren—bottles containing slivers of human tissue soaking in formaldehyde. Too faint-hearted to lie limp obstructing the door of a clinic. I admit it, I had never come to grips with the issue other than to agree verbally that it was wrong. But weren't there—there must be—times, like with Angie, when life and death cancel each other out? Questions, questions—as bad as Sister Cleo. Except for this question she would have all the answers. And Siluvas were not Maryknolls: I knew enough to keep my mouth shut around the mother house.

Across the hall the Misson's well-baby clinic was in full swing. The doctor from the Public Health Service and a county nurse were coping with a roomful of kids. Mothers yelled above whiny toddlers, babies screamed. It occurred to me to go in there and help referee. I got up and shut the door instead.

I returned to my desk, and swung my chair to the window facing the parking lot. Heat waves snaked over the asphalt and the air conditioner droned at low speed. Maybe my "yes" had done Angie wrong. Not a philosophical or political wrong, because I hadn't beat the drum for doctrine. But a more personal one; because I had chosen oneness for her just as I had chosen it for myself. Because the world of babies was as alien to me as the surface of the moon.

People say that in order to do something first you have to be able to imagine yourself doing it. At no time in my entire life had I pictured myself a mother. Or a wife either, for that matter. Before I went into the Siluvas, friends had hemmed and hawed, then come right out and said things like, "You'd be terrific with kids." Or, "Come change of life and you'll be sorry." I was waiting for someone to suggest, "Have one, then take vows." Like people think a dog should have one litter before it's spayed. I never bothered explaining, because it grated on my nerves, how people make so much out of the abstinence aspect of religious life. Celibacy fascinates everyone except the celibate. Abstinence comes with the deal, that's all, take it or leave it. A few months before I moved into the mother house on a trial basis, I knew I would take it and never look back.

I had moved in with the Siluvas the September after I graduated from Mountain State. Scott and I had broken up the winter before, and, looking back, I realize his rejection of me had precipitated a clinical depression. As soon as I had turned in my last term paper, I had taken to bed and slept until noon each day. Activity—going to Kroger, the library—took every ounce of bodily strength. All I could think of was Scott and everything I had done wrong. Not only the social relationship, mind you, the sex, too. What he knew about my person. Things I had done to him. What I let him, or rather, wanted him to do to me.

My stipend was over, and I had to find a job, fast. But getting out of bed at the same time every morning seemed as probable as my climbing Mt. Everest on a regular basis. The everyday world seemed impossible to negotiate, and I took a fresh look at supermarket checkout clerks, policemen, ordinary people who amazed me with their self-discipline and drive. Where did they get that stamina? What did they eat? I told myself that depression was only guilt talking back; enough self-help and it could be licked. There were the paperbacks, their covers embossed in irridescent lavender, titles like *Kick the Traces* and *One Upsmanship and Above*. Then I tried transcendental meditation, which turned out to be a bust, as were yoga, guilt annonymous, depression and affective disorder support groups, and a low-sodium, high-fiber, low-fat diet. I discovered my student Blue Cross would cover the services of Dr. Celestine Norton, a sister of Notre Dame Noir who practiced psychology on campus.

"How did you feel when you cut up that waterbed? Get it out. Get it all out," she said, perched at the edge of her desk chair. She wore a tie-bow blouse and a beige suit with a tiny gold cross pinned on the lapel, probably a remnant of her habit. Her hair was clipped up the back of the neck, and frizzed in erect ringlets over her forehead like a salon-groomed poodle's.

"I was mad."

"Get it all out."

"Mad as hell."

"Get it out."

"I just did."

She drew back and stared at me under her pale green eyeshadow. "Why are you resisting treatment?"

I cancelled my next appointment and went to confession instead. This was on a Saturday afternoon in March, in the middle of a sleet storm, the kind of day sane people stay indoors. The Jesuit who served the Mountain State Chapel and I were alone, just as I planned. Father's breath quickened during my rundown of sins, but, pro that he was, he asked no questions and granted absolution if I promised abstinence until the sacrament of matrimony. I strolled back to my off-campus apartment thinking I was home free. But the next day I discovered my ten-rosary penance hadn't put a dent in my ruminations.

Again I tried to lock out the thoughts. Thoughts like: I destroyed Scott, who, after all, claimed he had never been impotent before he met me and now he could never have children; I had in a sense murdered him; my coveting of his mother's Williamsburg placemats—the symbol of everything I suppose I secretly wanted—had turned into revenge of a have-not against a haves. Scott was right. Of course I was a pervert. Not your standard type. I must have been getting something out of those weekends.

I worked to lock out these thoughts, but they crept in through the windows, under the door, though cracks in the wall, distorting my every move, every decision. Like taking a job in Seattle, hoping a change of scene, being a counselor at a CYO camp would do the trick. But instead of working out the anger against myself, without meaning to, I deflected it onto the kids. The camp was coed, and the boys slept in cabins across a stream. At night I patrolled that creek like a sentry on the Rhine. I told myself I was only saving the girls from heartbreak. They hated me.

The season over, I found myself with a plane ticket back to Charleston, a hefty paycheck, and two weeks to kill. I wasn't ready to face the world, so I bought deck passage on the Alaska State Ferry. After hanging around Sitka for a few days brooding and looking for eagles, I decided to check out the Alaska Highway. The cheapest car in the rental fleet was a rattletrap Pinto that looked like something the Russians had left behind for Seward. Its odometer showed only a few thousand miles, and I wondered if the people up here burned out as fast. I inched the car into the hold of the ferry, then, the following afternoon, down the gangplank at Haines. The next morning I struck out for Whitehorse, 250 miles northeast of the Chilkoot Pass.

By evening, I was farther from civilization than I would have been on Mars. The highway was nothing but a wide track with oil sprayed on the gravel to temper the dust. The ascents into mountain passes were long and gradual,

a seven percent grade they would call it back home. But
the St. Elias peaks were no West Virginia mounds and hollows. These were mean giants, monastic old men with stiff
white hoods erect over rocky faces honed wind-
sharp. What on earth would this place be like in winter?
The ridiculus Pinto crunched up and up through the dusty
stones. I was mounting a staircase in the center of a ballroom, the wide plains in full view on either side, a river
looking more like it would from a plane than from any
road I had ever been on. Then I noticed the evergreens
stood farther and farther apart and that the higher I
climbed, the smaller the firs; an inverse relationship
between the height of the trunks and the distance to the
sky. Or was I getting bigger, taller, as the sun pulled me
toward it. Suddenly there were no trees at all, only mead-
ows of scruffy gray-green plants: actually dwarf birch and
conifers that had adapted to the harsh altitude. The road-
bank sloped into hillocks of frozen mud, zig-zagged with
streaks of creamy snow. A few miles of the jagged flash of
white and brown and my eyes burned. I parked on the
shoulder, slipped on my parka, and stepped onto the
crusty earth.

Low silver hills surrounded me in every direction as far
as I could see. Except—it took a minute for this to regis-
ter—these were not hills at all, but the tops of lower
mountains. I was a giant, my elephant feet crushing bon-
sai limbs, twigs and trunks on top of the world, my arms
long enough to reach the peaks below. Dazed, high, I felt
a coming into light, the way you must feel when you're
born.

I zipped up my jacket and hiked along the foot of the
cliff. About a mile beyond the highway, the terrain
became too steep, and I rested on a rock. The long day
had caught up with me; I leaned back, closed my eyes.
Images of snow and mud, white and brown, circled my
mind slowly as the hand of a clock. Creamy white bricks
outlined in brown grout. A building in—where had it
been? In New Martinsville, on that street overlooking the
Ohio River. The Carlton Arms, built in 1941, the date

chisled over the archway. I had been eight when Tillie, Ralph and I moved to the third floor. I pictured the thick sunbeams streaming through the leaded panes of the windows of the sunporch, crowded with my parents' queen-sized bed and my cot. The official bedroom had been turned into Tillie's sewing center; a joke because in spite of courses from the community college and the Singer people, she couldn't hem a dishtowel. Nevertheless, the room had been taken up with her machine, two K mart dressers and a card table piled with crumpled tissue-paper patterns and butchered yardage.

The porch faced the river. Nights, and the beam atop the red-eyed channel marker blinked on and off, on and off. Steamers pushed barges from Huntington to Pittsburgh, gold shining from their cockpits, their wake a foamy white V. Next-door, the neon sign for the FOB Hall slanted green light onto the bed. That, plus the street lamp, lit the room like sunshine filtering in through moss.

Ralph's shadow was a giant frog on the wall. He would be whimpering, the bedsprings yip-yipping as he moved back and forth over Tillie, her face covered with a pillow. I was supposed to watch, wasn't I? Ralph would step up the pace. The pit of my stomach quickened. Then he would be sucking air, Tille swelling beneath him like a dampened sponge. My own skin felt hot, itchy, and wet. The top sheet turned to canvas, and I would shove it off, then reach down and pull it up to my neck wondering if anyone was watching me the way I watched the bed next to mine. All of a sudden the springs would stop, and Ralph would roll on his back. Tillie would slide the pillow from her face, prop it under her head. A minute of silence, and she would say something like, "What did they charge for the tune-up?"

Sometimes I wanted to shout. Do anything to remind them I was breathing not more than ten feet away. Sometimes right in the middle I would get up, step over their shoes, go into the kitchen and bang around, come back with a Coke and a bag of chips. They paid me no mind; the beat went on.

We stayed in New Martinsville for about a year, then moved on to Parkersburg. The end of the Carlton days marked the end of their exhibitionism. Later, when I was old enough to understand perversion, I assumed the three of us had it. I look back on New Martinsville as the one and only time they needed me.

An icy breeze from the Arctic Circle cut through my parka, and I opened my eyes and rubbed the small of my back. What on earth had made me assume Tillie and Ralph needed me then? Or ever, for that matter? Come to think of it, no one had officially cut me in on their deal. Say, for example, by turning on the lights. Or yelling at me to go away to make sure I hung around.

I slipped down from the rock. Maybe they hadn't needed me at all. Maybe everything looked like exactly what it was, and why hadn't I thought of indifference before? I paced between the bluff and a muddy ravine streaked with snow. For an instant I felt lost, cheated. But then everything inside me seemed to turn to face a different sun, like a plant following light. As far as Tillie and Ralph were concerned, I hadn't been in that room. Or was, but as a picture on the wall, a stick of furniture. I was that tree falling in the forest, and if no one saw me, had I ever been there? No, came the answer, sharp and cold.

Suddenly the wind was a solvent for my blood, now running blue-white and fresh. I floated from one hillock to the next, buoyant, a balloon cut free. I knew I should be moving on to Whitehorse, but I couldn't leave. Back at the Pinto, I opened the trunk and found a half a bag of Grandma Utz potato chips and two cans of diet Sprite, leftovers from my gas station stop at Milepost 33. I was able to carry everything from the car, including my sleeping bag, in one trip.

I finished the chips and saved one soda for breakfast, then wrapped myself in a blanket and stared at the ruddy clouds, thinking, look at me, here I was, alive and well in this no-man's land where nothing you could eat could grow. Me, needing no one and nothing. Vida Zedonis, a survivor.

The next morning I awoke staring straight at the Timberlands of a Canadian Mounty. He glanced at my can of Sprite, then went to his Range Rover and returned with a thermos of coffee. Eyes on the lower mountains, he ran down the dangers of irresponsible camping and described each and every one of the frozen bodies he had found. Minutes later, he was opening the car door for me while explaining the merits of all-terrain vehicles. Then he started up the Rover, waited until I pulled onto the main track, and followed me for the next few miles, just like the cops do in West Virginia after handing you a ticket.

I hit Whitehorse around seven that night and bought a take-out order of sweet-and-sour pork and a sixpack. Back at the motel it hit me that at no time during the day had I reviewed my past sins or fought a crying jag. I stood on the crumbly cement balcony. The breeze smelled of pine and wood smoke. That had been it, the air, the air at the top of the world, that thin air had done the trick. I lifted my Bud toward the ridge of mountains, a pale blue line a hundred miles away.

LaVerve's voice—my mind snapped back to the well-baby clinic. "They're all through in there," she called through the closed door. "And Father Kozakas called asking for his truck. I said you'd call him back. Can I go home now?"

"Have a good one." Suddenly I realized the time, and that Hunt was due in half an hour. I turned off the air conditioner and remembered to lock the office behind me, and the front door, too, since this was Stella's bingo night.

Upstairs, I reached in the closet for the gray gabardine slacks. They seemed heavy as felt; outside it was ninety degrees in the shade. Of course a short-sleeved blouse could be worn loose over the waist. I pictured the linen shirt hanging over the top of the pleated pants, looking like maternity clothes. I crossed the attic and opened the window. A warm breeze lifted the curtains; the smell of honeysuckle, those last few flowers that pop out in the fall. I turned back to the closet.

There was nothing in the Order's dress code against

wearing jeans in public; it just wasn't done. I pulled my
one and only pair from a coathanger, stepped into the
pants, held my breath and pulled up the zipper, then
reached for the blouse. Even with Levis it looked stupid
both tucked in and loose. I went back to the closet and
rummaged around. It was still there, the t-shirt with
"Rockdusters" written across the front I had won at the
St. Stanislas raffle.

I felt strangely light as I moved around the room gathering my bag and car keys, scooping the coif off the lampshade. Then it dawned on me that the veil wasn't going to
work. It would look absolutely absurd with the rest of the
outfit. But going without it would be breaking the one
mandatory, inviolate rule of dress. Should I retreat to the
gabardines? They hung from the hanger clips like large
dead fish.

I lifted the veil to my head. Then lowered it onto the
lamp and carefully straightened the cuff over the rim of
the shade. Suddenly I felt entirely too cool, too free. Was
the shirt too thin? Did the chemise hide enough? I went to
the mirror and examined my reflection in profile. The
capital "R" drew all your attention, I decided.

CHAPTER
12

Hunt pushed open the glass door to Suds City, and I was hit with the smell of boiling Clorox and Bounce. Before we left the Mission, he had asked if I minded waiting for him to finish the load he had left in the launderette. It seemed that morning a waitress had spilled orange juice on his lap and with two more days of meetings, he said, he might need those slacks. I had agreed, and why not? He had been a good sport about going with me to Pops's instead of us having dinner at the Steer and Surf as he had planned.

I pulled up a spindly plastic chair while Hunt went down the aisle between rows of machines. He paused and with his thumbnail fired a wooden kitchen match. Then he lit his slim cigar and balanced it on the edge of a washer.

"The motel probably had a cleaning service," I called out.

"I noticed this place right across the street," he said, lifting the lid of the Maytag. "The problem is I guess I'm not used to people doing for me."

"You sound like my grandfather." I watched him draw a wet shirt from the tub.

Suds City was empty but for an old woman at one of the special tables for sorting clothes. Osteoporosis had gathered up her shoulders, and her head seemed too small for her body. She moved from a dryer, then back to the table, a fragile gray bird folding towels. I wondered if she was getting enough calcium and tried to think if she had ever been to Meet-and-Eat. My eyes focused on the curve of her spine. But something grated on the back of my mind, something wrong between Hunt and me. The way he had assumed I wouldn't mind stopping at the launderette. The way he had just gone ahead and left his stuff in the washer. Would he have brought anyone else here? I mean, any other woman? But this wasn't a date, was it? In fact, I had thought to carry enough cash so we could split a check if need be. So why did I feel taken for granted? He tossed a shirt into the dryer. "I thought the problem was slacks," I said.

"Running one piece is a waste of hot water."

"Why didn't you throw in the motel towels and sheets while you're at it?"

He held a towel midair. The overhead neon cut deep shadows beneath his cheekbones and alongside the high ridge of his nose. "It sounds like you're saying I shouldn't have asked you to come along. It's just that the place closes at—"

I held up my hand. "No big deal."

He slammed the dryer door and dropped a quarter into the slot. Then a minute later asked, "Why isn't it humming?"

I rose and joined him at the round window. "Hit it." I looked around for instructions. A sign hung over a stationary tub, "Mining clothes in the last four machines only. Please."

Hunt smacked the metal with his palm.

A few dryers away the old woman drew out a bundle of scatter rugs. She nodded at me and shouted, "A quarter."

"I put one in," Hunt replied.

"Tell your mister it's to get one more."

That word *mister*, and all at once I felt self-conscious but oddly enough at the same time safe, pro-

tected somehow. Hunt groped in his pocket, fed the
machine and instantly it rumbled and clicked. "Highway
robbery."

I wondered if he had caught that mister, too. Now I
was embarrassed, probably for my feelings the minute
before: unearned. I put my hands in my pockets and
slouched forward so that "Rockdusters" hung more
loosely. "Imagine what it would cost if you had kids." I
hoped my voice sounded matter-of-fact. "And came here
twice a week." I strolled back to my seat, Hunt behind
me.

He motioned to the row of vending machines. "Want
something cold to drink?

"You could see if they have Nabs."

"You're sure you don't want to go to the Steer and Surf
before your grandfather's? They say it's the best in Shackle."

"Pops always fixes food. Besides, ever been to the
Steer? Cornstarch gravy and a salad bar; canned chick-
peas, all you can eat."

Hunt laughed and headed towards the far corner of the
room, and I studied his back, his tight hips in khakis. In
the car he had taken off his jacket, and now his blue shirt
stuck to sweat between his shoulder blades. I thought of
Mountain State and of his one long braid. These days his
hair was collar length but every bit as sleek. Sleeker in
fact, curled neatly over the nape of his neck.

Evening sun filtered through the streaked picture window. My head felt light and warm without the veil. All of
me felt exposed, loosely wrapped, gradually becoming less
sensitive to light, as if being out of the habit my skin was
working on making one of its own.

Suds City was the anchor enterprise in a strip of stores;
a video outlet, a cut-rate drug and a pizza carry-out. I
watched a couple cross the parking lot. The man glanced
in my direction, and I wondered if I came across as an
everyday person. A housewife, say, in these jeans. Or
would I strike him as being what I was, a nun in the
wrong clothes. I sure had fooled the old woman. The man

lifted his head, and my stomach sank. Angelo—what was his last name—from the Rights Alive committee. I quickly moved to a bench behind a sign on a tripod. The couple walked straight on by the door, and the muscles in my stomach relaxed. But why had I panicked? So what if Angelo recognized me, what would he do? Other than point out to Mrs. Angelo that he had never seen me in street clothes, and that I was fatter, thinner, whatever, than what he had thought.

Hunt handed me a package of crackers. "Why switch seats?"

"Someone from the parish was outside."

"So?"

"I'm in regular clothes."

Did Hunt draw back? Or did I imagine it? "I noticed right off. Only I thought you told me you left," he said.

I bit open the cellophane. "I said I was in the process, the process, of leaving." I held out the crackers, and he took one. "There's been a glitch," I said. Then I told him about Vinnie and about Mother Silesia. "I'm between a rock and a hard place."

He pulled a cigar from its narrow box. "Are you still coming to Matewan?"

"How do I know?" I said too sharply. "I'm sorry, the thing's making me crazy."

The door flew open, and a fat woman lugging a clothes-basket marched into the room followed by a pale skinny man, probably the mister. He balanced a duffle bag on his shoulder. One of their kids dashed to the Pac Man machine and started pounding on its frame. The other kid yanked his jersey up over his head, plowed into a washer, and screamed, "I can't see, I can't see."

"I'm going to belt you one." His mother swatted at him and missed.

Suddenly a group of teenagers filled the entrance, and a brown dog was tearing around in circles sniffing the floor. The man pulled a boom-box from the duffle bag and set it on a table. "Right down memory lane, Hank Williams singing 'Waitin' on you,' " the announcer said.

"It's making me crazy," I repeated.

Hunt dented the Coke can with his thumbs, stood, then headed toward the trash barrel.

"I can't see," the kid yelled.

"I'm going to belt you one."

The announcer went on, "Eighty-seven degrees." I strained to hear the rest of the weather report, but all I caught was "Fog."

Hunt closed the lid of the trash can and walked to the change machine. Two of the teenaged girls in shorts and halters moved around him to the bleach dispenser. The one with frizzy hair waited until he turned away, then nudged her friend. The girl looked him up and down and nodded slowly.

The child, shirt still over his face, reeled against Hunt's leg. "I can't see," he yelled.

Hunt bent, whispered in his ear, and the kid rolled the jersey down over his waist. Then Hunt scooped him up and held him eye-to-eye with George Washington's picture over the slot for bills. The child stared at Hunt's dollar disappearing into the machine, then shouted, "Twizzlers." Hunt lowered him to the floor, and he galloped towards his mother.

I leaned back and listened to the radio drone on with the mine openings, "Number Eight Emerald Shaft. Report to work midnight shift." The announcer worked his way down the list.

Hunt slid onto a chair beside my bench. "You might be going through what I did when I decided to leave the reservation."

"To go to Mountain State?"

"Later. After my pediatric residency and stint for the Public Health Service in Matewan. You remember."

What made him think I had been tracking his life? "I lost you," I said.

Hunt held up his hand and moved his index finger. "After Mountain State, I paid back my tuition by working in Matewan." He raised his middle finger. "Then I signed on with the Indian Health Service on the reservation." He held up his fourth finger. There was no wedding band, not even a white circle where the ring—if he had ever worn one—had been. I knew he and Penny had been divorced, and I wondered how long along ago, and if it would be rude to ask. "That was a loser," he went on. "So I decided to go back to Matewan and open a practice."

"What was a loser?"

"The Indian Health Service. Lousy Reagan appointments. The new Maternal and Child Health guy was a Navajo." He paused to let that sink in. "I take it you don't know tribal politics," he said. I nodded. "Budget cuts, and I wound up with one dietician and one RN six months from retirement," he continued. "Then they took her slot. Kids with fetal alcohol syndrome, worms. I tried to fix it, couldn't, and split."

Hunt turned to watch the skinny man empty a miniature box of Tide into a machine for mining clothes. I felt Hunt was waiting for something—my reaction, maybe my approval.

"Bobtown, Shanahin Number Two," came from the radio.

"Why do the poorest people buy soap from those expensive machines?" I asked.

Hunt studied my face. "You're blaming me."

"What do you want?" I said. The man looked up and I lowered my voice. "Three cheers for walking out on sick kids."

"I tried Jessie Helms. I tried—"

"You think big shots care about Indians?" I folded my arms across my chest. "Where have you been lately?"

Hunt loosened his tie, then slowly pulled it off. "West Virginia, and that's enough," he said. "Cost containment, DRGs, I could be making four times as much in the real world."

"Still, no one up and leaves a commitment."

He carefully folded the tie into thirds. "Why not? If you're dead-ended where you are?"

"It's"—I struggled to think of a reason—"disloyal." The word sounded old-fashioned. "I mean, it's too easy."

He slipped the tie into his hip pocket. "Are you telling me that? Or yourself?"

I unfolded my arms and drew my palms back and forth across my thighs. Could be Hunt was right. Maybe I was judging his decision by the standards I set for my own— my own what? Commitment? Or lack of it. And that "easy" had popped out of nowhere. Did that mean I was hung up just because I was too dumb or too stubborn to take an easy out? "You got it right," I said.

"The dryer should be done." Hunt said. He slid back the chair. "Funny, I've developed this sixth sense about time. Since living by myself, that is."

Here it was, the opening I had been waiting for. Or was Hunt baiting. At any rate, I went for it. "Where was Penny when you were on the reservation and all that?"

"She left Cherokee a year before I did. She wasn't alone," he added.

"Are you. I mean, have you—"

"Not unless you count my cat Custer."

I followed him into the aisle and waited while he folded his wash into a neat pile. He tucked it under his arm, and I headed toward the door.

"And I built a house, too," he called from behind me. "Did most of the work myself. Had to go clear to Charleston to get the thermo-glass."

I inched around the old woman, now carefully hanging a drip-dry housecoat on the bar of a rack on wheels. On impulse I asked her, "Do you live near here?"

"On Monongalia."

Her street was a block from the Mission. "Do you know about the programs at St. Michael's Center?"

She studied my face, and suddenly I realized that without the habit, I was just an ordinary person and that my question must have struck her as odd. "I go there almost every day," she said. "Mostly for the meal club."

Any minute and I might be recognized. I smiled, then hurried to the door: one step ahead of her memory.

CHAPTER

13

Hunt and I drove to the farm separately—a waste of gas. But one of us had to bring Pops's back from Bayloukas's and my pickup only sat two. We could all have ridden in Hunt's wagon. Except Pops believed cars always roll over and he refused to ride in one.

I pulled up next to the barn, and Hunt parked his Subaru a few feet away. The school bus sat beside the asparagus patch, chained onto a flatbed that was hitched to a bright blue truck. The word "Peterbilt" was in raised letters across each mudflap and someone had painted a view of the Rockies across the back window. Cigarette smoke rolled from the cab. I walked toward it, and Hunt followed. The door swung open and Pops, in the driver's seat, rested his foot on the running board and tapped the ash from a Lucky Strike. "You're late," he said. Then he groped for something beside him, probably the Gatorade bottle he used as a flask.

I shielded my eyes from the setting sun. "How can I be late when I never said what time."

He turned and held up the whiskey. "Kill the nerve?"

"No."

If he noticed how I was dressed, he didn't show it. I stepped aside and motioned to Hunt. "Julian Hunting Sun. Remember? Matewan County?"

Pops tipped the bottle toward Hunt. "Made from my own organic corn, Doctor Sun. Could I interest you?"

I raised my hand, ready to call Pops on the organic corn business—the corn being those rotten potatoes he bought half-price. But then the old man smiled, and I dropped my arm. Hunt didn't understand our relationship, and I could come across as bossy, the type who wants the last word.

Hunt studied the bottle a minute, then put it to his lips and tilted back his head.

"Sveikas," Pops said.

Hunt gasped and wiped his mouth on his sleeve. "A hundred fifty proof, at least."

Pops crossed his arms across his chest. "A man's drink."

I was thinking about a salami sandwich on rye with tomato and mayo, and how the sooner we got to Bayloukas's the sooner we would be back. "Let's go." I glanced at the bus. "You sure that thing's tied on right?"

Pops shrugged. "Check for yourself."

I examined the cable holding the bus wheels to iron stanchions on the flatbed. Hunt came up beside me and tested the tension on a chain. "Seems okay."

"Ready?" I called to Pops.

The door to the cab clicked shut. It swung open, and clicked again, louder this time. Then the door opened a few inches and slammed shut hard enough to rock the cab.

"He's drunk," I said.

"No wonder." Hunt smiled.

I went back to the cab, stepped onto the running board and rapped on the driver's window. Pops wound it down. "You're in no shape to drive," I said.

He reached for the keys on the dashboard.

I turned and shouted down to Hunt. "How about I take the truck, and you and Pops follow in your car."

Pops thrust the key towards the ignition and missed. "I'm in enough shape not to roll over."

"Don't give me a hard time."

"Mind your beeswax."

My lips trembled, and I pressed them together. Here I had sacrificed what might have been a pleasant evening to come all the way out to the farm to help the old man, and what thanks did I get? What thanks had I ever gotten? I glanced at the faded yellow bus. "Get down this instant."

Pops rolled up the window.

I smacked the glass with my palm. It left a damp circle. I raised my fist to knock, and Hunt called up, "Leave him alone."

"He'll kill himself." I stared at the rain-streaked pane, then slowly stepped down. The engine of the Peterbilt sputtered, roared, and a cloud of diesel smoke swelled up and over the barn. I turned to my pickup. "Your judgment is as bad as his."

Hands in his pockets, Hunt strolled beside me. "He's his own man."

"Only I'm the one who always has to pick up the pieces."

"Hack them up?"

I stopped dead. Hunt's eyes were impossible to read. "I expected you to forget—the waterbed. That whole business."

Hunt raised his eyebrows.

"At least you didn't have to bring it up."

He opened his car door. "Get real."

All the way down Route Seven I wondered what he had meant. Then I decided it wasn't worth worrying about and turned on the radio. More mine shift announcements, then BeeGee Hollis, the only good, really good, country-western singer to come out of Shackle.

Minutes later I turned into the entrance to Bayloukas's mobile home in Copper Run Hollow; the shore of Copper Creek was about twenty feet from the trailer's corrugated metal skirt. The stream churned high and fast with yesterday's rain: thick orange water, runoff from Shanapin Number Two. Another foot and the entire hollow, a quarter-mile stretch, would be flooded. It happened at least three times a year.

Hunt was lost somewhere behind me. Pops had parked the Peterbilt alongside the galvanized Quonset hut with no door that Bayloukas called his garage. I pulled onto the driveway, two strips of flat grass, and cut the motor. There it was, as I remembered, Bayloukas's yard with one of every single object ever made by man: a galvanized tub, wringer washer, Ford chassis, a TV set with no screen, the hull of a fiberglass runabout. I hadn't been to his place for a few years and now saw that the trailer was worse for wear, those strips of sun-bleached aquamarine paint peeling around the picture window, poison oak crawling beneath the deck used as a porch. A few feet from the trailer, a rusted-out VW wagon nestled among tall spikes of goldenrod. A goat stood in trunk. The hatch door had been taken off and replaced with a plywood ramp runing from the wagon to the ground. The goat wore a collar and was tied to the door handle with clothesline. I stepped from my pickup into a clump of burrs and started towards the porch. Halfway across the yard, I was sidetracked by a cloud over the washer and changed my course. Gnats—the little zingers—whizzed over the rim into my eyes. I waved my arm and looked down at what must have been a thousand grapes packed inside the tub—shriveled blond kernels and limp stems. The rollers on the wringer were stained light brown, flecks of stem dotted the pitted rubber. I recalled that Bayloukas made his own champagne. Second to none, he swore.

A squawk, a rustle of wings and I raised my head. Chickens milled around inside a fenced-in yard. Instead of a coop, a cap to a pickup rested on the ground. One window was open, and a chicken sat on the ledge.

At first glance Bayloukas's place was a mess. But once you got onto it there was a logic here. Except the old man was as poor as a church mouse, so the logic didn't produce. Maybe he spent too much time worrying about the little things and forgetting the big picture, perfecting the wrong details. A man buried in his own ground rules. I stepped around a galvanized tub filled with vermiculite and mounted the steps.

Bayloukas's voice floated from behind the screen. "You got to know the style of your particular groundhogs." I paused on the landing. "Then take old rags and stop up all their holes but their chief one, and take the hose that you already connected, like I said to, to your Toyota tailpipe, stick it three, maybe four inches down that chief hole and stuff anything, straw, plastic bags, around your hose to give it a good seal. Then gun 'er."

"So far, so good," Pops replied. "So long as one don't croak under my cellar. "

I knocked, pushed open the screen and closed it behind me. Not that it mattered; any fly that cared to could walk straight in through the jagged tear in the bottom panel.

Pops and Bayloukas sat at the built-in table, Lump asleep at their feet, dead to the world. An island counter divided the kitchen from the living room that was furnished in early American plaid. The sofa faced an over-stuffed checkered chair. The maple cocktail table held a small plastic barrel with imitation ivy trailing down the sides. My eyes adjusted to the light, then I braced myself and glanced at the far corner, where the six-foot-high circular pen sat. I knew it was filled with snakes.

"Sister," Bayloukas called out. He must have noticed the Rockdusters shirt, for he added, "You don't look like yourself."

"It's after hours." I laughed.

"Come sit anyway. I got salami, fresh rye, dry-roast nuts, anything you want."

"Groundhogs," Pops said. "They're animals."

As Bayloukas was pulling out a kitchen chair for me, footsteps sounded on the deck. "Here's my friend now."

A few minutes later, Hunt, Pops, Bayloukas and I stood around the wire pen. Lump paced in front of it. "She's jealous of my doing for them," Bayloukas explained. "And seeing to seventeen snakes does keep a man on his toes."

Bayloukas had turned the inside of the cage into a forest. A section of tree trunk rose amid rocks, branches, and a piece of gutter pipe bent to look like a creek zigzagging between potted plants. The old man motioned to a blue coil under a philodendron leaf. "There's Kissinger, one of your racers." He rocked his hand back and forth. "Or could be a coach-whip." He nodded at an orange rope lying flat along an overhead limb. "Come on down, Jack Kennedy, say hello." He turned to Hunt. "Them copperheads play hard to get, every damn time. Sorry, Sister," he said to me.

Hunt touched my arm and pointed. Inside the pen the tips of the ferns quivered, then a long—incredibly long—gray and black striped S lifted its head, or, rather, its upper part and out came the tongue, flickering left-to-right, right-to-left.

"Hey, Hoover," Pops shouted.

I cringed.

"Gained weight, the little sucker," Pops said.

Bayloukas crossed his arms across his chest and smiled.

"How long is it? About nine feet?" Hunt asked.

I closed my eyes.

"Nine and one-quarter of an eighth, as of two p.m. yesterday," Bayloukas said. I turned to the wizened old man who was smiling into the pen the way I had seen new fathers smile into the glass of the nursery at Valley General. He stepped closer to the wire, placed his index and middle fingers in his mouth and whistled three longs and a short, an owl hoot.

Hoover whipped into a W and froze.

"M" for Mountaineers," Bayloukas said proudly.

I squinted at the black letter.

Bayloukas must have caught my expression. "You're standing upside down is why it looks wrong," he explained.

"I can't believe this," Hunt said. "Snakes have no external ear structure."

Bayloukas whistled again, three barn-owl notes and Hoover slithered into a C, but with his tail erect and curled slightly inward. "Governor Gaston Caperton,"

Bayloukas announced. "Now here's the kicker." A whistle
and the tail hooked sharply inward. "Gorbachev."

"Yet he does it all from sound," Hunt said.

Bayloukas shook his head, "No, it's my whistle. Three
years it took before he got the hang of it."

Hunt walked slowly around the cage. "But an indigo—"

"Hoover's a thundersnake," Bayloukas corrected.

"—is a predator," Hunt continued as if to
himself. "Why doesn't he do in the rest of them?"

"I give them good eats," Bayloukas said, and motioned
for us to follow.

I found myself in a bedroom that had been turned into
a rodent kennel. Bayloukas pointed at the cages filled
with white baby rats. I couldn't face those pink eyes.

"See, Dr. Sun, " Bayloukas said, "if everyone gets what
they want they don't want anymore."

Hunt nodded thoughtfully.

We sat at the kitchen table, which was covered with
platters of bread, cheese and meat. A potted ruta plant
served as a centerpiece. I arranged my feet around Lump's
tail. "She's at the end of her rope," Bayloukas said. "I got
all ten of her babies shut in the bathroom, wall-to-wall
newspaper, giving the old lady time out."

"I told Sister about her puppy," Pops said.

Bayloukas turned to me. "Pick of the litter. Soon as we
eat, you'll see for yourself."

I reached for a slice of Baltic bread.

"You work in kids, Dr. Sun?" Pops asked.

Hunt started to answer, when suddenly Bayloukas spun
around, held a napkin to his mouth and coughed, horri-
ble, choking spasms tearing his lungs, phlegm clogging his
throat, making him heave again and again. Veins on his
temple swelled. Everyone in Shackle knew someone with
black lung and could tick off the symptoms: the blood
running soot instead of oxygen, the kidneys go, then the
heart. Bayloukas was dying. Mother of God, let him be
taken painless and quick. Like Vinnie? I drove the thought
from my mind.

Bayloukas gripped the edge of the table to steady him-

self while he struggled for breath. Hunt laid his hand on
the old man's arm. Pops twisted a corner of his paper napkin, and I stared down at my folded hands. A breeze filled
the crisscross curtains, and suddenly the room smelled of
sewage.

Bayloukas straightened, wiped his eyes on the sleeve of
his flannel shirt, then passed the bottle of Four Roses to
Pops. He filled Bayloukas's glass, his own, Hunt's, then
mine.

I tried to recall where Bayloukas's married daughter
lived. "Does Ruthie come by?"

Bayloukas lowered his glass and smiled. "Her mister
drove me the Peterbilt down from Hagerstown." His
voice was harsh from the cough. "She followed in their
Escort with little Mark. The kid's eating solids, already
taking on cabbage. Ruthie says come, come live near
us." He studied the rim of his plate. "At the senior citizens'."

Pops flashed me an odd look, and I wondered if he
knew what I had been thinking the other morning. When
had it been? Monday, after Baccalotta's visit. How I knew
that Pops could not survive one second in a senior citizens' high-rise.

Bayloukas went on. "But I can't throw over the snakes
museum. Hoover's trained and ready to go. All's I have to
do is fix up the bus, then stand by and watch the money
roll in."

He caught his breath. "Of course I'll advertise, have to
tap the tourist arket. I got this here sign—."

"Forget Great Snakes and rest yourself," Pops said.

Bayloukas went on as if Pops hadn't spoken. "Then
every month like a clock I'll send them a check." He
leaned forward. "Lithuania's almost her own place
again. The way I see it, every nickel here helps Lam-
bergeiris over there. The third world," he added, and
drew back.

I looked at his shirt hanging limp, his chest blown hollow from coughing out his guts.

"You sound crazy as Vito Pucas," Pops said.

"That's because he's right," Bayloukas replied softly.

I turned to Hunt. "Vito's the president—"

"Grand Master," Pops corrected me.

"—of their lodge."

"Which reminds me, you be at the picnic?" Bayloukas asked Pops.

"Don't I every year?"

Bayloukas turned to me. "You come too?"

I tried to recall the last picnic I had been to. When was it? Ten years ago?

"She's going to play the accordion." Pops announced. "She's—

With my foot, I nudged his ankle under the table, afraid he was going to spill the beans of my leaving to Bayloukas.

"Accordion?" Hunt said.

"She does 'Lady of Spain,'" Pops said. "You wouldn't believe, it's like you were there."

Hunt raised his eyebrows. "Really."

I gave him a steady look. "What's wrong with that?"

"You, too, Dr. Sun," Bayloukas said. "It's to be at the Teamsters' Hall, this Friday night."

Hunt nodded politely. "I'm here for a meeting and was planning to go back Friday afternoon."

"It's a benefit." Bayloukas urged. "For my cause."

"Thank you. I'll see how the day goes," Hunt said politely.

While Bayloukas drew a map to the Teamsters' Hall for Hunt on a napkin, I wondered how long it would take me to get over feeling like a fool. The accordion. What on earth had ever posessed me to take lessons? I had been thirteen years old for one thing, I recalled.

Bayloukas reached for the butter. His fingernails were rimmed coal black although he hadn't been in the mines for at least ten years.

"Do you go to Valley clinic?" I asked, relieved to be changing the subject.

Bayloukas shook his head. "My union policy wants a fifty-fifty co-charge."

"Pay and be done with it," Pops said.

Bayloukas studied the ruta plant. "I got priorities."

"What's this priorities?" Pops snapped. "Forget Lithuania. Your money's a drop in the bucket anyway. You talk like that snake's going to bring in enough to float the whole goddamn country."

Bayloukas glanced at Pops, then at me. "Watch your mouth."

"Sister wasn't born yesterday," Pops said. He slapped his palm on the table. "Face it. Vilnius is over. Kaput. Washed up on the beach." Then his shoulders loosened and he said in an uncertain voice. "Besides, there's more to live for."

Bayloukas leaned and pinched off a dead ruta leaf, then crushed it between his fingers, and I caught the scent of bitter mint. "But not to die for."

Hunt excused himself and slipped down the hall toward the bathroom. Lump struggled to her feet and followed.

"The Mission has a van now, for medical transportation," I said. "Let me set you up at the free clinic in town."

The bathroom door opened. Hunt appeared in the hall, disappeared, then suddenly reappeared chasing a brown puppy that was scrambling into the rat room. "The dogs are out," he yelled.

Bayloukas leaped to his feet. All at once the trailer was filled with puppies, jumping, yelping. Lump tore from one end of the room to another. Her tail hit the curtains and knocked an ashtray off a stand. Small wet circles darkened the rug. I went for a black pup backing away from the coffee table, shaking its head, a sprig of plastic ivy in its mouth. Pops, on his knees, groped beneath the sofa.

"Over here," Bayloukas yelled.

A cluster of puppies stumbled around the pen. Some stood on their hind legs, their front paws braced against the wire. Lump, her head thrown back, danced back and forth barking at the cage.

I ran down the hall, set the black pup in the bathtub,

shut the door, then went to help Bayloukas. One side of the pen rested against the tree in the center. raising the bottom about a foot from the floor. A slender green snake whipped under the wire, across the carpet and under the couch. Inside the cage, two puppies drank from the imitation creek. A black flash shot along the baseboard, then was gone.

"The hole in the screen," Bayloukas yelled. Hunt, a dog under each arm, swung the storm door closed with his foot.

I joined Pops in the hall and pointed to the bathroom. "They're all in?"

"I need two more."

Hunt came up holding two squirming dogs against his chest. Pops positioned himself with one hand on the doorknob. "Ready?"

Hunt knelt and Pops inched open the door as Hunt pushed the puppies into the crack.

I turned to the living room. Except for the whimpering in the bathroom, the trailer was strangely quiet. Someone had uprighted the empty snake cage and set the furniture back where it had been. But I sensed eyes, snake eyes, glinting from behind each curtain, each chair. I walked into the kitchen imagining fangs, any minute sinking into my calf.

Bayloukas stared into the sink. He lifted his head and motioned to the cupboard under the wall oven. "Don't nobody reach for the pressure cooker. Kennedy's behind it." He walked to the table and carefully, as if every bone in his body had been broken, lowered himself onto a chair. "Hoover's gone."

It took me a second to grasp the meaning of what he had said. The snake was his world. If his dream of a museum, no matter how foolish, was over, how on earth could he recoup? I sat next to him, as if somehow I could buffer him from the blow he had already suffered. "Maybe he's under something," I said, resisting the urge to draw my feet up onto the chair.

Pops shook his head. "I seen him on the porch, only I

had my hands full."

"It's my fault," Hunt said. "I wasn't thinking and the puppies shot out—." He stopped, probably knowing an apology was useless.

"These things happen," Bayloukas said gently.

No one in the room knew what to say. I tried to think of something, anything. Loss hung in the air, like the smell of dried cologne on an old party dress. A feeling of helplessness settled inside me, a sort of despair that nothing in the world could go right for anyone, ever. I looked at Hunt as if he had an answer. Missing my glance, he rose, walked to the window and looked into the darkness.

Then Pops slapped his knees and stood. "We got to round up the rest of the herd."

Bayloukas stared at the table.

"Come on, George, snap out of it."

Hunt turned from the window. "Maybe I can find him. I have a lantern in the car."

Bayloukas raised his head, and I could have sworn there was a hint of new color in his cheeks.

"I'll be right back," Hunt said. He strode across the room and onto the porch, carefully closing the storm door behind him.

Bayloukas turned to me. "Can he do it, Sister?"

His voice was so eager. It would have been easy, too easy to give him false hope. "He's going to try to find a black snake in the middle of the night. What do you think?"

"Except"—Pops held up his index finger—"you yourself told me he's a Cherokee Indian."

"So what?"

"Them people do miracles with horses, birds, you name it, snakes. They know the woods like the back of my hand."

Hunt returned carrying a Coleman lamp. He set it on the kitchen table, lit one of his wooden matches and fired the wick. "It's a long shot," he said, adjusting the flame. "But get me something to put him in."

Bayloukas jumped up and and rummaged in an Atlas

moving carton beside the refrigerator. He handed Hunt a folded burlap sack and a forked stick. "You want I should go along?"

"Finish your dinner," Hunt said. "One person's best. And I might be gone awhile," he said at the door.

Pops turned to Bayloukas. "So I guess it's up to you, me, and Sister to collect the rest of them." Pops leaned on the kitchen island and seemed to be sizing up the living room. "Here's how we do it. We get one of them rat babies, and, like in Africa when they tie a goat to a tree to catch a lion, we tie that sucker—"

"Gross," I said. "Absolutely gross." I felt my lips whiten.

Pops shrugged and held up his palms, "How else?"

I shoved aside my plate. "Only a monster—"

"Grow up," Pops said. He looked at me and shook his head, then turned toward the rat room with a set to his shoulders that told me there was no arguing.

"I'm getting out of here." Giving the lower cupboard wide berth, I hurried to catch up with Hunt.

14

I stood on the rickety front porch. Earlier, on the way to the farm, wisps of fog had been circling the higher elevations. Now it had nestled into the creek bed and floated in milky shreds lit by the spotlight over the garage. The fog, plus the darkness, and Bayloukas's place could have been a junkyard on the moon. I tried to make out the objects creating the shadows that zigzagged across the drive. What was that T square beside the boat? **The eliptical thing near the oil tank?** A break in the mist and I spotted the white glow of the washer, then Hunt crossing the track to the garden. I joined him at the compost pit.

"I'm staying out of my grandfather's way," I said. "He's using a baby rat as bait."

"It won't work. The snakes are too well-fed. They only eat once or twice a week, you know."

"No, I didn't."

Hunt played the Coleman light over the hull, the truck cap, then the ramp leading into the VW trunk. "Bayloukas uses it for a pen," I said. "The goat must be inside."

Hunt swung the lamp around the asparagus rows, the patches of yellow straw mulch, the tall silver stalks. I looked up at the lacy foliage and thought of Pops's cash marijuana crop. Then I thought of the money I had been

banking on that very well could be lost. The feeling of
helplessness that had come over me in the kitchen swept
over me again. Was the universe at a dead end or just my
life?

Hunt held the lantern over his head and kicked aside a
mound of mulch. "Homeostasis," he said. "Body temper-
ature is as important to a reptile as food."

"You realize this is a colossal waste of time."

Hunt rearranged the straw with his foot. "Hope. Not
as good as Hoover, but better than nothing, I say."

"Leading him on like this is just plain cruel."

Hunt moved away and became a voice in the mist.
"Humor me, will you? I'm doing something, anything to
feel better about having messed him up. Besides, no one
knows for sure what will happen until it happens." The
circle of light moved toward me, and Hunt said softly,
"Believe."

"I believe you can't find a black snake in the middle of
the night."

"Okay, have the last word."

"You sound like the housekeeper at the Mission.
Another one working on my character." I picked my way
along the walk to the back porch.

A ditch behind the trailer divided Bayloukas's yard
from Allegheny Mountain, one of those conical peaks
you're more likely to see south of Charleston than here
between the panhandles. Allegheny wasn't particularly
high, but rose so sharply it seemed if you didn't watch
where you were going you would smack straight into the
slope. Years ago I had trailed Bayloukas and Pops up and
down these woods, Bayloukas checking that the trees he
had marked and sold to the sawmill for pulp were the
ones actually cut. Hunt pointed to the track leading up
into the pines. "My gut feeling is Hoover would go for a
high place."

I followed Hunt along the rim of the ditch, skirting the
propane tanks under the kitchen window. A ray of creamy
light streamed through the curtains. Pops's singing carried
through the screen. "Namo, Namo," Bayloukas's quivery

voice joined in.

"Pops's third stage of drunk," I said. About an hour before he passes out."

"How will we get him home?"

"He'll come around long enough to fall into my truck. Then sleep it off in the tool shed."

Hunt shone the lamp on the path, held aside a tangle of Rosa multiflora and watched me maneuver around the thorns. "Why don't you wait down here?"

"As a kid I knew every inch of these hills," I said, confidently moving in front of him.

The trail, a swath Bayloukas cleared with a brush hook, was a carpet of spongy leaves. I leaned into the ascent and paced myself for the long haul. For a few minutes I wondered why I was doing this. Then putting one step in front of the other took all the steam I could muster. The higher we climbed, the thinner the fog became. Either it was lifting, or, as sometimes happens this time of year, it had settled only in the hollows. The air was muggy and warm. Mosquitoes strafed my ankles and bare arms. I slapped at my skin and quickened my step hoping a moving target would throw them off. Halfway to the top my feet felt heavy, and I realized my sneakers were soaked through. I stopped to catch my breath and look for Hunt and discovered he had been right behind me. "I couldn't hear you," I said.

He smiled, a flash of white teeth, and pointed to a lop-sided pine a fair distance ahead. "Almost."

I pushed on. Up here the path was overgrown and I strained to see where it led. A tingling in my calf and I stopped. "Wait, there's something on me." My hand on a tree trunk, I leaned and felt the back of my leg. "Ticks."

"Can I—"

"Got it." I flicked the insect onto the ground, straightened and suddenly and lost my balance.

Hunt's arms were around me, his body hard and warm. "Careful." He smelled of cigar smoke and a hint of what I had always thought of as juniper. But this close it was something different, herbal, like cardamom. "Stupid of me." I quickly pulled away. "It should have been burned." I brushed off my t-shirt, and stepped forward. The pressure of his hands lingered on my shoulders, and for some reason my knees shook.

"Burned?"

"Pops puts a tick on toilet paper and lights it."

Approaching the peak, suddenly the branches and needles were etched sharply against the three-quarter moon. Below, a foamy mist covered the lower trail making it seem as if Hunt and I were standing on a cloud. I tried to spot the light from the trailer. "We might be the only people in the world," Hunt said.

Then we were at the top, in a circular clearing about an acre in diameter that was filled with tires. Short, tall, columns of them in straight rows—a gigantic bar graph. Some of the pillars had tipped, and the tires lay on the ground, spikey weeds shooting through the holes in the center. Moonlight cast long round shadows on the tall grass.

"A rubber Stonehenge," I whispered.

Hunt walked to the nearest stack and ran his hand along the edge. "Retreads."

I pictured this field as it had been years ago, filled with wildflowers. "In daylight you can see clear to Pennsylvania. Why doesn't Bayloukas clean up this mess? It's as bad as his yard, a pigpen."

Hunt hooked his thumbs in his back pockets and strolled along the row. "I bet he sells them."

"You saw that hill. No one's been up here. And there's not enough wind in the old man to make it himself."

"Maybe that's why he can't clean it up."

"He can pay a teenager a few dollars. That's the trouble with Bayloukas, my grandfather, maybe it's West Virginians in general. Instead of stocks they invest in stuff." I pointed at a truck wheel with a vine curled over its rim. "It's their dream of some day a fortune, success, happiness, whatever."

The wet edge of my sneakers was rubbing my skin raw. I ran my finger between the canvas and my heel.

"Come to think of it, they probably don't see the trash they throw around as trash at all. They use auto grave-yards the way normal people use banks, old washing machines as a trust fund. Something they'll pass on to their kids. Junk is their legacy."

"Those are saleable tires."

I dried my finger on my jeans. "And there's something wrong with you, too." I walked over and sat on the edge of a Goodyear and unlaced my Keds. Hunt watched me a minute, then turned and ambled along the columns, here and there shining the Coleman lamp. "Lots of luck," I called out. He returned, set the lamp and burlap sack beside the tire and sat down.

I was trying to dry my shoe with a Kleenex. The feeling of helplessness was beginning to creep back. "Anyway, the mosquitoes are gone." The Kleenex was not working, and I set the sneakers beside me, soles up.

Hunt felt his breast pocket for a cigar and reached for his matches.

Just then Bayloukas's dying, the snake, something inside me seemed simply to roll over and give up. I closed my eyes. The match grated, hissed, and Hunt exhaled. "What's wrong?"

"I can't handle it."

"What?"

After a few minutes I said, "There might not be enough words to get it across.

"Try me."

I leaned against a tire that was resting halfway across the Goodyear. Hunt drew on his cigar, then twisted around and tapped the ashes into the center. "I blew it," I said. "Couldn't pull it off. I'll be ninety-two years old, slaving away in the Order and still trying to find a way out." I motioned to the clearing. "I'm my own living junkyard. A life that never got off the ground."

Hunt studied the lit end of the Tiparillo.

"I'm not smart enough, to get around the obstacles, that's why." I ran my finger along the metal rim of the wheel. "The atoms, molecules, congealing to make a force, a negative energy field closing in on me. Children feel it too; helpless," I added.

"Sometimes," Hunt said slowly, "people think too much. After all, things change. Maybe your stint in the Order is over. Simple as that. A rope is only so long."

Immediately I thought of Magus's saying, "The world of the Son is over." But I wasn't sure, or ready to hear, what Hunt was getting at, so I let the words pass and continued my line of thought out loud. "It's like time, weather. A sixth dimension. Impedimenta, the Church calls it."

By now, any logic I had to start with was down the tubes, but I went on anyway. "What blocks a beatified from becoming a saint." I lowered my voice. "Not that I wanted to be a saint anyway. And everyone's struck down by it in the end. Look at Vinnie. Super-victim Vinnie. Bayloukas can't sell his tires because he's half dead. Now the snake. Forget the merits of the museum, it's the best dream he ever had and—"

"I do feel like two cents."

I put my hand on his arm. "No, it's not personal. You're not getting my gist." I looked around the clearing, at the fog drifting up the slope. Without moving my hand, I explained master plans, destiny, all the while becoming more and more conscious of the warmth of Hunt's skin. He put his hand over mine.

I paused for breath, then resumed, "The wonder of it is that anyone tries."

Hunt gently rubbed the nape of my neck. "Cause and effect," I said weakly. The muscles in my back loosened. He drew me to him. "We all might as well crawl in a hole," I added.

My head was buried in his shoulder, and I wondered if he could hear me. "Are you doing this just to shut me up."

He was kissing my forehead, my eyes, temples. "I don't know."

He was kissing my mouth. His tongue tasted of cardamom, and I ran my hands over his chest while he stroked my thigh, then reached and unclasped my braid.

The barrette fell into the center of the tire, in with the ashes, and I could have cared less. He worked my hair loose and trailed his fingers through the length of it, then slowly drew away.

In one motion he turned, lifted the burlap sack and walked to a grassy knoll. Mist, ragged slices of it, circled as he spread the sack on the weeds. Barefoot, I came up beside him. The air smelled of moss. In the back of my mind I knew there was a list of reasons why I should beat it back to the trailer. But reason didn't seem to matter.

We held each other as he tossed my shirt, then his shirt and khakis on the ground. His hands on my hips, he stepped back. The tip of his sex shone, and I knew it would be wet to my touch.

We were on the ground. "Stop me," I said, pulling him closer. "Please."

He covered my mouth with his hand, then moved it away and kissed me. Suddenly my scalp felt like it was being scraped with an ice pick. "Hair," I screamed.

Hunt jerked back.

"Don't move."

"Christ, my watchband." He carefully held his wrist to my head as we sat up together. "I'll work it free. Take me a minute."

A twist and I gasped, then held my breath as he untangled the section near the crown. "Can I go ahead and cut this last part?"

"Just do it," I said.

"Only I need you to get my knife in my pants pocket." He motioned with his free hand.

He leaned with me as I groped through his khakis. I felt the outside of his pockets. Curious, I pulled out a large coin. "My lucky deutsche mark. You ever see one?" He asked.

I handed him the Swiss army knife.

"Pry up the blade."

"What's lucky about it?"

"The Tribe gave me the knife at my farewell dinner."

"I mean the deutsche mark?"

"Hold still."

Thwack, and I shook my hair free and rubbed my scalp.

Hunt drew his slacks over his lap and slipped the knife in the pocket.

It dawned on me what had happened. I bit my lip. "Don't you feel it? How it went wrong? It's ruined."

"It'll grow back."

"It's all ruined."

He looked up and must have seen my face. "Not for me," he said softly.

"Proof nothing works." The damp air suddenly felt uncomfortably cool, and I reached for my t-shirt. It was inside-out. "Proof. Sure-fire proof." My eyes burned and I pulled the sleeves through the opening at the waist. "Maybe God meant for us not to—" I couldn't think of the word.

"Do you believe that?"

I crossed my arms, ready to slip the shirt over my head. Then I lowered it onto my knees. "No." I stared at a spider web stretched between two weeds. Somewhere in the distance a dog barked. Hunt leaned, as if about to reach for a cigar, and I gently took his hand and held it, palm up.

Callouses ridged the base of his long tan fingers. I slowly traced the crease slanting from the top, the crease in the middle, the curve around his thumb.

He took a sharp breath and shifted his weight.

I drew a circle, kissed it, and held his palm to my lips.

He lowered me to the ground. My throat went dry, and I realized I was breathing through my mouth. "Do you want to?"

He was on top, sitting upright as if on his heels, his knees straddling my thighs. For an instant his face was hidden by a wisp of fog, then I caught the dark shadows under his cheeks. He moved his hand slowly across my stomach, probing, pressing small circles on my skin, as if trying to feel himself inside me. I grasped a corner of the burlap and twisted it around my wrist. All at once my muscles, the ones beneath his fingers, locked. I let go of the burlap and without stopping Hunt lowered himself onto me full-length and buried his head in my hair. I arched my back just as the heat of him flowed through my veins.

The moon lit the weeds with a bluish glow. I turned my head. A whitewall lay a few yards away, its paint peeling and chipped. Hunt's trembling eased, and I smoothed his hair from his temple.

"The first time I saw you, you were in the Mountaineer Bookstore," he said quietly.

"Near the stadium."

"I loved you ever since."

I didn't know what to say, as if I had been handed a gift and did not have one good enough to give in return. "I never knew that."

"Neither did I."

The barking started up again. "Probably the old man's dog," Hunt said. "I've been thinking about getting one myself." He shifted half off me and ran his hand along my hip.

"You have a choice of nine."

I lifted a strand of his hair, wrapped it around my finger, around his ear.

"Wait till you get to my house," he said. "It's up on this hill. I cleared the trees all the way down to the river. Nights you can see the McDonald's arch in Logan and the power plant."

"You sound—lonely. As I was. Am," I added.

He eased his body over mine. "Not lonely. Patient."

We made love again, and when our breathing calmed I realized the burlap now lay a few feet away and my leg was touching the whitewall. I sat up. The sky was clear, a star or two biting the dark.

I groped for my jeans. "Pops must be wondering. Reach me my top, will you?"

Bayloukas, a dishtowel slung over his shoulder, greeted us at the door. "No sweat, Dr. Sun, I got it all figured out."

"I couldn't find him," Hunt said.

Bayloukas turned to the kitchen. "Who finds a black snake at night? Especially not knowing where to look."

Pops slept in the Easy-Time, his head resting against a doily pinned onto the headrest. Bayloukas, whistling, went to the sink and picked up a dish. I took it from his hands. "Go sit down."

"But Sister—"

"No buts about it." I nodded to the living room. "Keep the doctor company."

"The snakes are all here," Hunt called. He moved toward the kitchen and must have caught Bayloukas's face. "But for Hoover."

The old man pulled out a chair. "He'll show in a few days when he's hungry enough and wants to do Gorbachev." He pointed to the window. "Bet you he's back up on Allegheny where I first found him. Where Statler stores his tires."

"Whose?" I held a Brillo pad above a skillet.

"Statler's. Chuckie Statler's. He's got a franchise with Mountaineer towing. Rips off tires from cars totaled on the interstate. Says one of these days he'll have enough to open a used tire lot beside his gas station, then he'll be in the money. You know his station, the one sells pop free with a fill-up. Diet or plain."

"Statler rents the clearing from you?" I asked.

"Why should he rent? He owns it."

I rinsed the pad and laid it in the soap dish bolted above the spigot. "No, he doesn't. I remember for certain, you, Pops, and me shlepping up and down checking Xs painted on trees to make sure which ones you sold."

The trailer was silent. I polished the countertop with the dry dishtowel. Bayloukas cleared his throat. Suddenly it dawned on me the old man had been stealing the trees, and I had been a fool not to have seen it before. Hunt looked at his watch, at me, and I nodded. He lifted his jacket from the back of a chair.

"I'll wake up my grandfather."

"He's not asleep," Pops yelled from the living room. He bent and fumbled for his shoes. I hurried across the kitchen ready to steady him when he got to his feet. "You catch the snake?" he asked. Without waiting for a reply he said, "You been gone long enough."

I folded my arms over the grass stain on my tee-shirt. "Let's get cracking," I said.

He rose, waved me away, and lurched proudly across the room. Minutes later he leaned against the pickup while I opened his door. The instant his head hit the back of the seat he was asleep. Or had passed out. It was hard to tell.

Hunt, holding a cigar, was waiting for me on the driver's side. He dropped the Tiparillo, ground it in the gravel under his heel, then pulled me against him. I checked to see that Pops was still out of it, then rested my head on Hunt's chest. "Come back to Matewan with me Saturday."

"I thought your meeting was over Friday."

"The fund-raiser. Whatever it is. I owe him that."

My mind raced. "If I ride down with you, how will I get back"

"Don't get back, ever."

His jacket was rough against my cheek. "Let's think on it." It took every ounce of willpower in me to move away.

"Wait." Hunt rummaged through his pocket and handed me a plastic envelope with a few tablets on the bottom. "I had my bag in the car. For the old man when he wakes up. Time's the only cure for a hangover, but this will cut the nausea. As needed."

"Absolutely not. If he is ever going to straighten out, he'll have to deal with the consequences of—"

"How old is he?"

I laid the pills on the dash.

Pulling out of the driveway, I checked the rear view mirror. The headlights of Hunt's wagon flashed against the trailer's metal skirt.

Just as I turned onto Jacob's Ladder Road, Pops sat up and wound down the window. "Give me one of them pills."

"Now?"

"They're right in front of you."

"But—"

"I don't need no water."

CHAPTER
15

Everything about Caraveggio's Mortuary—the sandle-wood air-spray, the taped organ music of "I'll Never Walk Alone," the embossed Leather-True visitors' book—warned me that Vinnie's funeral would be as down and out as his life.

I had not taken the interstate but had chosen the old route to Port Shirley through Uniontown, Elizabeth and Clairton. Past rows of two-story houses facing the road and desolate commercial strips of mattress outlets and unisex beauty shops. Past statues of Our Blessed Mother sheltered in upright bathtubs, arrangements of plastic flowers at Her feet, reminiscent of the roadside shrines in the old country. I crossed the bridge over the Monongahelia River with the steel mills on both banks. Overhead a mixture of ore dust, diesel fumes and coal smoke hung perpetually trapped between the ozone layer and the hills. The locals called it sky.

I found Caraveggio's on a side street off Saw Mill Run Boulevard. You could tell by the fire escapes that at one time it had been a multi-family dwelling. Canyon stone—pink, yellow and gray boulders—sided the facade of the old house. Mr. Caraveggio (I assumed this was a one-man outfit) opened the door. He wore a maroon tie and a dark tweed jacket that complemented the stubble on his jaws. I followed him through the vestibule and into the room marked "Visitation Suite." Vinnie's coffin was closed. "And will remain so for the memory celebration," Caraveggio informed me. The suite was decorated in Victoriana. Rosewood-framed sepia photos of corseted ladies and children in sailor suits were propped on cabriole-legged stands. Wall-to-wall oriental-style carpet matched the wine velveteen drapes. "Coffee, Sister? Tea?"

I looked at my watch. I was an hour early. "I'll wait."

"Of course. Yes." Clearly he had no notion of what to do with me. I started to lift a folding chair from a stack in the corner. "Let me, please." He snapped down the legs. "Where would you like this?"

"Beside Mr. Le Clair."

He made an elaborate show of checking the sturdiness of the seat before he let me sit down. I crossed myself, lowered my head and felt his silent sigh of relief as he glided away.

"Sister Zedonis?" A tall heavy-set woman in a black satin dress with a crumpled bow at the hip stood over me. I was suddenly afraid my slacks and jacket (the only black garments I owned) might be too casual. Enormous earrings, silver spoons, brushed her padded shoulders. Orange permed hair flamed from her head, and her eyes were hidden behind pink-toned glasses. "Cindy Le Clair," she said. She nodded to a pudgy man in cream-colored polyester—his only suit, I suspected—who came up beside her. "This is Leroy Shultz," she said, then, urgently, "Did you square things away?"

Jesus, Mary, and Joseph—where was this woman's mind, discussing Vinnie's effects in front of Vinnie? I rose and ushered the two of them into the foyer. Caraveggio slipped around us and shut the door to the visitation room.

"You got a priest to do the service?" Cindy asked.

"I'm sorry. I thought you were referring to your uncle's belongings," I said. "Father Kozakas can't make it. But he called the Diocese and the parish pastor will serve Mass. I think arrangements have been made between Caraveggio's and St. John's.

Cindy nudged Leroy. "Connections. Me not being Catholic, the snotty secretary wouldn't spare the time of day."

"The Church has considerations," I said.

She turned to me. "I can come to Shackle and pick up Vinnie's shit—stuff, I mean. We got us a pickup."

"We need a truck for the store," Leroy explained. "Stitches 'N' Snitches—crafts. You been there?" He beamed at Cindy, and she smiled modestly. "A Hallmark franchise, too."

"Mr. Le Clair didn't leave much," I said. "It's all in a box in the Mission's van. One of the residents is driving it up."

The organ swirled into "Climb Every Mountain."

"You were close to your uncle?"

Cindy's eyes shifted to the wall. "Not uncle, exactly. He was, you might say, my mother's friend. Until she died, but I was finished high school by then." She opened her purse and drew out a tissue. "He was always full of laughs."

"A big spender, too," Leroy said. "Course I never met the man."

Yesterday—or had it been the day before?—over the phone I had explained to Cindy that Vinnie had been on the streets, and that in spite of his big talk he lived off Supplemental Social Security Income he was entitled to by being in terrible health. I glanced at the wreath of white orchids over the visitation record and at the gilt sign, "Vincent Le Clair, May ye rest in peace." Maybe Cindy missed the point.

"The Social Security Administration will only pay funeral costs to the widow." I said, carefully refraining from adding, or children of the deceased.

She stiffened. "It's no big deal."

"It's the least she can do," Leroy said awkwardly.

My throat tightened. People like Cindy weren't rich. But over the years I noticed that the families with the smallest houses were the ones who took in kids in emergencies. The poorest parishioners brought me Christmas gifts. I touched her arm. "You have a good heart."

Visitors lined up to sign the guest book. Caraveggio, now in a black suit, slid through the crowd like a thread drawn through silk. He entered the viewing suite and was about to close the door when I came up behind him.

"We'll be ready in a minute," he said.

"I'll wait here."

He shrugged and checked the brass lock on the walnut casket. "Is it because of the wound?" I said. "On his head?" I touched my vest. "I was the one who found him."

"The closing is the wish of the family. I, of course, could have restored Mr. Le Clair."

"I imagine it would be a challenge. The wound was fatal."

Caraveggio raised his eyebrows. "No, it wasn't. No, not at all. Cardiac infarction." He glanced around and spoke in a conspiratorial tone. "Smoking, booze, is what does it."

I wondered if he knew of any non-smokers and drinkers who would be spared. Then the impact of his words hit me. "You're sure it was a heart attack?"

Caraveggio's mouth tightened. "Mr. Le Clair came to us intestate. There are regulations."

"I was the one who found him," I repeated. "Someone looking for cash or drugs struck him with a lamp and killed him."

"Not killed. Injured, yes. But not killed." He turned and swung open the double doors.

I resumed my place beside the coffin and tried to get used to the idea of Vinnie having died from a heart attack. To recall if Kalisky or any of the policemen had explicitly told me Vinnie had been murdered. No, I suppose it had been my own theory. I even had sold it to the residents Monday afternoon. Of course, I wasn't entirely wrong. After all, whoever had broken in had caused the heart attack. Did that make the second-story man a murderer? I would have to ask Buccalotta.

The visitors stopped for a moment before the casket, then found seats. The room slowly filled. Who could have guessed that Vinnie had so many friends? Or had Caraveggio hired actors? The mourners sat on the Belter sofas and chairs and stared at each other. No one wept.

Manny, cowboy hat in hand, sauntered into the room followed by Pavel, LaVerne and Stella who wore the black dress she had worn at the Knights' but without the matching beads. The organ swung into "Bluebird of Happiness." After a half-hour of watching the viewers watch each other—the Memory Celebration, I suppose— Caraveggio, wearing a tan Norfolk jacket, was organizing the cortege to the church. He disappeared into the house and returned with an umbrella tucked under his arm. The low-pressure sytem that had stalled over the Mon Valley for the past two days had turned into a fine drizzle—acid rain, the radio meteorologist announced. My truck was fourth in line. Manny, Pavel and LaVerne went in Shultz's Taurus, Stella was to ride with me. She held onto the door handle as I bounced onto Saw Mill Run Boulevard, over the potholes the size of Mona Loa. She seemed distant, distracted. "Miss Cindy," she said finally, "a shark, that one."

"Wrong. She's providing for Vinnie's funeral. No matter what she looks like, she's a generous soul."

"I can tell she isn't married to that Shultz person."

My grip on the wheel tightened. "Which is nobody's business."

Stella turned to me. "You know what's wrong with you?"

I closed my eyes.

"You're going soft."

St. John's, a cinder block building, had the architectural features of a cardboard box. A shopping center sprawled on one side of its parking lot, a used car dealership on the other. I opened the steel door burnished to look like wood. I knelt, then followed Stella to a pew. Behind the altar a landscape of pale yellow mountains was painted on pink stucco giving the nave the dusty, outdoorsy flavor of the southwest. At least it made one feel dry, a relief in the humidity and what felt like ninety-degree heat. Father, a man with soft blond hair who appeared young enough to be my son, whispered to the altar boys. The pallbearers stood at attention around the casket, which now rested on a metal gurney. The altar was flush with the floor so that the Mass could not be followed from the back pew, where Stella and I sat. I fanned myself with an announcement.

"Mr. Le Clair dealt with his time on earth," Father said valiantly, "within the constraints of an alternate lifestyle." Electric fans on either side of the room raised, then lowered, the hem of his white cassock. He mopped his brow. "May this good man soon hear the words of words, 'Inherit the kingdom prepared for you from the creation of the world.'"

Prayer, then the service was over, and Stella and I followed the hearse. At the entrance to the cemetery a map encased in glass marked the various trails in colors: blue for "Our Lady," red for "Sunset," yellow for "Streets of Gold." The grounds went on forever, acres dotted with statuary, arched oriental bridges and brass plaques level with the turf.

Caraveggio's Cadillac, then the hearse drew up at a curve in the road. Doors flew open, and an electonic lift lowered the casket from the rear doors. The motors were kept running. The pallbearers, ignoring the drizzle, hoisted the coffin and slowly started, out-of-step, up the incline. The crowd straggled behind. For some reason I could not move from behind the wheel. I sat staring—at the same time trying not to stare—out of the truck window to the top of the rise. A green canopy covered plastic urns of flowers. A backhoe was half hidden behind a cluster of pines. I forced myself to look at the open grave, and, beside it, the slick mounds of fresh, thick red clay so heavy I felt the weight of it on my chest.

"What's wrong, Sister?"

"Nothing."

"Sit, sit. I'll go up the hill."

My eyes burned. I pressed my lips together to hold

back the tears and opened the truck door. The ground was soft, my heels sank in the mud. I walked behind Leroy, who struggled ahead. A row of cherry trees lined the walk. The trunks were peeling and gnarled. Brown leaves dangled from the branches. They would be filled with pink blossoms in the spring, I reminded myself.

A mat of synthetic lawn covered the ground beneath the canopy. Where the mourners stood in a circle was the narrow deep trench. I heard the hum of the hearse engine drift from the road. Cindy propped her glasses atop her head and wiped her eyes. Father faced a portable lectern. "Nothing is within our eternal grasp." He bent, slipped his hand beneath the mat, and straightened holding a fistful of dirt. Then he allowed it to trickle slowly through his fingers onto the imitation grass. "This life of this man is over."

In front of me the stalks of a red-twigged dogwood shrub glistened. Drops slid along the limbs, then splashed to the ground.

I bowed my head. When I looked up, Father was tucking his missal into a leather valise. I approached him.

"Didn't you bring a raincoat, Sister?"

"No problem."

Stella took my arm.

Father unfolded a super-sized golfer's umbrella and held it over the three of us. "Walk with me," he said.

Cindy had invited everyone to a luncheon in the basement of St. John's. The room was a mildew-smelling cave. Churchwomen fluttered around a folding table covered with overlapping paper tablecloths. A forty-gallon coffee urn sat among Styrofoam cups. I passed by the paper trays of Velveeta and bread and hunted for a tea bag. LaVerne, Manny, and Pavel huddled over sandwiches with three teenaged girls. Goodness knows what their relationship had been to the deceased.

I found the pot of boiling water, then joined Stella, who had a plate of potato salad and a ham on rye in front of her, at a table in a corner. "I heard something," she said. "You tell me if I'm all wet." She leaned closer.

"Rumor has it, a heart attack all along."

"I know what you're thinking," I said. "And I admit it. The talk I gave everyone in the kitchen Monday afternoon was premature, off-base."

Stella nodded. "That too."

"And you're thinking that Kalisky should have called us about the outcome. I agree."

"Sister, please listen to a person before making up what they're going to say."

I unwrapped the tea bag. "Sorry."

Stella glanced around as if afraid of being overheard. "If Vinnie didn't die by being hit, that means nothing happened."

I lowered the bag into the water. "Well, we can't really say it means nothing."

"It means it wasn't on purpose," she went on. "It was just another act of God."

"Don't be silly. Of course something on purpose occurred. His room was a mess. Someone was after something."

"But," she persisted, "maybe that someone wasn't doing anything wrong."

I glanced at her face. It seemed to be bonier, smaller, as if pulling inward. An image of Vinnie's yellowed skin beneath his aviator shades flickered across my memory. I leaned and picked a sliver of lint from the sleeve of Stella's dress.

"I would of said something Monday except"—she dropped her plastic fork onto the plate—"no one asked."

"Asked?"

"If I was in the room. But if Mr. Kalisky threatened the boys, I would have spoke up. In fact I wanted to because not saying anything is making me feel sneaky, gritty inside like someone wiped their feet on me." Her face flushed. "Don't look at me like that."

"Like what?"

"Like I'm wrong."

"Who said anything about your being wrong? Stella, what on earth has gotten into you?"

She placed her hand on her heart.

"Skip the Mother of God routine."

She dropped her hand. "Just suppose"—she paused—"I said it was me who threw the lamp."

"How could—"

"I'm strong as an ox," she said quickly.

At first what she said made no sense. Then I felt odd, disjointed, as if something fundamental, like gravity, had run amok. A second of panic, then an inner voice said if I was to set things to rights, I would have to get a grip on myself. I put my hand over hers. "Start from the beginning."

"It, the lamp, rolled around on the floor, I guess. After the argument."

This wasn't the beginning of the story, but for Stella it was a start.

"Then what did you do?"

"Do?"

"Do."

She slid back in her chair. "I had the banner to take care of."

"I'm not following you."

"You must recollect me hanging up the Knights' banner."

I ran my hand over my forehead. "When was all this with Vinnie?"

"Five, maybe six in the morning."

"What were you doing in Vinnie Le Clair's room at—" My mind boggled.

"A person has to live."

I swallowed some tea, then more to wash down the oily taste of non-dairy creamer. "What was the argument about?"

"'Loveboat' reruns." She coughed, patted her chest, and went on. "I say to him, 'You got the money. Let's sail.' He says what with the condition of his heart, a cruise and he would check out." Stella snapped her fingers. "Just like that."

She shoved her sandwich aside. "Then he says, 'But

everything I have will be yours, so after I'm finished take off.' I tell him, 'No way, José. The Medicaid will just add it to my pension, then take away my card. How about spending the money now? Sister needs it. We can fix up a few more rooms around here.' He hems and haws. 'Who you saving it for?' I asked him."

She leaned closer to me. "Let me put it to you, Sister. Who was he saving it for? Then today everyone says there's no money anyhow. You think I believe that? Me? In the old country they say flax in the mouth, linen in the bag."

"I lost you."

"Meaning Cindy's into him."

"Don't be silly. He was on welfare. I helped establish his eligibility."

"The welfare worker. She checks every nest egg?"

"Stella, do you realize you're talking about this as if it was a problem in estate planning? A man is dead."

"What estate?"

"Don't you care?"

"Care?" Her eyes seemed empty. Then I looked more closely and saw something in them that was steady and solid, like mountains far away. "It's this English language," she said. "Death is the other side of care."

I finished my tea and struggled to fit the pieces of what she said together. Stella and Vinnie; what would you call their relationship? Doing it? Yes, doing it, right there in my Mission, and I had never even suspected. Had known nothing about what was happening right under my nose. "How long had it been going on?"

"Since after the late news."

"I mean the—your—friendship?"

Her eyes narrowed. She opened her purse, pulled out a pack of Camels, a Bic lighter, and lit a cigarette. Then she turned her head to blow the smoke toward the open door. "I forget," she said.

I went through the motions of winding up my responsibilities at the funeral. I made Manny transfer Vinnie's belongings to Leroy's car. I thanked Father for the memorable service, Mr. Caraveggio for his thoughtfulness, the churchwomen for the lunch. Meanwhile my mind churned with the implications of what I began to think of as Stella's confession. It all boiled down to one question for me, should I speak up? I tore apart each pro and each con. No. Who could prove Stella's action was the direct cause of Vinnie's attack? And the wear and tear on an old lady wasn't worth dragging Kalisky back into our lives. Vinnie—the life of this man—was over. What was it Hunt had said last night? A rope is but so long. We had come to the end of it. Everthing one could say about the death of Vinnie had been said. *Res adjudicata*.

On the way back to Shackle, partly to put the funeral behind me and partly to see how Pops's hangover was progressing, I decided to stop at the farm. Last night I had dropped him off in front of the toolshed, then gone straight to the Mission. It had been after midnight and I assumed everyone would be in bed. As soon as my foot hit the steps, Stella swung open the door. I assured her there hadn't been an accident, that I had merely stayed late at my grandfather's, then shot up to the attic before she could offer her opinion on the Rockbusters shirt.

I pulled up beside the barn. Pops's truck wasn't in the drive. I pushed open the kitchen screen, and Lyda jumped to the floor. The table was covered with dried cereal, the box rested on its side. I helped Lyda out the door with my foot, turned, and spotted Tillie's fish tank. The aquarium sat on a platform of K mart walnut. Complex life-support systems, hoses and tubes ran from the wall to the floor, where something dripped discreetly into an opaque twenty-gallon can. An iridescent glow emanated from the green water. I stepped closer. It was like walking into a Jacques Cousteau film. The mollies whipped around submerged castles, towers, a plastic battleship with its stern in the gravel and its bow up. I examined the array of boxes on the fish's nightstand. Vitamins, eyewash, clarifier pellets, minerals for fins, calcium supplements. Then I noticed a smaller tank behind the cellar door.

The bottom held colored sand, and there were more toys per square inch than in the larger container. Three or four fish, I guessed one of them to be an angel, wove cautiously around the bubbles coming from a hose. An infirmary, obviously, to keep sick fish from infecting the others. Good show. God bless the old man. I smiled on my way out the door.

Pops's four by four was parked in the orchard. I pulled up beside the Toyota and joined him as he unloaded empty wooden crates from a flatbed. "This hot weather's lousing me up. First stem rot. Now this." He held up an apple.

"Looks good to me."

He pointed to a brown stain. "Rust. I got to get these babies in by today."

I glanced at the thirty or so trees. "A bit ambitious."

A ladder leaned against a trunk. Pops gripped the sides with both hands, swung it upright, and for a moment it wavered in the light breeze. Then he walked the ladder down the row of Jonathans and rested it against another tree.

"Your hangover must be okay."

"Can you get me more of them pills?"

"You have eight."

He made a circle with his thumb and forefinger. "Pinheads, that's all the bigger they were."

"Is there a substance, any substance you can get your hands on that you won't abuse?"

Hunt's words, "How old is he?" flashed through my mind. Let it go, drop it, I told myself. "By the way, I stopped at the house. Your fish set-up's not to be believed. That little tank, the infirmary's a great idea."

"What infirmary?" He picked a few apples and carefully lowered them into a crate. "No one's sick. I buy me a new fish from Mountaineer Pets up the Mall. Then figure the little sucker has to settle in gradual. It took me one year after the old country to get used to this West Virginia." He gathered an armload of fruit and eased those apples on top of the others. "Not that the guys will be in there that long. I adjusted everything down to fish time."

I laughed and moved to the pickup.

"Wait. You got a minute?"

It was two o'clock, ordinarily time for the Mothers Anonymous meeting, my child abuse prevention group. Only this week the session had been cancelled.

"If you're not doing anything—"

"Just for an hour or so." I took off my jacket. I draped it over the seat, then rolled up my sleeves. "When was the last time I picked apples with you?"

"Don't remind me."

"You using that other stepladder?"

"Take it."

"I'll finish the row across from you."

He shrugged and mounted the bottom rung.

The weather was beginning to clear, the breeze breaking the solid cloud cover into wheels and rolling them past the sun. Steam rose from the silky grass that Pops mowed to within an inch of its life. An apple dropped on the edge of a crate. It split, and the air smelled of autumn. I hung my vest on the corner of the flatbed, lifted an empty carton and carried it to the tree I was working on. Standing on the top rung, I discovered the ladder only went halfway up the trunk. Above me hung a dozen or so Winesappers, as Pops called them. Holding a branch, I inched onto a limb and sat with my legs dangling what looked like a mile above the ground.

From here you had a bird's-eye view of the entire orchard and, in the distance, the thin blue line of Geezer's Ridge. At least it looked like Geezer's Ridge. I squinted and shaded my eyes. Come to think of it, the line could also be a bank of low-hanging clouds. All at once I found myself wondering if my judgment was as astute as I always thought it was. I stretched to pick an apple, polished it on my thigh. Lately I seemed unable to interpret one single thing that was going on around me. As if I had lived on this earth thirty-five years for nothing. I bit into the Winesap, then studied the random yellow grain on the skin. The discovery that I might not have the foggiest idea of what was going on around me should have been unnerving. Instead, I felt light, agile, as if a weight had been lifted from my back. A warm moist breeze lifted the loose hairs around my forehead. A kestrel whirled above the trees, and I pictured a field mouse, undercover, watching the bird spin circles in the air.

A few minutes later I pitched the core and wiped my mouth on my sleeve. I checked that the ladder was propped securely against the bark and started working my way down.

CHAPTER
16

Whenever I'm awakened by a ringing phone, my first thought is I'm late. Then, what have I done wrong?

Friday morning, half asleep, I lifted the receiver.

"Peace in Christ, Sister Vida."

Sister Arnette was speaking in her power-broker voice, and I gradually woke up to the fact that she was ordering me to the mother house. Now.

"But our regular staff conference is this afternoon. Mother Silesia and I can have a one-on-one afterwards. Besides this morning I have other plans."

"The Mother General told me, if you said that to tell you this meeting's mandatory."

"What meeting?"

"You'll have to ask her."

"Put her on, please."

"She's to Daybreak Prayers for Peace."

"When will she be back."

"In time for your meeting at seven."

My digital clock read five a.m. In all the years I had been in the Order I had never gotten used to the hours. For some reason rising before dawn (what normal people call the middle of the night) had become mixed up with Siluva virtue. I come from a tradition of fine sleepers. Tillie could clock down eleven hours at a stretch. Pops swore by sleep as a cure for everything from head colds to Alzheimer's. Owl power, he called it. He evaluated a night's sleep the way a food editor would review a restaurant. "Everything was humming along okay until that damn whippoorwill kicked on."

I stumbled to the closet and reached for a skirt. There was nothing for it but to show up at the mother house and get—whatever it was—over with. Could it have anything to do with me, my leaving? Probably not. The appointment with Crumrine was coming up Monday, so my defection would be put on hold. Sister Silesia would never risk taking a position that might be shot down by the bishop, weaken the image she held of herself as a corporate magnate, the Lee Iacocca of the Siluvas.

In the kitchen I snapped on the overhead fixture. Every ceiling crack and chip in the linoleum blazed to life. What is it about the quality of indoor light just before dawn? I lifted the kettle in the nick of time, before the whistle went off, and found an opened can of milk in the refrigerator. My eyes felt grainy, and my senses were totally out of synch. Unless I could sneak in a nap, the day would be shot.

Weaving through traffic along the business stretch of Route Nine, I couldn't believe the number of vehicles racing their engines at intersections, their lights on, wisps of exhaust curling over the fenders. What kind of people elected to work these hours? I mulled over remedial social policies, composed a letter to the Labor Department that I would never write.

The parking lot at the mother house was empty except for Sister Silesia's Chevette and a black Ford wagon. The front door was locked. I rapped on the glass. Sister Arnette appeared behind it swinging a key ring the size of a small Frisbee.

"A good thing it isn't cold out here," I said as she opened the door.

"Are we running late?"

"You tell me." To my credit I did not add, "and I'm sure you will."

I opened the dollhouse door and brushed past the L-shaped secretarial desk. Voices drifted through the partition of Sister's office, one of them a man's. "Go on in, the Mother General's waiting." Why did Sister speak in the third person? The Mother General. She was a human being, not a position.

Sister Silesia's office was as I had last seen it except the International Year of Women poster had been replaced with "Stop a Family Tradition: Child Abuse Prevention Week." She sat, legs gracefully slanted, at one end of the tufted Naugahyde sofa. At the other end sat a trim balding man wearing a navy three-piece suit. His black beard, clipped close to the jaw, was shot with gray.

"Sister Vida, Mario Sonaro."

Brother Sonaro, Society of Jesus, rose. I knew him only by reputation—had heard Sisiter Silesia refer to him as the Cardinal Ratzinger of the West Virginia Diocese. Sonaro was Bishop Crumrine's right hand, the conservative arm of the Charleston See. After serving with the Jesuits in Nicaragua, Mario had moved straight into Crumrine's good graces, chairing CREP, the Coalition to Restore Educational Prayer. (As opposed to, say, recreational prayer?) A few months ago the *Star-Democrat* featured Mario in the Sunday supplement. He lived in a restored mansion in Beckley and his hobby was collecting Ethno-Americana, whatever that was.

"Please sit down."

Did Sister mean me? Or Mario? He sat and crossed his legs revealing high black socks. I moved to the canvas-backed captain's chair beside the coffee table.

"We were just discussing my work," Sister said.

"*Saints Alive* should do well," Mario said.

"There's certainly a need for it," I said.

How long would it take for Sister to dispense with the overture and get on with the meeting. I caught her eye and smiled.

"The funeral went well? I briefed Brother Mario on the incident at the Mission."

I looked over her shoulder as I spoke. "I think you

should know that Mr. Le Clair died of a heart attack."

The room was silent. Why no reaction? Sister's worry about a Vinnie scandal had just been put to rest.

"Let me remind you," I said. "This means that nothing happened. That is—"

"I know exactly what it means. I spoke with Detective what's his name, begins with a 'K,' a few days ago. He told me about the cardiac infarction."

I stiffened. "The funeral was okay. As these things go."

"I mean, were the residents of the Mission able to work through their grief? Express their feelings of loss, abandonment?"

"Yes."

She turned to Mario. "Critical in crisis intervention. Confront loss and cut it."

"Confront loss and cut it," I repeated. "Well said, Sister."

She smiled. Then frowned. "On to other things. Bad news. Sister Cleo cannot, absolutely cannot, work at the Mission."

I concentrated on my face muscles, don't let them smile: keep everything impassive, still.

"Her asthma. That old house without a central vacuuming capacity. And I'm not having any luck in finding someone else." Her voice took on a helpless tone that I had never heard before. But then I had never spoken with her in the presence of Mario. "Can you go on handling it alone?"

She must have forgotten that the coming of Cleo had been exclusively her own idea.

Mario nodded at me. "As we were discussing earlier, before you got here, the entire diocese is short staffed." He laughed shortly. "Now, of all times, when Catholics United Against Poverty decide to stage another candlelight vigil. This one's at the Peace of Bread shelter in Beckley. Same contingent that brought newspeople out in droves in Fairmont, Weirton, Martinsburg. We can't keep up with them." He stroked his beard and added. "The homeless, I mean."

Sister glanced at her nails, as if not sure where to look. The silence was awkward. I thought about saying something about the militant homeless gaining ground, decided to keep my mouth shut.

Mario draped his arm along the back of the sofa. "Having said that, let me just say this, Sister Vida, that the bishop is thrilled and delighted at the way you handled the incident at St. Michael's."

Thrilled? I folded my hands in my lap and lowered my eyes. What the son of a bitch meant was that if Kalisky's accusations had come true—drug-crazed shelter residents kill alcoholic victim—if there had been a messy investigation as to the quality of social services provided by agencies affiliated with Catholic Charities, if Vinnie had not conveniently checked out with a heart attack—I would have been in the soup. "Thank you for passing that along."

Mario brushed at his paisley tie. Sister stood and walked to her desk, and I reached for my bag on the floor beside me.

Then she sat back down and swiveled a half-turn. "The purpose of our meeting this morning is—"

She paused while I lowered my bag.

"—to clarify the relationships between and among Religious, the Mother General, and the diocese."

This was going to be a big one.

"Having said that—" she paused again. Had she caught herself echoing Mario? "I was amazed that you felt compelled to make an appointment with the bishop." She leaned towards me. "Whatever for?"

During my career—as a bureaucrat that is, not necessarily as a Religious, although one wonders sometimes at the distinction—I had noticed that under stress we move like knights on a chessboard. One step forward, lurch.

I smiled at Sister and turned to Mario. "About my rights as a Religious requesting dispensation."

"Any questions, I can answer," Sister said quickly.

"Why didn't you put in papers for me?"

She shrugged.

"When I submitted a request."

"I wasn't convinced that the petitioner was of sound spiritual disposition at the time."

"That was four days ago. The circumstances have changed, what with the crisis of Mr. Le Clair's death put to rest. So I'm asking you again."

The intercom buzzed, and Sister leaned to answer it. She tilted her head and whispered, "Ring her through." She picked up the telephone and covered the mouthpiece with her hand. "I have to take this one. I won't be long."

Another observation of bureaucratic behavior, leadership in initiating the small talk demonstrates excellence in the player. "Is it as hot in Charleston as it is here?" I asked Mario.

"That, and fog. Wednesday night they closed the bridge over Route Four, visibility was so bad."

"Wednesday night," I repeated thoughtfully.

"A fluke, heat, this time of year."

Mother Silesia's voice rose. "Good show. Mail him the roster, attendance forms, and an adjunct faculty guide to St. Elmo's. Copy me. For the record." She added before hanging up. She nodded to Mario, "You're all set for the winter semester."

I studied her face for signs that she knew that I knew she had sold out. How many times, in this very office, had she sworn she would never allow Bishop Crumrine's teachers to infiltrate St. Elmo's. "Let one in, next thing you know the Siluvas are out on the streets," she maintained.

"I found you a classroom with a window." She spun her chair from Mario's line of vision to mine. "Now. Where was I?"

"You were about to agree to my request for dispensation," I said.

She turned a pen slowly in her fingers. "This decision hurts me far more than it does you. But I'm not convinced that at this point in time your motivation is without spiritual pathology, and I can't allow you to do something you might regret for the rest of your life."

"I could come back."

She twitched once, irritably. "Not viable."

"You're still refusing?"

"Why can't you understand?" Her voice went soft, and she crossed her arms across her chest. "My hands are tied."

I faced Mario. "Monday I have a meeting with Bishop Crumrine to ask him to waive—"

Mario held up a finger. "His Eminence delegated this to me before he left for the west coast. Sister Silesia and I agreed on sitting down with you together to clarify our respective roles."

A set-up if ever I saw one. But it couldn't hurt to try once more. "Fine. I'll mail you a written statement. You sign my release and send it back."

"Except for the Rule," Sister said. "You forget your vows included obedience to the Siluva Code as expressed in the Constitution of the Order, meaning that without my concurrence, you have abandoned your vocation, which by Siluva standards, means your Church." She carefully laid the pen on the blotter. "Excommunication."

Again I faced Mario. "She's talking about an archaic phrase in the Rule that no one bothered to delete after Vatican II, that's all. It's meaningless. It won't hold up in this post-Concilliar climate."

He ran his finger around his collar. "It's not my judgment call."

"Then whose?"

He closed his eyes, then opened them. "There are so many issues here. So many. The hierarchical relationship between the Siluvas and the diocese, the fact that the Order was founded in Lithuania, where the records of the original Constitution will be hard to come by, the conflict of individual conscience over community rule. All, all of these questions must be interpreted in the context of the Concilliar Committees."

Catching my breath was becoming a problem. "I've been to Rome, and the Committee reports aren't just in filing cabinets. We're talking rooms, here. Rooms and rooms of records.

"It could take some time."

My skin felt clammy. So be it. I would tough it out. Beat them at their own game. Mirroring Sister, I crossed my arms across my chest. "What do I do next?"

His answear came too quick. "Write a justification for a release of vows. Include relevant—and only relevant citations from the Siluva Rule. Also, put in a thorough discussion of your interpretation of the language."

"And send it to?"

"Me," Mario said.

Silesia smiled.

"I'll put it through diocesan clearances and forward it to Rome," he added.

I looked around the office and this time saw it through the eyes of a visitor. The rooms separated not by drywall, but by sheets of dark brown knotty pine. The doorknobs of brass plate. The dieffenbachia on the windowsill, over-watered foliage yellow at the stem. I would beat them at their own game. The fan stirred the brass cord hanging from Sister's desk lamp. "A rope is but so long." Beat who at their own game? The Order? The nuns, so quaint, like the blacksmiths at Williamsburg. The Church? But the language, the beauty is gone. The Church is over. Everything ends. "This life of this man is over. The world of the Son is over."

"Have you any questions?" Sister asked.

Suddenly I was aware I was standing. "No."

"How's the budget coming along?"

"I'm leaving." The words sounded as if spoken by someone else.

"Eventually, yes, I know. But meanwhile the area agency will need the carryover figure in order to authorize spending."

"Now." I turned to the door.

Sister Silesia stood and moved from behind her desk. "Are you serious?"

Mario struggled to his feet. "Think what you're doing."

"I'll clip a briefing note on each of the current files. That way my replacement won't have much downtime. After I pack, I'll drop off the keys with Sister Arnette." I couldn't trust my voice to say more.

"You can't just walk out," Mario said.

"It's over."

"You must, absolutely must, give us a written justification."

My hand rested on the doorknob. "Why?"

"For the record," he said stiffly.

"And who is that?"

In the outer office I paused, waiting for my knees to stop shaking. Sister Arnette blew on a streak of whiteout. "Is our meeting finished, Sister Vida?"

Either she hadn't been listening, or was doing an unusually good job of faking it.

"Father Kozakas called. Someone at the Mission told him you might be here."

I rested my knuckles on her desk.

"He wants for you to return the truck. I said I'd call him back. What should I say?"

"I have to speak to him anyhow."

"But what should I say?"

"I told you, I'll call."

"What will you say?"

I moved toward the entrance. "Never mind."

"Don't forget the cookout," she said. "In the cafeteria. Sister Jo Ann and Sister Cleo worked up a skit, 'Our Lady of Siluva, the First Thousand Years.' Do you have a program?"

I shook my head. "No."

She handed me a sheet of paper with a computer design on top and text printed in script.

"Why didn't you get a program? I sent one over to the Mission in the weekly packet I always send to your girl, LaVerne. Did she lose it? Maybe it was lost—"

I closed the door behind me.

The Teamsters' Hall, a white clapboard single-story

building, sat on the spur of land where Hazel Creek flows into the Shackle. The river was about a mile wide at this point, but the channel cut so close to shore you could almost count the lumps of anthracite on the barges sliding by. Inside, the Hall was a gigantic dance floor of gleaming oak, a stage, a vinyl-topped bar, and enough coatracks to accommodate an army. Outdoors a pavilion sheltered picnic tables and barbecue pits. A section of water had been roped off as a swimming area, complete with a gravel beach raked smooth as sand and a lifeguard seated atop a tripod. A fleet of aluminum rowboats bobbed beside the dock.

It was seven in the evening. I handed my ticket to Mrs. Piaschi, who was manning the door. She tore it in half and dropped the pieces in the wastebasket. Before I realized what was happening, she stamped an ink pad, then my wrist. I wiped off the black *x* with a tissue.

On the stage, the band was setting up the drums, "Polka Punks" scrawled across the skins. The clarinetist wore a leather vest, but, instead of a shirt, ropes of seashells covered his chest. Despite the heat the Punk fingering the accordion sported knee-high fringed suede boots. No sign of Pops, so I crossed to the pavilion, made my way around the tables, and down the steps to the beach.

A few couples basked in the setting sun, metal rock thrumming from boom-boxes resting on Ninja Turtle super towels, while nearby, preschoolers buried a litre Pepsi bottle in stones. The lifeguard blew his whistle at a teenager about to dive from the dock, and I turned to the river, then shaded my eyes with my hand. What in heaven's name were those bright discs drifting on the water? It took me a minute to realize they were hats. Hats worn by ladies of Stella's vintage (Stella, in fact, was among them), who each year especially for the picnic bought bathing suits, beach robes, and floppy sunbonnets only to stroll waist-deep in the water and talk to each other. It's entirely possible that not one of them had ever swum a single stroke in her life. Now, in the soft evening light, the brims could have been water lilies floating over the waves.

Pops wasn't in the picnic grove. It occurred to me that he would head straight for the bar, and I retraced my steps. Since leaving the mother house this morning, I seemed to be in a fog. Ride it out, I told myself.

The dance hall was filling up. Men leaned on the bar downing boilermakers. Those who were Knights wore narrow red silk scarves around their necks with what I assumed was the crest of the Lodge embroidered above the fringe. The Knights' banner hung in all its glory over the door, the metallic threads shining softly.

Along the wall, women sat on folding chairs and sipped beer from plastic wine glasses. Mrs. Kovelesky, Mrs. Koleck, the Spassky twins, both married to contractors who made a good living, Mrs. Walecki, whose son had fought in the Persian Gulf. The air smelled of bay leaves and fried pork. Tables flanking the stage were loaded with steam trays filled with cabbage rolls and sauerkraut bubling aound tiny white potatoes and wedges of scarlet kielbasi. Vito and Bayloukas worked the bar, Bayloukas with a dishtowel tucked in his belt and Vito giving orders. He glanced my way, but there was no sign of recognition. No wonder. After I left the mother house I had stopped at Montgomery Ward. Now I was wearing a sundress with a wide skirt, thonged sandals, and teardrop earrings—fourteen carat. The jewelry was bought on impulse. Who was I kidding? The entire shopping spree was an impulse. Where on earth had my mind been? I glanced down at the miniature roses and violets on the skirt. Was the print too gaudy? For someone younger? Older? All at once the world seemed incredibly complicated. How long would it take to figure it out?

Bayloukas circled the bar with a quart of beer in his hand and refilled Mrs. Koleck's glass. Then he headed in my direction.

"Mr. Bayloukas?"

"You look nice, Sister. Where's your old man?"

"I'm waiting for him. About the other night—Hoover."

Bayloukas glanced around the room and spoke in a low

voice, as if afraid of being overheard. "There are signs he's cracking. Soon enough, he'll come crawling home."

A call for a refill, and Bayloukas hurried away. Someone bumped my arm, and I turned to face Mack Jeruski, a beer in one hand and a shot glass in the other. "Sorry, Miss." He lumbered toward the doorway, laughing, then called out, "Hey, Zedonis."

Pops, dressed to kill, leaned over the ticket table. He was decked out in a white shirt, string tie, and a navy jacket with the Knights' scarf draped over the collar. I went up to him.

"Your accordion's in my truck. Where did you get the earrings?" Then he looked down at my shoes. "You be warm enough in those?"

"For heaven's sake, it's ninety degrees in the shade."

"You look like a princess," he said softly.

A clash of cymbals, a chord on the electric guitar and the Punks swung into the "Take Me to West Virginia Polka." One-two-three-four—the walls boomed in four-four time. "That's where I long to be." The lead singer was too close to the mike, and the amplifier crackled like buckshot.

Sammy Koleck tugged at his wife's arm and pointed to the dance floor. She turned to Marie Spassky, laughed, and pretended to pull back just as Sammy whirled her onto the polished wood. A few more couples stomped past the bandstand.

I touched Pops's elbow. "It's over."

He pointed to his ear.

"Over," I shouted.

"Come outside."

We found an empty picnic bench facing the beach. The sun had slipped behind the mountain, but the water was lit with high-pressure sodium lamps above the dock. Under the bulbs tiny insects treaded light. The lifeguard slapped at his thighs. The women in hats had drifted to the ankle-deep section roped off for toddlers and I could guess why. The lights lured catfish to the surface, six-foot long tigers with sharp whiskers and thick, muddy skins. Stella, in a wide-brimmed orange number, was holding a drink and bending Mafalda's ear.

Pops swung his foot on the bench and reached into his breast pocket for a cigarette. "Everything's settled?"

"Sister wouldn't sign, and I walked out."

Pops stared at my face while he fired a wooden match with his thumbnail. "I'm surprised. How were you able to do that?"

I drew my feet up on the bench and struggled to find words to fit the thoughts. "The old me would have drummed up a hundred sensible explanations. Except down deep I know the real reason was simply because I couldn't have done anything else." I raised my heel and watched the leather strap of sandal tighten against my foot. "They say people control their own lives. But it's not true, not true at all."

"I never said that."

"Oh sure, the picayune day-to-day stuff. But the big ones come from—" I motioned to the dark pines beyond the clearing.

A teenaged boy and his girlfriend stolled by, his arm draped across her shoulders, her arm around his waist, her thumb hooked in his belt.

I drew a line along the edge of the picnic table. "A rope is but so long."

Pops nodded slowly.

"You know what else? Tillie and Ralph."

Pops dropped his cigarette and ground it out with the toe of his boot. "I'll never change them. That's over too." I mustered a weak smile. "Listen to me, I sound like Vito Pucas, 'The Second World's over, bring on the Third.'"

The three-four beat of a waltz throbbed through the muggy air. Someone shouted, "Hey, Arnie, we're down here."

"There's only one problem."

"Damn straight. Pucas goes around talking as if Arafat—"

"Not that. Me. I've been sheltered too long. The world seems strange now, too hard to negotiate." My voice broke. "As if I've just been born."

Pops reached and touched my hair, the first time in my life he had done anything like that. His hand felt skittish and rough. I looked up at his face, creases darkened by ingrained coal-dust, weathered by underground wind. "How will I live?" I asked.

His arm dropped to his side. "You seen me do it."

A shadow moved in the trees behind Pops. A twig snapped, and he turned. "Dr. Sun."

Hunt stood, his seersucker jacket slung over his shoulder. "It's hotter than hell."

"You eat yet?" Pops asked.

"I've been looking for you. There must be a hundred people packed in that place. I can't believe the dancing."

"You want a kielbasa sandwich?" Pops asked me.

I shook my head.

"What's wrong with this family?" Pops said. "No one eats anything, like birds." He started toward the pavilion and motioned to Hunt. "You and me get a bite and bring it back here. A person can't digest Punkers."

It occurred to me that Pops was itching for a drink.

"Vida?" Hunt said.

"We'll fix a plate for her. I'll show you how."

I watched them disappear into the crowd around the steps, then turned to the river and tipped back my head to catch the breeze. All at once a sweeping bright light, and a barge rounded the curve. Kids in bathing suits shrieked, jumped, and raced up and down the beach watching the black hull slice the current. Then came the steamer gliding before the dock like a homecoming queen on a float. Cockpit lights twinkled amber and orange. Flags—West Virginia's, PAW's, and the Stars and Stripes clapped from the flying bridge. The children shouted, and a man on deck touched his cap. I watched the ship until the red glow of the stern lights disappeared upstream. The V of its wake spread wide, wider. Stella and Mafalda swayed slightly as the waves lapped at their calves.

Killing time, I slapped a mosquito, then reached in my bag for a tissue. My fingers brushed a folded piece of paper, and I drew it out. The program for the cookout, "Siluvas: The First Thousand Years." The first paragraph was printed in tiny slanted letters. I held it up to the light.

Long ago, long ago, so very long ago, as Lithuanians say, the town of Siluva was famous for its grand cathedral. Then Protestants came, tore down the church and planted rye where the altar had been. One day shepherds saw a woman wearing a golden crown sitting on a rock.

She said, "At this place my son was worshiped while now they plow here and sow. Some think crops are monuments. That to worship is to feed the poor, do good works, conserve fuel. But duty is inferior to faith. Love is a spendthrift. Pour wine on Christ's feet. Dig up seed beds and plant cathedrals, gold chalices, jeweled mitres, cupolas with spires so tall they reach the stars.

"So, you ask me. How will we get clothes, water? How will we live?

"Say what I say when sickles whirl and seeds fly. God gave me teeth. He'll give me bread."

I slipped off my sandals and headed toward the women in the wading pool.